THE SUN CHAMPION

CUT THORN
THE SUN CHAMPION

Book One

BY GENESIS BRILLANTE

This book is a work of fiction. All characters, fantasy lands, creatures, places, names, and events are fictional and from the author's imagination. If there is any resemblance to any actual persons, living or dead, any firms, situations, or sites it is a coincidence.

ISBN: 978-1-7366941-0-7

To my family,
who encouraged me to write.

"Time is infinite and definite, but only a rose expresses true fidelity as it grows and shoots upwards rising towards the Sun, deep in the heart and mind of a hero."

DRIED FLOWERS

They shrink and depreciate

We belittle them
Cast them aside
Like tossing a fresh bouquet
The only difference
No one catches their fall

Their demise means nothing to us
Except an empty vase to fill with
Fresh Flowers,
Symbols of blossoming love
But when death and decay set in
They are dead to us.

- ***G.J.B.***

The purple crystal belongs to the territory of Miezul Noptilandia.

The orange crystal belongs to the Horizonia Empire.

The blue crystal belongs to the Gardium Kingdom.

The green crystal belongs to The Terrace Gardens of Nominia.

The black crystal belongs to the Crystal Common Grounds.

The red crystal belongs to The Volcanic Village of Humberia.

The yellow crystal belongs to the Kingdom of Terraminionium.

The pink crystal belongs to the Kingdom of Dalium.

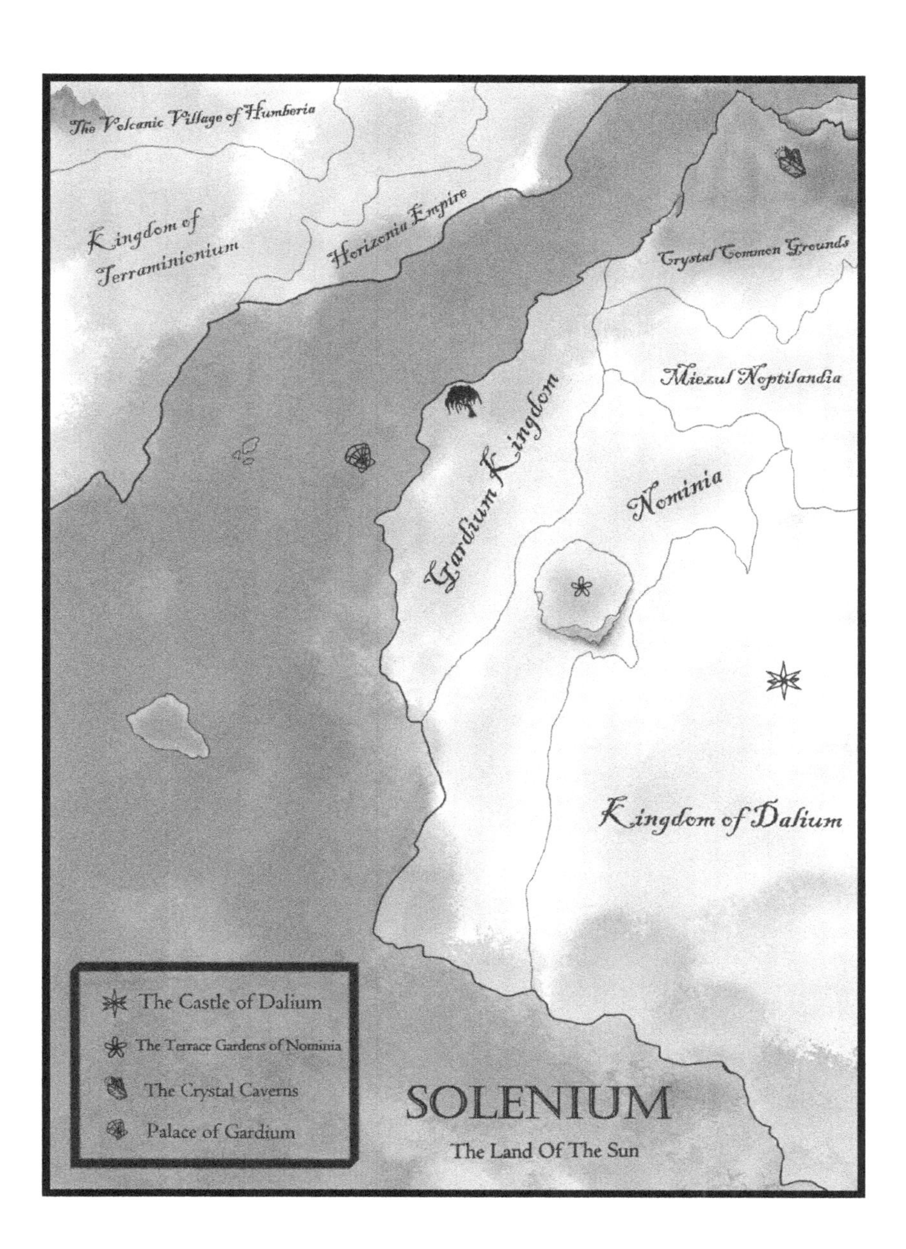
The Volcanic Village of Humberia
Kingdom of Terraminionium
Horizonia Empire
Crystal Common Grounds
Miezul Noptilandia
Gardium Kingdom
Nominia
Kingdom of Dalium
The Castle of Dalium
The Terrace Gardens of Nominia
The Crystal Caverns
Palace of Gardium
SOLENIUM
The Land Of The Sun

Table of Contents

Prologue
The Sun and Its Champion

The Sun brought life to the land of Solenium through light. The warm rays of the Sun first touched the land that became the Crystal Common Grounds. The heat of the delicate light created a fierce mountain, for crystals grew under the barren rock. Within the Crystal Caverns there formed the very first creature of the light. The Sun created a Crystal Being that roamed freely across the Sun Lands. The being created new life by treading on the ground to make soil. Its breath created the wind. The tears of the Crystal Being created the ocean. The mighty flapping of its wings molded the meadows, fields, trees, and mountains. The Crystal Being's wings painted the night sky. Thus, life was brought to Solenium as a result of the Sun's creation.

From the soils sprouted the plants and then the animals. The animals each reflected an aspect of the Crystal Being, built to mirror the Sun's purity. Then, mankind was formed. From the divergence of man created division and hate. Different clans were formed based upon the differences in powers and gifts. In the beginning mankind sprouted from the nutrient rich soils, softly baked in the light of the Sun. The first civilization formed in a region that came to be called Dalium. Although the people that lived there did not possess any outwardly gifts they created a powerful kingdom. However, as a result of traveling and the use of different resources across Solenium, the groups of man became divided through different gifts. Those who lived close to nature in the forests had a bond with the plants that grew there. They learned to fly by watching the golden eagles. They became the fairies of Nominia. Others that lived by the sea took an inclination to swimming. From the ability to tread water as fast as a fish they adapted to survive both on land and beneath the waves. Thus, the territory of Gardium was born. Even then, there formed a special type of man that could innately wield magic. Those who have magical powers to control the elements of the earth, such as precious metals and fire, are exceedingly rare. Following the creation of the Nominians, Gardium people, and those with magic all different groups of mankind emerged.

The Sun was proud of the Crystal Being and the land of Solenium. To praise the light of goodness and kindness, the warmth of life, the Sun decided to bless an island in the ocean that could act as a bridge between Solenium, the mortal Sun Lands, and the Heavenly Sun Lands of the Everglades. This way when the Sun's creatures died they could rejoice in the Heavens above. Thus, the Sun formed an ancient passage to connect both the spiritual world and the physical. The passage, known as The Mountains of the Sun Blessed Everglades, was to be kept hidden on the secret island. This way life and death could be balanced.

The Crystal Being brought life to Solenium on the behalf of the Sun, and all was flourishing. Until, the Sun realized there was a shadow spreading across the Sun

Lands. The balance of light and darkness, life and death, was being ruined through violence. Mankind battled over their different gifts and fought over the free land of the Sun. Chaos spread and darkness corrupted. The Sun was abhorred in the discovery that its own blood could give life to such destruction and evilness. It feared for its first creation, the Crystal Being. To protect the Sun's first born creature it broke the Crystal Being's body apart. To separate the creature's remains, the Sun gifted the eight crystals to eight separate regions, forming five territories ruled by the regular man, one by the fairies, one by the people of the sea, and the last territory remained common to all. There was a ninth crystal shard, but it is said that the Sun kept that crystal piece hidden for itself. The Sun Crystals, as they became known, brought prosperity to all eight regions of Solenium. Thus, forming seven mighty kingdoms across the land to rule over the territories. Yet, each Sun Crystal is still alive with the blood of the Sun coursing through the hollow center. Although they were formed in the Sun's reflection to create the perfect Crystal Being, there is still darkness in its core. The temptations to use the crystals, if not tamed, could corrupt the people of Solenium. Thus, where there was light, shadows of corruption also blossomed. The common land of the eighth territory, The Crystal Common Grounds, quickly became a harbinger of darkness, for foul creatures were drawn to the strength of the crystals in the caverns, and even more so to the power of the unclaimed Sun Crystal hidden deep within.

The Sun realized this and thus created an ancient tradition of selecting a Sun Champion and assigning a fate to the mortal possessing promising traits. Loyalty, integrity, strength, courage, and love. These are the qualities that make up a Sun Champion. The traits of a hero are most sacred and rare. The champion's faith in the Sun must be strong. Therefore, a Sun Champion is only chosen in the most pressing of times to which the qualities may be found in a living being of Solenium. Thus, the selection of a Sun Champion is rare and many centuries pass between the times in which the Sun chooses a person to represent the land of Solenium on a given quest. The quests are dangerous and perilous. Those who are selected rarely return alive and the missions are daunting. Yet, the Sun Champion is the guardian of both light and darkness. They restore order to Solenium for the sake of bringing prosperity to all lands when chaos arises from the shadows. Therefore, it is significant that the chosen hero discovers their fate with an ambition to succeed and live for the sake of bringing peace to Solenium.

Chapter 1
Solenium's Past

The sun lowers over the western plains of the Kingdom of Dalium. A gentle breeze blows through the village, carrying the crisp cold air across the many fields and to the doorsteps of the small meek huts. The green blades of grass are laced with ice; the dirt path frozen over. The fountain is still, the water frozen mid air as though in trepidation. A horrendous crash sounds through the distant mountains as snow piles over the remnants of a house and a cloud of catastrophe arises. Autumn's harsh, cruel, cold breath hits the villagers as they open their doors to see winter at their doorsteps. The shallow breaths of scared adults follows a succession of synchronous shrieks from the children. The ground shivers underneath the cold eerie figure, who stands next to the fountain. It is as if the world has frozen over, leaving nothing but darkness and death among the shoulders of Time. The figure is wrapped in a light blue cloak. It moves from side to side, but remains huddled by the fountain, weeping. It cuddles the corpse of a baby, and is lost in the bittersweet thoughts of remorse. In a final moan the weeping figure presses against the fountain, clutching the baby tightly to its chest. It shrinks behind a red flash of light as another shadow of a more prominent figure, whose hands are bathed in warm blood, materializes.

The greater figure with bloody hands takes its time to observe the petrified village and glare at the mounds of ice, before turning its attention to the weak form of the lesser figure. It dares the other to move with eyes like sharpened daggers, but as hard set as stone and as dark as night. The bloody hands reach out to grab the baby. The other figure screams, but the child is wrenched away and tossed aside on top of the fountain rim. The cloaked figure covered in blood moves to the frozen water and lays a hand into the basin, then pulls away to watch as the ice turns into vibrant crystals and begins to spread. A hollow laugh comes from the shadowed figure as it stands happily watching the maroon and violet crystals cocoon the baby's body within, entangling the fountain, and spreading its rock solid fingers outward, slowly reaching for the rest of the village.

The villagers slam their doors shut and hush the children, extinguishing their lights, all silent in prayer. Yet, from the outskirts of the village arises a hero, the Great King Russleton. The Castle of Dalium fell three days ago to the creatures of the night, and the monarch was said to be dead, killed by his own daughter. However, to the surprise of the two figures, the one with bloody hands and the other weeping shadow, the king is very much alive. He is tired, beaten, and solemn, yet his heart beats with a renewed ferocity and burning passion. King Russleton approaches the shadowy figures and draws his sword, dragging his boots limply against the frozen ground. He does not dare look directly at the wicked figure with maniacal hands; rather, he looks up at the sanguine sky. The king is old; his beard grey, face unshaven. His soft emerald eyes are wet, and he bears no armor. However, King Russleton is very much alive.

The clinking of the King's metal blade against the scabbard animates the wicked figure. It turns viciously on the old man, slicing at him with bare hands. It is as if the air has turned on him, the whole world rejects him. He falls hard against the rough broken ground, stumbling to get up. The monstrous figure laughs in bitterness, its hands drip with the King's warm blood. King Russleton hits the demonic figure with his metal sword, but it rises above him as his blade turns dull. The metal starts to drip from his wounded hand. It clings to his neck and hardens with just enough space for him to take light breaths while choking in his own blood. The shadow of the wicked figure emerges from the darkness and casts aside the dark burgundy cloak to reveal the figure of a woman, Medaia. A tall beautiful woman with dark hair and darker eyes. She stands over the king for a second, observing and judging him to see if he is worthy to live. A silver blade hangs from the brown leather belt wrapped tightly around her waist. The eight Sun Crystals in the crossguard of the silver blade, each shining a different color, pulsate to the king's diminishing breaths. Medaia unsheathes the sword from her scabbard, and raises it above old King Russleton's chest.

She pauses in hesitation while watching the man gasp for breath and whispers, "Revenge is a blossoming rose," then she lets her blade drop. The eight Sun Crystals glow a furious shade of red as she wrathfully presses the blade down into the king's stomach. King Russleton draws in one last shocked breath as his hands move out to trace the silhouette of the weeping figure, his eyes longing to make contact. However, by finding no satisfaction in meeting another human hand, he releases his breath and collapses to the side. His face crashes on the rough ground and his once brilliant glowing eyes fade, becoming like ash. The extinguishing of the Great King's strength causes the violet crystals to sprout from the fountain like wildflowers and spread throughout the village.

Everything erupts into chaos, as villagers cry out in pain over the death of their king. The wind howls and the frozen air lashes out to combat the spreading crystals. Medaia screams too. Not for what she had done to the Great King; rather, as she wrenches the sword from his chest, the crystals lining the crossguard burst into a red flame that begins to engulf her. The red flame stretches up her leg, across her torso, and up to her neck, then sprawls across an eight-pointed star necklace. The necklace and the red flame disappear into the hands of the weeping figure. The crystal bearing sword now ignites into a vibrant white flame. The Sun Crystals on the sword burn brightly too, each in their own color, and then they vanish in retreat to their rightful owners. The Sun Crystals return to the eight great regions of Solenium, safe in the respective domain of each territory. The sword's warmth radiates across the village, stopping the spread of the fountain's crystals.

The meek figure approaches Medaia and throws the star necklace into the fountain, where it fades away. Covered in shadows, Medaia is pulled into the crystal mass she had created and she too disappears. The remaining figure reaches into the crystal cocoon surrounding the fountain. The figure's light blue cloak slips away, revealing a young and sorrowful face. Her cheeks are pale, her dark brown eyes glitter, and her breath is shallow. She pulls the child free from the cocoon and hugs the baby to her chest. The blue tint of the baby's skin begins to glow as the figure rocks the child gently in her arms. The chilling coolness of the baby's small hands makes the figure shiver. She presses a warm hand against the baby's frozen cheek. Her long black hair falls forward and tickles the lifeless form of the baby. The figure turns her back on the fountain filled with Medaia's wicked crystals and walks away, smiling and humming as the villagers peek out from behind the doors.

Only when the figure disappears behind the shrinking Sun do the villagers begin to sigh a breath of relief. They come out one by one to talk of their misfortunes, mourn their many losses, and pity King Russelton's corpse.

Over the ensuing days, flowers are laid beside his body and fresh bread is placed around him. A funeral is held on the third day and his body is set on fire. Each villager looks towards the embers and stays by King Russleton's side until the cold air chills their bones. The pale moon begins to rise, while the glorious Sun hides behind the mountain ranges. The ashes of King Russleton are scooped up by children and streaked onto their foreheads as a blessing to cure them of Medaia's presence as soon as the first star rises into the night sky.

Eerie silence follows the village for ten days after the death of the King of Dalium. Each day the villagers sing in the evenings, holding their cream candles out of their windows. The wispy smoke from the candles blows with the breeze in the same direction that King Russleton's ashes were carried out. They pray at midnight for the Sun's grace. The eleventh day of mourning and prayer brings forward King Russleton's cousin, who is next in line for the throne. The king had only two daughters, both said to have been lost as a casualty of war. Thus, his cousin became King Charles the first, who had the castle rebuilt within a year's time and the fountain rehabilitated to honor the many losses that the Kingdom of Dalium had faced. Ceremonies are held across each land in the entire world of Solenium to honor the heroes of the Great War, who stopped Medaia's shadow from spreading.

Medaia, the shadow sorceress, had turned on each entity ruling in all the lands to harness the power of the Sun Crystal for herself. She stole the eight Sun Crystals and killed mercilessly. She caused chaos to spread across Solenium and was at fault for the monster attacks. Medaia was the traitor that had caused many deaths in the ensuing war for the Sun Crystals. She and her shadow beasts had killed heroes, she slayed the Great King Russelton of Dalium, and brought misery to all the lands.

Thus, great panic arose when the word spread from the Kingdom of Dalium to all the lands in Solenium that Medaia had vanished into the crystal pile of the fountain, following King Russelton's death. At once the remaining rulers set out to search for a sign of her. For years they were unsuccessful in their search, for there was no trace picked up by any kingdom, nor any sign of her dark magic. Eventually, by using the power of their Sun Crystals, the surviving rulers of each land picked up a slight trace of her being that led them to the Crystal Common Grounds, a place of vile temptations. Dark creatures brood in the everlasting night of the deep mountainous caverns, waiting for their chance to end the light of the Sun for good. However, it was a stroke of luck that they were able to find Medaia, for even the shadow beasts had remained dormant until in a remote village within Miezul Noptilandia a shadow beast sighting had occurred. Each ruler used their crystal to seal Medaia in the deepest part of the Crystal Caverns on the mountain of the Crystal Common Grounds. Thus, she was of little concern for any of the regions because nothing could break the power of the crystals except the Sword of Eight. Although, even that would require all of the eight crystals from each region to have enough strength to free Medaia of her imprisonment.

The recent war resulted in great losses for every region. However, like a tree destroyed by a ravishing forest fire, new life will emerge from the past. Thus, throughout the entire world of Solenium, hope spread like wildflowers. Each region celebrated and mourned. The fairies from the Terrace Gardens of Nominia mourned over the loss of both the King and Queen, who left behind a single daughter, Chlonia. The Gardium Kingdom commemorated the crowning of Prince Nautilus to King Nautilus. Miezul Noptilandia celebrated freedom from the reign of the night monsters. The Kingdom of Terraminionium reclaimed lost territory. The Crystal Common Grounds grew darker as the monstrous woman retreated further into the caverns high on the mountain. Humberia's small village erupted with excitement and tears as they rejoiced that the end of the war was among them. Yet, the loss of the Great King Russelton was heartfelt throughout Solenium for he was highly regarded as being benevolent to all. However, the territories did not just lose their heroes, they lost their crystals as well. As soon as each remaining ruler finished sealing off the Crystal Common Grounds, the crystals vanished into thin air. It was said they returned to the Sun. Nevertheless, each region felt at ease after a year had passed with no monster sightings. The crystals' disappearances were not of importance seeing that they were no longer needed and each region returned to a peaceful state.

The following days in the Kingdom of Dalium following the loss of King Russelton, rebuilding of the Castle of Dalium, the coronation ceremony of the new King Charles, resulted in a time of celebration. The rebuilding of the village was a priority, but trade had picked up, the market had grown, and facts turned to legend. The story of the Great King of Dalium was written down into the sacred book of the Sun, which contains the history of the Sun Lands, and all was glorious throughout Solenium.

Chapter 2
The Kingdom of Dalium and the Sun Laws

Twelve centuries have passed since the tragic event in the Kingdom of Dalium. In the meantime, both life and death flourished. The village prospered and grew into a great city surrounding the glorious castle. The walls were built stronger, the roads repaved, and the towers lengthened. Everything in the Kingdom of Dalium had been made new. The fountain, although it was rehabilitated, became a memorial of Dalium. The cracks, broken basin, and original features were left mostly the same to honor the past. However, the fountain still spews out gentle water that occasionally drips over a modest plaque honoring King Russleton. Below King Russleton's name is an inscription that reads, *In honor of the brave saviour of Dalium, our hero of legend.*

The current king of the land is King Charles Noapten XVII, who has reached the age of thirty-one and is hosting a grand wedding celebration. The bride is Penelope Chards of the Kingdom of Terraminionium. They are a perfect match; she is resolute and beautiful and he is a powerful king, who is related to the ancient king of legend, King Russelton. Hours of laughter and hope for the world settles in as each member of royalty throughout the entire land of Solenium is welcomed into the Kingdom of Dalium. They each bring gifts for the king and his chosen bride. In addition, King Charles XVII gifts Penelope a pink crystal he found buried near the churchyard. Queen Penelope presents to her husband gems from her land, as a promise to further prosper the Kingdom of Dalium. Together, they lay in bed enjoying the late hours of the night.

The following morning concluded the wedding celebration. Each ruler offers their well-wishes for the newlyweds and the entire Kingdom of Dalium as they make their final congratulations before leaving. Then, the drunken citizens stumble away through the palace gates and the Castle of Dalium enters a short-lived state of tranquility. The air is fresh and the clouds a tender grey. The songbirds begin to sing a soft welcoming tune. The morning Sun rises high into the brilliant sky, the light strikes the fountain, and a soft glow erupts from the fountain's basin. The Sun is golden and gentle in the sky and the dew of water is laced over the beautiful stones of the fountain. The light pulses to the beat of a human heart as rain begins to fall, everywhere except on the fountain. The citizens gather around, puzzled. Nothing is in the fountain except the gentle water, nor is anything surrounding it as a possible source for the light.

Trumpets blare and the knights scramble forward as King Charles XVII emerges from behind the castle walls bearing a heavy crown upon his head and an even heavier, drooping red royal mantle. Queen Penelope scurries behind him in a white lace nightgown. Her lengthy brown hair is undone and blows in the chilling breeze. They march in silence through Dalium until they reach the center of the kingdom and spy the glowing fountain. Queen Penelope gasps at the sight of the burning light.

"What does this mean?" She whispers with wide eyes and trembling lips. "Is it an omen?" King Charles XVII places a warm hand on his wife's cold shoulder. She shivers at his touch.

"It is nothing. It means nothing," King Charles XVII says in a hushed voice. He then addresses the growing crowd, "Return home for there is nothing to fear. This *light* is a gift of good fortune from the Sun. It is nothing more than a blessing to our good health."

The crowd mumbles and slowly the people of Dalium retreat from the fountain. King Charles XVII throws off his royal mantle and passes it to his trembling wife. "Here." He commands with a gruff voice, implying for her to put it on. She lifts it over her shoulder and drops her eyes, before taking one last fleeting glance at the fountain. Penelope shuffles away and a group of five guards follows behind her. She pauses and spins around, letting the white lace of the nightgown glide against the ground.

"King Charles!" She glares at him and drops his royal mantle, letting it fall against the wet ground. Queen Penelope declares in a loud voice, "What cause would the Sun have to bless us so eagerly? You know that this is no gift. What if it is a curse? We should be prepared to act if–"

"My dear lady," he interjects with dangerous glaring eyes, "There is absolutely nothing to fear. Head to the Castle of Dalium, secure yourself within the walls. This union is not cursed."

The knights rush up to Penelope at King Charles XVII command and grip her arms with their rough gauntlets, forcing her back to the Castle of Dalium. King Charles XVII glares at all around him, before taking slow and heavy steps to lift his mantle off the ground and follow after her.

As the Sun sets, the fountain begins to glow brighter. Light bursts from the fountain and strikes through every crevice of each house, shop, and even the Castle of Dalium. The newlyweds stride outside onto their balcony to watch in fear of what is to come. The wind picks up swirling around the castle of the Kingdom of Dalium. It prods at the gates and knocks on every door in the kingdom. It twirls around Queen Penelope, lifting her dress and twirling her like a doll. It smacks against the king and shoves him aside. Yet, nothing besides the light comes from the fountain memorial. King Charles XVII sends his guards to scour the city for any signs of a shadowed figure or shadow beast. Nothing comes from the search. However, eight days later, the glowing light fades and a weeping toddler is found sitting on the rim of the fountain. No one knows where she came from, but she bears the eight-pointed star necklace, the mark of the monarchy, and a gift from the Sun. The king and queen grant the child into their lives within the palace of Dalium, for she bears their symbol. At the sight of the toddler, Queen Penelope removes the necklace and buries it within the pocket of her gown. The necklace has never been seen again.

Vicious rumors follow the uptaking of the child, they mainly consist of twisted lies that accuse the two royals of an illegitimate child. To protect the royal family from the rumors of an alleged affair, the queen and king claim the girl to be their own, born before the marriage and that the child the queen is now expecting would be second-born. Thus, came an end to all the rumors and the kingdom seemed to enter a time of providence yet again.

***

Years have gone by since these events occurred. The past was long forgotten by the people of Dalium by the time the young girl, Linum, turned seventeen and her brother, Charles, turned sixteen years old. The day the Kingdom of Dalium fell, the old king, and the shadowed figures soon became legend; then myth, then fairytale. Medaia and the war only remain as a fictional story of legend in their hearts and minds.

A new day dawns over the Kingdom of Dalium. There is peace and prosperity throughout the land. The city is full of bustling citizens, hurriedly carrying out morning tasks. The castle stands shining over the many stone buildings and great wooden towers, watching each person scurry along their daily paths. From within its walls, the young princess Linum sits on her bed, willing the day to move forward and for tomorrow to bring with it a grand adventure. She looks out of her window only to see the citizens hustling along, free to go anywhere, to converse with anyone, to do anything they like. They appear like ants gathering food for a queen, only they are humans gathering supplies for their own survival and the monarchy is ruled by the strict Charles XVII and his wife, Queen Penelope. Linum is the first-born and rightful heir to the throne, according to the Sun Laws.

The Sun is sacred in the lands of Solenium for with it comes light and protection from the creatures of the dark. The laws of the Sun are written on a parchment with ink that only appears during the day or when light is held up to it. Thus, they are called the Sun Laws. Linum, as well as the rest of the royal family must ensure that the laws are kept within the castle walls and reinforced when necessary. Therefore, each member of the royal family must memorize them during their teen years. Each time a monarch is brought to the throne of any kingdom in Solenium, they have an option to create new Sun Laws, in addition to the three original laws of the Sun. Most do not take the offer and leave the laws to be, for they are sacred and only may be changed in the uttermost pressing of times. The three original laws read:

> 1) All creatures who claim their will to the Heavenly Sun Land of the Sun Blessed Everglades shall render themselves responsible to the prosperity and well-being of the providential land of Solenium. The heir to each throne is decreed by the separate laws of each respective kingdom.

2) All kingdoms shall appoint a guard for each sacred Sun Crystal, protecting the land from invading forces.

3) Power shall be split among the eight great regions of the world through the use of the sacred Sun Crystals:

The purple crystal belongs to the territory of Miezul Noptilandia.
The orange crystal belongs to the Horizonia Empire.
The blue crystal belongs to the Gardium Kingdom.
The green crystal belongs to the Terrace Gardens of Nominia.
The black crystal belongs to the Crystal Common Grounds.
The red crystal belongs to The Volcanic Village of Humberia.
The yellow crystal belongs to the Kingdom of Terraminionium.
The pink crystal belongs to the Kingdom of Dalium.

Three more laws were added to the sacred Sun Laws. Solenium has a history of violence by divisions among the kingdoms. Loyalties are often tried and tested through the differences between the eight regions of the Sun Lands, and eight different kingdoms. Thus, three more laws were created. They are:

4) Any creature of magic yielding powers that is not of the Terrace Gardens of Nominia will face the judgment of life and will receive fatal consequences for their abilities.

5) Magic beings and creatures of myths are to be welcomed into society by their own choice of being.

6) A woman may not yield a weapon in any of the great regions, especially women in royal standing.

The fourth law was created by King Fangtooth of the Gardium Kingdom who surrounded himself in the complete darkness of his thoughts. His advisors were executed weekly for any sign of weakness or possession of magical abilities, although his kingdom is well known for their magical gifts. The people of the sea were at war with those on land and thus the prosperity of Solenium was divided not only by the breaching sea, but the division of beliefs. The fairies of the Terrace Gardens of Nominia sought the help of the Kingdom of Dalium to protest against the added Sun Law. The Kingdom of Dalium may have been the first kingdom the Sun had formed, but it did not satisfy the others in joining the fairies as an ally. The Kingdom of Terraminionium bonded with the Kingdom of Dalium in support of the fight against rule number four. However, the Gardium Kingdom, Horizonia empire, and Miezul Noptilandia remained in support of the new law.

Magic has been a force of destruction in the past and it has brought new life. It has been viewed as both a blessing and a curse. However, with King Fangtooth's fear and evil heart, the creation of law number four became an enemy in itself. Magic users either perished or gave up their gifts. Protests over the law grew violent, until a full scale war broke out and divided the land of Solenium. A compromise was reached at the end of the war to edit the fourth law, for the original did not make an exception for the fairies. However, great distrust remains among the Terrace Gardens of Nominia and the Gardium Kingdom. Thus, this war over King Fangtooth's fourth law of the Sun, occurred years before Medaia's shadow war.

The fifth and sixth rules were added within recent years. The fifth followed King Russelton's adoption of two girls that both had magical powers. He created the law to protect them from law number four, which states that any creature containing magical powers will be killed. He was a king of legend before his early death from the dark figure of fairy tale, for he believed all creatures deserve a life of prosperity, whether human or not. Thus, to protect the two girls from receiving the same fate as their mother, he adopted them with the creation of rule number five. Yet, some people in Solenium still scorn his addition of rule number five due to the war against the shadow sorceress, Medaia.

Linum, a strong minded female, has always leaned away from the idea of being a princess of grace and gentleness. She preferred the idea of becoming a knight. A warrior of honor, a sword slinger, an adventurer, a hero to all that called upon her. However, fate was against her as her father, Charles XVII, had placed a new law stating that women may not yield a weapon and thus may not become a knight. Therefore, rule number six was devised and followed strictly in the Kingdom of Dalium, whereas other territories take scarce notice of the new law. Rather they choose to ignore it so war does not break out yet again.

Chapter 3
A Hero's Lost Cause

The Sun glows magnificently in the sky, high above the castle of the Kingdom of Dalium. Hope glitters in the air for, like everyday, it is a new day full of light and wonder. The birds sing new songs and gossip among each other. Even the far off cries of the mountain may be heard, if one listens intently with keen ears and a pure-heart. The people hustle to and fro from every direction within the boundaries of the kingdom. Children play in the lush green grass of the fields on the outskirts of Dalium. The clouds dance across the brilliant blue sky. However, behind the grand castle's walls, in a dark corner in a small grey room, there is a young woman sitting upon a dull bed. The rigid planks of wood creak with each movement and if a slight creak of the floor boards is loud enough, or the soft thud of the teen's body against the ground is audible, then the guards would burst through the heavy door. Thus, limb by limb she must lift her body from the tattered bed and move onto the broken desk. This is the teen's daily ritual within her prison cell, her bleak room. She stretches her tan legs across the desk, avoiding the stack of papers, and lifts with her arm to push off onto the hard surface. A quill rolls, trembling the ink jar beside it. She freezes in fear and flashes a quick glance towards the door. The black quill slows to a stop hitting against the brass inkwell. The ink drips steadily upon the parchment containing meaningless handwritten copies of the Sun Laws. She flashes a quick glance at the corner of her room. In the corner is a small crack in the floor, a hole no larger than a human finger. She smiles slyly, and looks up. Above the dark desk, on a brooding shelf, lies a small silver box; she reaches for it and pulls it stealthily towards her. Leaning back, she pulls herself from the desk and moves back to the bed.

She pulls out a mahogany key from the box, and sets it in her hand, stroking its spine. The teenager is Linum, a young seventeen year old desperate for freedom and adventure. She has been working on the key for months trying to fashion it to fit her door. She draws the sharpened kitchen knife from beneath her brown tattered pillow and sets to work yet again.

The key is by far her greatest possession. It was only last year she had gained the right to go to the Churchyard at the far end of town without a guard by her side. Thus, this key will make quite a difference in her life. She just turned seventeen and yet her brother, Charles, who is sixteen is allowed to travel anywhere without supervision. Fear is the reason she is kept behind bars. Fear for whom, she wonders, but fear is the answer. Doctors are paid to diagnose her as weak and fragile. Her contact is limited. And she cannot bear it for much longer.

Linum is trapped in her room. The grey walls glare at her day and night. The citizens are free; the birds that sing outside the castle walls are free, but she is not. She feels trapped. Like all the goodness in the world is gone. Like there is nothing left but to waste away in the dimness of her prison cell. She lives, but in a nightmare that caresses her great fears and follows her like a shadow. However, she was not always locked away. Thirteen months ago she could walk freely anywhere with a guard. That is until murders started to occur within the kingdom. On the very outskirts of Dalium, the villagers were going missing in their sleep; their looming eyes looking for peace, but their bodies were found unscathed. The bodies were firm and rigid with fear, and cold like ice. Yet, the strange shroud of death has since spread to cloak the entire Kingdom of Dalium. Within the city walls, citizens have been found with eyes shaded by eternal darkness, while their chest still beats, but their bodies are frozen. Even if the hearts of the lost citizens are carved out from their bodies, the organ still beats with unnatural prowess. The lips of the citizens still tremble and if a doctor presses against the victim's face, they will feel a chilling breath being drawn in and released in utter silence. Death stalks the Kingdom of Dalium. Mostly the murders have occurred after midnight. Although, in the outer villages away from the city gates, a strange figure has been reported during the hours of daylight and after it vanishes, a villager is found dead. Thus, King Charles VXII has ordered a complete lockdown of their borders, increased the castle guards, and forbade Linum from the outside world, until the Midnight Persecutor is caught.

Her long black hair falls across her brown eyes. Her face drops, she leans down, and her eyelids darken. She resembles the room itself. Both are dark and brooding with a forlorn longing for something to come its way and make sense within the dreary borders. An opportunity to prove oneself and to be freed of some burden placed among them both. The key dangles, taps her thigh gently, and she awakes yet again. Her knuckles crack as her hand firmly grasps the key, her mouth stretches and her shoulders fall back, but still she chips away at the key while her mind wanders.

She longs to fight, to venture out into the open arms of freedom. She has never experienced true freedom before, always a guard in silvercrested armor standing beside her. Her life in a prison cell, in a world where people fear everything and everything is a threat to be feared, is dreadful. The rolling scraps of wood glide off the rims and onto the bed. The key is finished. It is like holding freedom in her hands. No longer would she have to wait until the Sun reaches the highest point in the sky to be let out for meals only to be forced back in her room in the late afternoon.

Linum has made numerous attempts to get out beforehand, but none have prevailed. Even in the brief hours of "freedom" she has, liberty does not stand well. It evades her. The guards observe her every move. Even before the murders began in Dalium, she was followed constantly. Her guards would leave her at the Church and descend down the grassy slope to watch in secret from the tavern.

She has tried to run from them and make it into the forest, but she is always caught by the brim of the great pine trees. At least the Church is upon a hill, overlooking nature's canvas of rolling hills, brooks, streams, and ponds. Linum is able to watch the Sun rise and set and ponder over what lies in the distance. She knows that somewhere, far beyond what she can see, is the mysterious dark lands where crystals are said to grow. Based upon every description she has read or heard of it, she desires to travel to that place. The very mention of the Crystal Common Grounds excites her. She feels compelled to visit it. When she stares off at the distant horizon and imagines what the mountain of the Crystal Caverns looks like, she feels as if it is staring back at her. Beckoning her and whispering in her ear, with a promise of a new life. She has tried to reach it, but the Crystal Common Grounds are out of bounds for all and it is a dark, forsaken land.

Besides the natural scenery, the Church balcony makes for the best viewing point of the fountain. Most citizens keep their distance from it, but Linum feels hypnotized by the waters swaying with the wind. She may not touch it or come near it, but like the will to travel to the Crystal Common Grounds, she feels the need to approach it, lay her hand into the water, and touch the plaque dedicated to the past King of Legend.

The key holds her freedom. With the key, her fate is in her own hands. Linum slides off the bed and onto the cold floor, making the slightest of movements, as to not alert the guards beyond the heavy wooden door. She pushes herself towards the small crack in the floor and presses her head against it. Beyond the hours of her freedom, the crack in the floor is her way of communicating with her brother, Charles, and with her only friend, Judith, the royal family servant. Judith takes care of Linum; thus, she helps her to deliver messages to her brother by collecting the letters Linum drops through the crack in the floor.

Linum drops a slip of paper down the hole and it lands into the laundry basket. Judith always does laundry on the first, third, and last days of the week. The rough wooden key follows the simple note, it slides against Linum's fingers and falls down into the crack, hitting against the wood and stone until it lands into a basket of clothes. Her breath begins to quiver as she listens for the sound of Judith's light footsteps to come through, hoping that she will see the key and pass it along to Charles, so she may be freed. Five minutes have passed and nothing may be heard from below. There is no familiar clink of a knob turning, no thud of light footsteps, and no voice to reassure that her message and key have been gathered. Linum still sees the key resting comfortably on a stack of clothes in the basket. She waits intently, worrying as each second ticks on by. The shadows have begun to travel across her room since she dropped the letter. She begins to panic as time flies by.

What if Judith is ill or someone else is coming to get the laundry? She said she would be there on time to ensure it was delivered safely.

Linum's mind becomes a hurricane of doubt and fear. She worries over the possibility that the key could be found by the guards and that she would be further imprisoned. The threat of disobedience buzzes in her ear as her mind echoes the sounds of metal chains rattling in the wind. King Charles XVII has threatened her before with imprisonment in the dungeons. Linum remembers clearly how his face turned a violent shade of red the last time she attempted to run away. She was dragged into the courtroom by a guard and thrown at his feet. His greatest advisors only shook their heads, but King Charles XVII spared no mercy. When the guard informed him that she had nearly made it to the castle gate in a wild run, he burst forward and clenched his fist. King Charles XVII had dismissed everyone from the room and as soon as the doors slammed shut, he was on top of her. Linum's yelps of pain were only quieted when Queen Penelope strolled through the door. Penelope did nothing to calm him or diffuse the situation. She merely watched. However, at the sight of Penelope, King Charles XVII pulled Linum upwards and dragged her away. He forced her down numerous stairs and hallways until they arrived at the forbidding dungeon. He then pointed at a cell and warned her if she was to attempt another escape, she bound with the metal shackles against the grim wall.

Linum sits wearily on her bed. She hears footsteps approaching and she shivers. Judith never came to pick up the key. Linum knows punishment is inevitable. The door to her room swings open and she is let out into the hallway. Two guards shove her forward and push her into a dark corridor illuminated by glaring torches. Their faces stretch into shadows of cruel images as their forms morph into darkness. The guards use their shields to block Linum from running in front of them or lagging too far behind. Their feet move in a successive pattern, stomping against the floorboards, mechanically.

Normally, when Linum is freed, Judith is responsible for locking all of the doors up to the garden side of the castle. Linum is not allowed to exit from the main doors, for they are only used in times of rare family appearances. Not to mention, Linum is not invited to such family appearances. She is kept as a shadow behind locked doors. Very few knights deal with her transportation from place to place.

Judith was hired to be Queen Penelope's personal handmaiden, but she was reduced to the job of cleaning the clothes and hanging them to dry. She took a fond liking to Linum after coming across her three years ago. When Judith arrived in the Kingdom of Dalium seeking work, she was a traveler who bore nothing but the clothes on her back and a few scraps of bread when King Charles XVII found her outside of the castle gates. With her blonde hair dirtied to an ash grey and her face riddled with dirt, she appeared desperate and alone. He invited her into the palace and offered food, and that is when she proposed that she might work for him in return for the service he had done for her. Charles XVII had no means for another servant, but his wife Penelope saw reason behind the offer. She proposed that Judith could be her own personal handmaid, in return for a place to stay and food. The deal was agreed upon and life for Judith seemed to improve. She had a place to bathe and warm food to eat, and although the quarters were tight and shared among the other maids she found a way to sustain herself.

Judith's origins were never clear and when asked about her past, her answers were always muddled between searching for something lost and having no home of her own. She is a beloved servant among all, the favorite of the queen, but still treated harshly. Penelope uses Judith daily for simple tasks, but never gives her any special treatment.

On one of her laundry trips she ran into Linum, who was fencing with her brother, Charles Noapten. She set down the basket and watched the two for some time and just as Charles was on top of Linum, she stepped in and informed Linum her stance was incorrect and guided her blade. Linum then disarmed Charles and, satisfied with the instruction, craved to know more. From that day forth, Judith would meet Linum outside in the gardens to show her some tricks with the sword. And it was of late agreed upon that Judith would help Linum get out of her imprisonment with the invention of the mahogany key. It was all Judith's design. She measured the keyhole, gave Linum the sharpened knife, made the plans and instructed Linum to drop the key down the crack in the floor, so she would receive it during her laundry routine. Then Judith would cause a distraction while Charles unlocked Linum's door. Yet, Judith did not appear as planned.

Linum and the guards move deeper into the castle where the heavy wooden door with the great silver metal hatches stands in place. She can see the delicate roses and the grapevines dangling from the outside pillars through the grand windows surrounding the garden door.

However, Linum notices something quite odd. Another door to the right, normally locked and heavily guarded, is cracked open just enough for her to slip through. Her eyes widen, but she tilts her head upwards facing the intricate ceiling and only takes a few seconds to sneak glimpses of her guards. Their eyes are distracted and their focus leaves her for a moment. She takes the opportunity and runs for it. The bewildered guards scream and chase after her, but Linum is ahead and she bolts through the door only to trip on something inside. Scrambling to her feet, she manages to lock the door behind her with its key mysteriously set in place. The guards beat on the door outside, warning that if she does not open the door, she will be punished.

She hollers back at them, "Being with you is a punishment!"

They jab at the door with their spears and she hears the scraping of wood. Linum breathes a sigh of relief. Her hand gently slides off of the great metal handle while inhaling and exhaling steadily to calm her beating heart. She removes the key from the lock and examines the freshly carved wood. The familiar carved edges, the gentle handle, the rough edges, all of which she had just finished crafting in her room. It is her key.

Her dark eyebrows furrow and she tightens her grip on the mahogany key. Linum takes a step back, but her left foot gets caught on something on the floor, and her right foot twirls back and knocks a basket aside. She tumbles down, but instead of hitting the cold stone floor and feeling its hard surface smack against her, she lands on a much softer surface. It is much warmer and sticks to her skin. She pushes herself up by clinging to it. Linum's arms are drenched in *it*. The red liquid, sticky and warm, embraces her. It trickles down onto her body. Her eyes widen, her dark eyebrows shoot up, and a realization floods her mind with foul thoughts. Clinging to the walls she draws in a deep breath of the cold dry air. Linum trembles as if lightning has struck her. Linum knows what broke her fall. She can see the once sweet smile and bright eyes turned dull, cold, and hard, staring at her. Rigid before her is Judith, dead.

Though she keeps muttering, "It cannot be. It must not be," she knows it is her.

The guard's voices fall silent, a drumming noise starts to pound at her ears. Her heart skips beats. She trembles at the horrendous feeling of the blood soaking into her clothes. The key slips from her hand and crashes against the cold, unforgiving floor. Linum looks at Judith's limp body, the empty eyes, and solemn stare. She releases a heartfelt scream and Linum crumbles down once more. Her body gives way and the world goes dark as the guards voices become audible again, growing louder and louder, and then muffled.

The door bursts open and the guards dart in, they drag her away from the body. Linum's head rolls and her hands slide against the smooth ground, her legs dangle as the guards hoist her up. They march to her room while a few stagger behind to oversee the situation. Guards shout commands yelling at one another and instructing maids, who shriek in terror as they see Linum's bloody dress. A maid with tight hair and a stern face exclaims, "Oh my!" and hurries off to inform the queen. She disappears behind the dining room door and reappears moments afterward, followed by Queen Penelope. Penelope rushes forward, her lace purple gown swishes around the corner and her spiked crown bounces on her head. She meets the guards in Linum's room, excusing the maid with a wave of her hand. The maid glances at the blood once more and mouths her surprise again, before hurrying away to gossip with the fellow servants. Penelope cradles Linum's bloodied hand and whispers softly to the head guard to summon the doctor.

She then turns to the unconscious Linum and flashes a stern look, her icelike eyes piercing into the soul. Queen Penelope faces another guard and whispers, "Keep this quiet. The King will not be informed. Clean the room and do away with all traces of blood. I will not have panic spreading throughout this castle. If anyone questions, say Linum injured herself. She is *very* fragile as you *must* know."

"Yes madam." He marches off, directing the five other guards to follow.

Silence. Dreadful silence ensues. Penelope's face twists and turns to the waves of frustration with tears of great fear accumulating even after she looks up and wipes at her eyes. Yet, when Linum stirs she resumes her cold and distant self. Linum jumps to life, the color returning to her ghostlike skin, her eyes reviving to their full color, and she gasps for air. It was as if she was thrust into the vast regions of the universe and told to breathe in the empty void of space itself. Her head pounds and her heart races. Her hands shiver and she has no words.

Penelope looks straight ahead, her eyes transfixed on the plain wall before her. She claps her hands together in nervous agitation and rubs them against each other, then whispers intently, "You were supposed to go to the garden."

Linum tries to mouth a response, but her lips fail to move. Her voice is strained and her body languid against the soft blankets overtaking her gentle features and sporadically increasing the pain she feels inside.

"Linum! You should never attempt to run from your guards. Where would you go? What would you do on your own?"

Linum's mouth quivers and from her lips escapes a single name, "Judith?"

Penelope's grasp hardens around Linum's bloodstained hands. Her nails penetrate the skin, as she speaks through clenched teeth, "You are an insolent wretch" and like a lion pouncing on distant prey she jumps upright, "You are a disobedient insolent wretch!"

And with that, Queen Penelope storms from the room, leaving behind an exhausted and pitifully confused Linum, who lies on the bed while exasperation settles onto her raised brow. Slowly her eyes drift off into another world.

Chapter 4
Valediction

When Linum awakes, she is alone, enclosed in her room. Her hands have been cleaned of blood and her clothes have changed from a simple grey dress to an olive green gown with lace running up her arms. The dress dangles at her feet and shimmers as she moves from side to side inspecting her re-energized form. The evening is beautiful. The sky is painted soft colors of blue, pink, orange, and then there are the red streaks across the sky. The red breaks between the bright oranges and light pinks and cuts the blue down the middle, interrupting the peaceful haze. The clouds are blood red in its reflection, they appear to soak up the sky. Linum turns away, gasping in remorse. Leaning back and choking on tears, she notices a pair of eyes watching from the door cracked open just slightly. They are eager eyes, full of greed and self-conceit. He shuts the door and shuffles away as fast as his small body can take him. He is the family physician, gone to fetch his master and tell her of the urgency of the situation. However, Penelope does not run to Linum's room in the ensuing moments, rather one of the numerous maids comes by to inform Linum that her family awaits her at dinner.

Linum pushes the door with trembling, tentative hands and peers out, only to be called upon by three new guards in silver armor. They escort her to the room where her family is waiting, marching right foot, then left, then right, then left again, in a succession of repetitive movements. She is shuffled along like cattle and transported, her head hanging low in defeat and her long gown sweeping the floor.

The knights line up beside the mountainous doors of the dining room and push them open, presenting Linum as they would a foreigner. Daylight pours over the table and the smiling face of her brother, Charles, awaits her across the empty chair on the right. The room appears to brighten further. Penelope sits in the shadows at the far end of the table, her hands tied in a knot of self-conceit while her face stretches into a cynical smile. The king sits disdainfully slouched upon an elevated chair with gold rimming. His face is either half lit by the shining light of the Sun or glowering in the shadows, as he sways back and forth rocking in his chair. Dinner is fresh and steaming on silver plates containing rare choices of meat and the table is strewn with an array of produce. Their chalices of glimmering gold are filled to the brim as are all the plates. Linum steps forward. The sound of her feet is the only audible noise in the glamourous room. The attendants rush in after her and napkins float, lifted upon the soft air. The attendants pull back Princess Linum's chair in somber silence.

The king and queen whisper across the table, making empty conversation meant to fill an eternity with boredom and meaningless words.

Charles nods at Linum and dares himself to quickly glance at the king and queen, before venturing for conversation states, "Father I am not confident in joining you tomorrow on the fields, for I have never been successful at riding a horse."

Penelope chimes in, "Perhaps, another month of lessons will serve him better."

The King turns solemnly to his son and mutters something about the horses, but all Linum hears in the great room is the echo of Judith's motherly voice calling out to her on the lonely evenings. She watches her memories of Judith float by in her head. Judith hangs over her like a shadow pulling her back into sorrow at each moment, setting sparks to a greater fire within her. Yet, Linum must not cry in *their* presence. Thus, she pulls her chalice to her lips and faces the ceiling, looking for hope or the Sun's pity.

Linum could not ignore the conversation for long as her father erupts like a bursting volcano from his chair and slams his fist down upon the table, making all the plates jump.

His eyes dash from the queen to Charles and back again. He slumps down once more, and with a booming voice changes the topic, "So, Charles how has your sword fighting been. Have you improved? *Or* were you once again beaten by a scribe?"

Nearly choking on his sausage, Charles responds, "It depends on what you mean by beaten. If improving is memorizing bountiful new stances then yes, I have improved greatly," he pauses and a witty smile appears across his face as his eyes glow from pure amusement, "Otherwise, the scribe may have the upperhand seeing that he has had all that practice of quick hand movements from writing."

"No son of mine is beaten by a scribe! For the Sun's sake, a *scribe*, Charles! A scribe," bellows the King, his eyes daring anyone to challenge him, to speak.

Charles's face reddens and his eyes take one cautious look at Linum before dropping down deep into the comforts of his food. He frowns, but after mashing his potatoes, he respectfully looks up at his father and asks to leave the table.

Yet, Penelope intervenes with an affectionate glance to Charles and an endearing flash to her husband. She yawns and leans back slightly in her chair, speaking softly, but loud enough to be heard by all, "They *need* to know. You can't keep the secret from my darling son and this wretched girl for much longer. You have no right doing this; you cannot do this. You are no coward, but you don't have the men or the weapons for it, so let me take the children. Let us all leave or you will be a coward!"

King Charles XVII's face is ridden briefly with confusion, but as fast as his confusion settles into his mind it leaves, and he lashes out, "The knights are prepared. Charles is prepared, he is nearly a man now and has had enough practice. This is his chance, his time to become a man. Penelope, you will be fine. Our castle walls have been built with the finest materials, and we have the best guards, and–"

"But people are dying! The citizens are found dead in their sleep and we expect the murderer to just disappear into thin air! And what if it is true, then what?"

The king begins to shake violently, "This is no matter. Charles is ready and *will* accompany me and my best knights on a hunt tonight under the light of the full moon to track down this alleged killer. You will have Linum's company, my dear Penelope, and the most attentive guards at your door."

"It won't be enough."

"You clearly did not trust me enough to inform me immediately of any news, thus, your word is nothing to me."

With that Penelope sinks into her chair, her eyes redden and brim with fresh tears. She lowers her face, and when her eyes meet King Charles XVII's glaring face again, there are no tears in sight. Queen Penelope resumes her cold mask of indifference. Her hands claw at the edge of the table and she resigns herself with a simple, "Do as you like."

Linum watches the defeated Penelope sulk in her chair. The king declares, "Children you are dismissed. I will talk to the queen alone."

Linum feels the need to mention her name, to throw it out once more into the universe. Mustering her courage, she blurts, "What about Judith? Why am I being punished for a crime I didn't commit? Why are we kept out of these important conversations concerning our lives and livelihood?"

The king glares at her, with his furious eyes. He warns, "You will not have a life to be concerned about if you speak again. Now go!"

Linum laughs. The Sun presses against the side of her face, as she rises from the table and yells, "I do not have a life here in this castle. The people of Dalium hardly recognize me and not all the knights know of my existence. It is like I do not exist! How do you expect me to one day become queen if I do not gain the people's respect?"

The king slams his hand into the table again, his face completely enclosed in the darkness of the shadows, and he grumbles, "You are ungrateful, you—"

"Do not call me that!" She harshly commands. The king falls silent and Charles stares at Linum with great concern. "What happened to Judith?" Linum matches his booming voice. Her face glows a bright red, matching the setting Sun.

"Get out, NOW! Judith died on her own accord. It had nothing to do with the Midnight Persecutor as Penelope suggests. But to be sure of it, Charles and I will go out tonight and end this nonsense." Linum begins to protest, but King Charles XVII intervenes sternly, "Let me rephrase what I just stated, Linum, *you* are dismissed, I will talk to the queen and Charles alone. *You* will remain in your room for the next two days and suffer whatever fate this castle may hold for you."

King Charles XVII nods to some guards waiting at the door and Linum is removed from the room. She thinks of Judith, her brother's assigned task, and of her invisible life. Frustration, longing, and an overwhelming force of remorse sends her to her room. She slams the door behind her before the guards can even lock it and faces the window so only the birds can see her tears roll down her rosy cheeks. The tears, the precious drops of water that hold her sanity, keep rolling down her face. Each drop comes faster and more violent as her figure shakes with rage. She longs for adventure. She longs for justice. She longs for a chance to mourn what was lost. Thus, the same girl that only just a short while ago dreamed of freedom and rolling down grassy hills, now longs for revenge. She pounds the door. Kicking with all her strength, scratching at the wood with her nails until she bleeds and her feet become numb. Hours later, she crumbles down onto her knees afraid to see the animal she has become. Her nails are mangled with blood and deep cracks, and the sight of her hands causes a rainstorm. She reaches up as if praising the great ceiling only to grasp her head in sorrow and collapse against the wood of the bed. She plugs her ears, as if that would end the pain, as she thinks to herself, *No one in the castle will see me. No one in the entire kingdom would ever want me.* She is alone.

Time spreads its eternal wings and clamors around the room in an idle rush, pointless and bored, but it has a lasting grip upon Linum. She has been lying against her bed for hours in an unsuccessful attempt to reassure herself. Her tears dry on her face. The blood sticks to her fingertips and her hair is a mess. She pushes herself up with shaking arms and hobbles to the mirror, tripping over nothing. She persists, stumbling forward foot by foot. She gasps for air and heaves in a shaking breath, yawning to fulfill her exhaustion. Her reflection is of a young woman, beautiful and strong, but trapped within a living nightmare. Her shoulders hang low and her eyes droop. She takes one last look before she stumbles to the door. She knocks gently against the heavy wooden door to ask for a glass of water. Linum's bed of crumpled blankets, a tangle of brooding despair, calls to her and so she collapses upon it and waits.

Sir Brandwyn, the head guard who is often appointed to watchover Linum, and bears a silvercrested chestplate with a bright feathery helmet, peeks into her room. He glances at her and frowns, then shuts the door quickly. He returns with a glass half full. He sighs behind his metal helmet and calls to her softly, "Princess Linum, may I do anything else for you?"

This is the first time he has shown her kindness or cared to ask if she would want anything more. The guards are normally silent and cold.

Unsure of his reaction, she asks with humble intentions, "A wet rag will do," and after some hesitation she adds in a quick, "Thank you."

Brandwyn leaves and she hears the loud bang of the door shutting and the click of the key turning in place. Her heart flutters in response to the simple act of kindness, but still she is prevented from smiling. It is as if Judith's death took away her smile, for all she can see and hear is death surrounding her and suffocating her.

Faster than she expected, Sir Brandwyn returns. He throws the rag to her side and appears to mouth, "I'm sorry for your loss," but then sternly approaches and addresses her formally, "Madam your brother would like to enter. May I permit him?"

Linum nods. Her eyes are grave and reddened from tears; however, with Charles's approach, a brilliant twinkle reappears.

"I thought I was to be alone in my room Charles, unless Mother excuses me?"

"I had to come."

"Sir Brandwyn, may I have a moment in privacy with my brother?"

Brandwyn wavers at the door, his brow frozen in a state of hesitation. His feet shuffle and hands twitch. He frowns and says, "A moment and that is all." He hurries out and shuts the door tenderly behind him.

Linum embraces her brother and whispers into his ear, "So you have come for advice, huh?"

He stammers, "Well more so to say farewell."

"So you have accepted a fate?"

"The Sun has given me none."

"Then, this will not be farewell!"

She hums indignantly and repeats, "Not farewell" with a quiet resolution.

Charles, rocks in silence, his weight shifting from side to side before turning to face the window. "Lovely evening wouldn't you say?"

Linum doesn't turn to look, she stares straight and carelessly replies, "Yes, it's nice."

"I have to go soon."

"Why?"

Charles grabs her shoulders with gentle apprehension. She looks down to avoid his hazel eyes, but the tension of his gentle grasp and the worry of his quivering body forces her to reconcile with his tender smile and his worried expression. She looks nothing like her brother Charles. His neatly stacked blonde hair glows brilliantly in the evening light, while hers turns to a midnight black and embodies her frown. His face is full of light. Her tanned skin and dark brown eyes contrast his light hazel eyes and light frame. Yet, the two understand each other perfectly well and rely on one another for the similarity of companionship.

He lowers his voice greatly and whispers, "Linum, I must join Father. You know why."

Linum breaks loose of his grasp and mumbles, "Charles I cannot offer any help or any advice, but the simple suggestion of not going."

He brushes this off with an impatient tap of his foot and is drawn to the window again. He repeats, "Lovely evening, but cold night."

This time Linum turns, her face darkens with a newly bestowed remorse. She softens her tone and sweetly begins to comment on the forest of pine trees, the distant glow of the villager's houses, and the soft sentimental hush of the wind. Brandwyn knocks at the door and casually calls for Charles.

Yet, Charles lingers. Then, to the shock of Linum, he leans in close and asks, "Tell me about Judith."

With her dark eyes facing his light galaxy and near-perfect complexion, she speaks with broken words coming from a hurt heart, "I thought Father knew. I thought everyone knew. But apparently Mother sought for it to be a secret." She pauses to collect herself, "a secret must be brought to light though; this is why Father addressed Mother in that way at dinner."

"Yes, but how was she killed? What am I up against?"

Linum turns to her brother and bites her lip. She pulls in close, but tears up and pulls back away on the bed before answering, "She was dead and that's all."

"Killed by the Midnight Persecutor?"

She shakes her head and sighs, "Charles, you know you cannot go on this hunt."

"I must prove my valor to our Father. Although I despise the sword and I cannot ride, I must prove my honor tonight."

And with a final hug, Charles marches out of the room. The door shuts and her heart sinks. She whispers "farewell" to the soft breeze carrying her voice up and down in a lyrical sensation, bringing a sense of solemn silence to the brooding room and despairing woman. Linum is a better fighter than her brother. The King, Charles, and herself are aware of it, but she may not accompany him. Thus, she lies in bed, pondering over the mysterious workings of fate and praying to the Sun that his farewell may be postponed til' some later time.

Chapter 5
Shadowed Dreams

Shadows stretch across the walls of Linum's room. The shadows twist and turn until her room becomes enshrouded in darkness. Linum's eyes, with reluctance, close and she drifts off into the sweet embrace of sleep. However, sleep often brings nightmares for Linum. In Solenium it is a bad omen if you are able to remember your dreams, even when you are awake. Dream remembrance is said to be a curse, for it is proclaimed to be the reluctance to awaken in the Sun's blissful light. Linum's remembrance of her dreams has always caused suspicion to surround her, and rumors to follow her like a shadow. However, while most of her nightmares may be pushed aside and easily forgotten, some stalk the late dreamer. Her nightmares are like predators hunting prey. Nightmares kill the weak with poisonous thoughts. Linum is not weak, but her mind is so often plagued with terrible visions that even when she is awake her dreams do not stop; rather, her dreams exist only in the form of a pounding headache that longs to get free and spill its demons into her mind, and into the world.

Her body begins to shake as she tosses and turns in the bed, writhing underneath the tattered sheets. Her eyes shoot open, but her mind is elsewhere. Linum's legs kick at the air and her mouth gapes at the dreary ceiling. She is in a deep sleep of torture that brings to life an overbearing despair to her hellish dreams. Her current dream is of the world in flames surrounding her while she is strapped to her bed. The key to release her dangles not far off, but just out of arms reach to taunt her. Charles sits upon a black horse, charging through the castle walls and leaping over the flames. He tries to grasp ahold of the key to free himself from the chains that bind his hands together. Yet, the horse rears and Charles tumbles down into the fire. Queen Penelope is there as well, watching Linum. She smiles, and hums a happy tune beside the bed. Queen Penelope gets up and prances to the corner of the room, and sinks through the floor. Linum lifts her head to follow Penelope's trace, and spots her through the translucent glowing ground. Penelope is beyond the premise of Linum's room and in a deep hallway behind a locked door. She is trying to show Linum something. Then, she frowns and presses a finger to her lips.

King Charles XVII bursts into her nightmare. He rushes forward in silver armor and swings at the air with a broadsword. However, a vile creature made of shadows launches at him from the darkness. It scratches with its right claw at his silver chestplate. Linum moves her head to the right. The creature thrashes his flesh with the left claw. Linum's body slides to the left of the bed. Then, the creature fades into darkness. King Charles XVII falls through the floor and is engulfed by fire. Linum's eyes watch as Penelope prances away into the night sky, out of sight.

Fire leaps onto Linum's skin and dances. The orange flames turn blue and caress her face, then it rolls off to sit obediently by her side. When she struggles to face the flames, they shrink away revealing an unrecognizable shiny object that appears like a silver heart. A hand reaches out from the darkness to touch the shiny heart. Linum's chest glows with a throbbing pain. She beckons the flames back, but when they return they turn orange. The violent orange flames crawl onto the hand protruding from the corner to dance a demonic dance and send sparks flying into the air. Smoke falls over Linum as she gasps for breath and shudders, still bound to the chains of her bed. The shadows that engulfed King Charles XVII hover over Linum with awe and after a startling brief pause, they attack. Everything goes dark and Linum is falling. Roses surround her as she collapses into the darkness. She gasps for breath. Then, the fire engulfs her entirely within a bright flash of light.

Linum bursts forward, breaking from the nightmare. Her eyes open. Her head aches. She is embraced by the desolate reality of the night, escaping from her imprisoned sleep.

She is awake in her room, on her bed, and as pale as the twinkling stars. Sweat trickles down her face, it falls from her chin, and splashes onto the bed. Her heart pounds in recollection of the nightmare. She flings her blankets off in a hurry, looking frightfully around her room. Linum feels the dew of moisture increase above her brow. She grabs the rag that Sir Brandwyn had brought her earlier. Linum dabs at her face in vain. Her trembling hands reach for the glass of water, but she knocks the cup to the ground. The glass shatters across the floor with a loud crack, piercing her ears and ringing throughout the room. She looks up.

Linum expects the door to fly open and the guards to rush in, but silence ensues. There is no noise coming from outside the door. Not even the shuffling of feet, the usual clinking of metal, or the occasional audible yawn. Nothing. There are no lights either. Linum's voice squeaks softly like a small field mouse. She manages to call out, "Brandwyn" into the silence. Yet, she hears nothing in return. Avoiding the glass, Linum attempts to open the door. However, she finds that it is still locked. Thus, she moves swiftly back to her bed.

Linum watches as the water from her cup seeps into the floorboards. She presses her nails into the dreary blankets of the ragged bed. Linum's eyes catch sight of a faint glow protruding from the corner of her room. She crouches on her bed. Her head pounds. Her body trembles. Her breath shakes. Her heart thumps against her chest. Linum lies half up and half down. She is afraid the mattress would reach out and strangle her. Time becomes slow as it appears like the seconds turn to hours. She gulps down the cold unforgiving midnight air.

Concentrating on the corner of her room, she spies movement. Her eyes strain to make out the shape. However, it springs into light before her. Within the corner is dust, dancing before her eyes. The dust shifts from side to side with the gentle breeze of the wind. It moves vividly against the darkness of her room. The floor begins to shake. The dust rises and slams to the ground with great force. It disperses quickly to all four corners of her room. Linum straightens herself in a curious manner. She is no longer afraid, but in awe of the movement. Then, from the corner of her room, where the dust had danced, emerges a shadowed claw of ivory. The claw is followed by a scaled paw and an arm as dark as night. Then, the face of the beast appears. It is so hideous and mangled that Linum could not help but to gasp. Where there should have been eyes is a single blue flame juggling between two sockets. A green tongue appears from the horrendous mouth of the beast, its saliva is a deep blood red. The teeth are like nails, some bent and some straight. Yet, all the teeth are razor sharp. A blue spark glows from the back of the beast's mouth. The light flickers and dives downwards into its stomach. Linum stares, frozen by the beast's dancing flame. Her eyes peer into the terrible face of the monstrous beast before her.

Linum's face lacks fear. However, when she opens her mouth to speak her voice comes out small and inaudible, weak. Again she tries and her scream turns to a mighty roar, echoing across the room as if she were in a deep cavern away from the castle. A distant response sounds into the night from beyond her door, calling in return for silence.

The beast looks her up and down, sizing her up. Its claw reaches forward, dragging itself further along the floor. It scrapes the wood and slowly lets out an ear piercing screech. Another claw emerges from the corner and the beast looks at Linum with greater interest. It licks its dagger like teeth. The abyssal eyes glare with a desired passion to kill. Reaching out its claw, it swipes at Linum's face. She jumps back, barely dodging the onslaught from the beast's other monstrous claw. Yet, its spiked tail comes forth and like thorns from a rose bush, its spikes strike Linum, hitting her left arm and cutting her skin. Her arm becomes a river of blood, which seemingly pleases the beast. Its flaming eye is no longer blue; rather, the flame has turned into a brilliant shade of violent orange. The creature licks its tail in vain, its jagged teeth dribbling with fresh blood. The orange flame pauses observing the inflicted wound and appears to scan Linum's face, before settling for her throat. The beast lifts itself up with an insidious growl that shakes the room.

Linum turns to face the door, unable to move. She hears the clamor of guards and the familiar clink of metal from beyond her room. The beast hears the guards too, as its narrow ears flash up to the dry ceiling. It snarls at Linum, licking its muzzle once more as the blue light returns to the beast's throat. The creature obediently opens its mouth letting the light dribble down its chin. The blue light hangs on the sick tongue of the creature. It observes Linum for a moment, determining her worth to live. The light then thrusts itself forward and into the beast's eye, making two complete flaming sockets. The beast jumps to life. Its claws swipe at her face, centimeters away from her cheek, but then the beast freezes midair. Linum winces and presses her back against the wall. However, the beast reels back to the corner. The monstrous form fades into the wall leaving behind no trace, apart from the gashing wound on Linum's arm. The floor, which was once marked and scratched, resumes its smooth and flat appearance. The dust sways and collapses innocently in the corner. It is as if nothing had made the dust move before, concealing a secret from the world.

Linum's door swings open and crashes against the wall. The room becomes a collage of silver and bronze as the guards rush in. Linum's stand on her bed, clutching her arm. The knights appear confused. A few glance around the room with wide eyes. The others await Sir Brandwyn's command.

When Sir Brandwyn enters the room, he gapes at the wound on Linum's arm. The deep wound scales up to her shoulder. Brandwyn raises his hand. His face turns callous. When he drops his hand and gives the signal, the guards like clockwork raise their spears and surround Linum.

Sir Brandwyn turns away from her and whispers to the guard on his right. He then yells, "A lesson must be taught here tonight. You have tried so many times to escape. What a fool we have been to allow it once, but not again! You are a wretch, an inconceivable wretch. Yet, you are the eldest and heir to the throne. You are frail and weak." He addresses his fellow knights, "Look how she bleeds." He takes a small knife and jabs at her arm. "Look how her skin peels."

Linum screams in pain. She cries out desperately, "Brandwyn, please help me. Please stop it. Please."

Brandwyn turns his back on her. He continues, "Her feeble mind is not capable of the outdoors. My fellow knights I believe we must become teachers. A lesson must be learned here!" Sir Brandwyn storms away and slams the door shut. He leaves Linum to the mercy of the other guards.

Rather than being treated as a wounded survivor, Linum is thrust off the bed and onto the hard floor. The heavyset guard with a deep frown stained onto his hardened face, makes the first move. He slams the butt of his spear onto Linum's back. She screams in anguish, begging for relief as another guard chimes into the torture by kicking her. She tries to move her right arm to cover her head, but she falls short as the bronze and silver armored men overwhelm her. Time appears to stand still as Linum rolls from side to side in pain. Her face contorts as she winces and yelps. The nights swarm around her. They jab at her wounded body like vultures. She is trapped, like a cornered bear with each dog taking a turn to bite at her.

After the knights have their fill of blood, Linum is dragged from the ground to a standing position. She hangs off of the frowning guard's arm. Step by step her bruised and aching body is forced to walk out of the room.

Linum trudges along, her head is drooped like a worn out animal surrendering to the predators, awaiting the final blow. They parade through many corridors, and with each breath Linum shudders. She feels a spike of pain in her lungs when she inhales the cold air. The walls become more elaborate the farther they go. The walls expand into great patterns detailed with the Sun's outline in gold. A glittering array of portraits hang on the walls.

Each subject in the paintings on the walls, has a dim face encased by the shadows from the light of the torches. The guards stop behind an elaborately carved door. One of the guards knock and a servant opens the door. The maid's face flushes as she catches sight of Linum. The maid bows to the knights and then scurries out of the room and then rushes down the hall.

Linum enters her mother's quarters. Penelope stands looking out of her window. The melancholy breeze blows the burgundy satin curtains back and Queen Penelope's wispy brown hair towards Linum. Her posture is straight as a knife and her gaze is sharper than the blade. Her lips curl into a strict sign of disapproval. She pays no attention to the bloody and bruised form of Linum; rather, Penelope smiles at the guards and thanks them for their service. Queen Penelope takes her time to dismiss each knight by name. The searing pain becomes unbearable for poor Linum, who collapses to the ground without any support; her eyes appeal to the queen, but she is briskly ignored. Linum may only stare at Penelope's frilled orange dress that sweeps the floor as she paces. Queen Penelope strides across the room, pauses at a drawer in brief hesitation, her hand taps against the mahogany surface.

Linum whispers, "Please help me."

Penelope remains still, her eyes stare at the contents of her drawer.

"What is happening to me?" Linum moans, and clutches her shoulder. She stares gravely at Penelope and declares, "I have had dreams of fire and now I have been attacked by a hellish creature." She drops her head and her voice rattles, "I am innocent."

Penelope stays there for some time listening to the wavering pattern of Linum's choking breaths, before rushing at her. She grabs Linum and thrusts her against the bed, pointing a small tapered knife at Linum's throat. She whispers discreetly, "So you came across it."

Linum coughs, her eyes plead innocence, but Penlope presses on, "Did you?"

Linum nods, her mouth is dry and desperate for speech. Penelope retracts her arm and Linum gasps for breath. Penelope paces from side to side, waving the dagger with quick swipes at the melancholy breeze. Submerged in brooding silence, Linum tilts her head to glance at the storming Penelope. Linum notices for the first time how many grey hairs are creeping through her long brown hair. Penelope's age is showing tonight and it seems to make her out as vulnerable. She wears it well though, almost as a disguise.

A crooked smile creeps onto Penelope's face and she speaks without warmth, "Well then, what a poor darling you are. Consider yourself lucky, for it is a taste of what is to come, that's all it was–" her voice trails off becoming inaudible for some time as if she is chanting curses underneath her breath. Penelope breaks the unbearable silence, she clears her throat, and she mutters, "And all along I thought Judith might serve as a lesson to you."

As if lightning strikes Linum, she bursts to life springing upwards with renewed strength, "Judith! What did you do to her!"

"Nothing, nothing, I saved her. Ended her. Did away with what was left of her." She looks Linum over with a disapproving scowl, "Did you really think of her as your friend? A mother perhaps? A monster can never be a mother! You should know that, you wretched girl." Penelope hurries over to the drawer and places the knife delicately inside. "Sometimes you impress me with your strength, but you will always continue to disappoint me and everyone."

Linum charges at Queen Penelope, clutching her wounded arm and yelling. As a result of Linum's injuries she is easily tossed aside. Penelope holds her down against the cold floor. Linum is trapped. Penelope presses down harder and Linum winces.

"You silly girl! You *fool.* You should be thanking me, you should be bowing down. I won't be your mother any longer, but you should be happy about that. You should be *overjoyed* to hear those words." With a sinister laugh, Penelope gathers her composure to state, "Judith is dead on my behalf and I am glad to say that I did it."

In frustration Linum yells back in anger and spite, "You monster! You monster..." Her voice trails off as her strength fails her and her head falls back. Linum's skin grows pale.

Penelope turns with reddened eyes and cheeks stained with tears. She leans in close and hugs Linum's exhausted face to her chest, "Perhaps, you will understand in time. This world is changing at every second, the curse has begun. I hope then you do not think so cruelly of me as you do now. There are reasons you are kept locked away." Penelope's mouth opens and closes as she tries to compose her strength. Her voice is hoarse, but she commands, "I did what had to be done for everyone's sake." She turns away from Linum and claps her hands together. The guards rush in and pull Linum out.

Sir Brandwyn yells out commands with a heart of stone. His pale eyes look above the gory display. "Lock her in her room, but do not let her try to deceive you." He catches a glance of Penelope and adds, "Runaways need to be punished."

Linum tries to fight, but she has no strength, her arms fall limp by her side. She is pulled away. The guards scratch at her back and she feels their nails dig into her skin.

She manages to whisper one last time, "You monster," as Penelope fades from her vision.

The sudden burst of energy is gone and Linum is left alone in her room, sobbing. She is weak and vulnerable. She sits on her bed dabbing at her wounds with the sheets. Linum watches the corner with mindful eyes, but in trepidation she dares herself to look at the door. Tentatively she waits, expecting the beast to reappear, but nothing stirs from the corner. The dust sits still, watching and waiting. With the sheets tied roughly around her arm, Linum closes her eyes. She feels the throbbing of her head. She wipes away the warm liquid from her hands. Linum hears the call of the nightingale and she gently turns her face to look outside. The stars appear painted in the sky, with the gentle blue and purple colors mixing together in a soft canvas. Slowly she lowers her head and drifts off into a restless sleep out of pure exhaustion and faintness of strength.

The morning is uneasily peaceful and is followed by a great feast shared among Linum and Penelope who sit in silence, ignoring each other's presence. The banquet table overflows with pleasant smells and fresh baked goods, but Linum refuses to eat. There is now a shadow falling across the empty chairs, where her father and brother had sat the night before. Linum's attention is fixed to the centerpiece of the table, a bouquet of roses. The flowers are brilliant, well cut and positioned with power. Their gentle pink, yellow, and orange petals all glow magnificently in the Sunlight. However, Linum is focused on the single red rose. The red rose is beautiful. However, the red rose is dry and limp. It hangs over the side of the metal vase with a serene appearance. Linum admires it for its beauty, but she pities it, for it has lost its vibrant color and strength. A maid traces Linum's locked vision to the single red rose. She sees that it is a dead rose, rushes forward, and plucks it from the vase. The maid's face flushes and she scurries away, embarrassed by the mistake of letting such a meek and unfruitful rose be in the presence of the two royals. Linum's dark eyes flash down in disappointment.

Spontaneously, the doctor enters. He waves his dainty hands in the air and struts up to the table. He smiles at Linum and glances at Penelope, then with a sigh reprimands the injury by repeating, "In the Sun's grace! Oh dear! Oh my!" as if this was new and unexpected within his profession. His beady self-approved eyes scan her body and his tongue clicks at every scrape he witnesses on her skin. Linum avoids his eyes as he unties the makeshift sheet bandage. She grows annoyed by each and every "Oh my," which increases in succession as he applies ointment. Her mind drifts off restlessly for a voyage that she will never undertake. Yet, Linum is drawn back to reality through curiosity, caused by her interest in the curious roses. The roses are trapped in the vase physically perfect. Although they appear blossomed and whole, they are dried of experience. The roses in the vase can never taste the chill of the cold morning dew, never know what the warmth of the Sun feels like, and never sprout from the nurturing soil. Other roses grow timidly outside with the blessed fresh air and faith of the Sun beaming on them.

The Sunlight falls across Linum's brown eyes making them glow brilliantly. The light lingers there, but Linum evades it. She gathers her composure and leaves the table. The doctor sighs and slams his dull medical kit aside. He takes Linum's seat, and embellishes the empty plate with the dazzling display of food. Penelope's cold eyes trace Linum as she leaves, but she makes no comment in objection.

No guards follow Linum as she walks to her room. Linum's long black hair grazes against the wound. She winces and tightens the cloth bandage before continuing her walk. Her room is empty, quiet, and warm. It welcomes her to take a seat on her bed and close her heavy eyes. She listens to the sounds of the birds chirping and tweeting of their endeavors. The sounds of the citizens actively bustling about. Time moves on like the morning birds taking flight, it jumps from here to there and soars all around the Kingdom of Dalium. Nothing stirs, which draws Linum's attention to the door cracked open, the way she has left it. There is no sound of metal clinking nor of maids hurrying about. Nothing. Linum lifts herself up and musters the courage to push the door, it wobbles and sways to her command. It opens with no one waiting outside, except the prospective freedom of the empty hall. In silence Linum shuts the door behind her, grimacing at each creak. She takes her first few steps out into the open arms of freedom. The floorboards echo at each step, bellowing like beating drums and thumping to the beat of her heart.

Linum moves across the hall with trepidation lingering in her fleeting glances. The castle appears asleep in the late morning as nothing stirs other than her. The gash on her arm still bleeds. The warmth of the blood trickles down her arm drop by drop, sending a cold chill up her spine. Her ears strain, for they are listening for any sound of knights shuffling to and fro. Yet, she hears nothing and her breathing becomes heavy. She stops, her eyes fix on a slow moving drop of blood, squeezing through the soaking bandage. It trickles down her arm, sending another cold chill up her spine, as it falls against the floor. More blood droplets fall to the floor, spiraling downwards. The blood droplets take the shape of a rose falling with great passion. The wound itself begins to churn. The bandage is stripped away as Linum's injury turns and twists into a blood red rose. Thorns emerge from the blood swaying and dancing before Linum. As if in a trance she chases after the dropping petals, trying to catch them. However, the petals only crumble in her hands. The petals pull her forward and the blood red rose glistens in morning light. Linum's surroundings darken. The familiar warm hallway of the castle turns brooding, cold, and dark before her entranced eyes. Linum's bloody fingerprints rest on the doorknob, watching as Linum runs away through the many halls. The thorns creep up across her arm, engulf her chest, and crawl up her spine.

Yet, Linum is unaware of all of this since the petals keep dancing before her, drawing her deeper into the unknown darkness. The stem engulfs her, tangling around her legs. Her eyes are covered in a milky white film as she smiles in a trance. Her body sways like the falling bloody petals. Her torso bleeds because she is covered by the thorns from the rose growing from her wound. The thorns jab at her. Her legs become twisted into the knot of a rose bush as the sharpened leaves and pointed thorns cover her neck. A petal falls and crumbles across her eyes. It creates a ripple of sparkling dust that explodes across Linum's face. The milky white film dissolves and Linum gasps for air. Her eyes return to a dark brown.

Linum awakes from the trance. She trembles in fear, for her surroundings are unfamiliar and dark. She is no longer in the Castle of Dalium. Yet, her strange surroundings, although eerie in its appearance, is appealing to her. There are lights flashing on the distant ceiling, blue, purple, grey, and a violent red. Each light display makes the darkness appear more beautiful. Linum attempts to move, however, the roses have her strapped down to the floor. She is stuck laying face up to look at the lights. The twinkling lights keep growing brighter. Their pulsating glow begins to blind Linum. The flashing becomes unbearable to witness as the lights turn menacing. Linum begins to struggle against the tightly coiled stems. She wiggles her head and yelps in pain. The thorns press down harder. Linum presses her eyes shut. She opens them and draws in a deep breath as a shadowy figure peers at her.

The figure stands over Linum, masked by the flashing lights and the surrounding darkness. Linum tries to make out a face but the light blinds her. She hears a distant voice call out. It is a gentle voice. The distant figure cries out in harsh grumbled words. Yet, there is a sense of familiarity in the tone of voice that protrudes a greater sense of fear over the blinded Linum. The rose on her arm stabs at her, the thorns jab, the stem grows, and it covers her face. Thus, the rose makes it impossible for her to see. The faraway voice grows nearer. She hears a distinct hissing sound as it comes closer. The figure standing over her, kicks at her leg. Linum bites her lip. She does not want to make a noise. The hissing sound stops abruptly. Linum can tell the other figure has arrived, for she hears the gentle voice.

It says, "This is the girl?" The voice laughs bitterly and it changes from gentle to harsh. It booms with a vicious intensity, "Step aside."

"She is not a fighter, she is weak. Gave in easily. I could have killed her there and then. My beast could have ended her. Mistress, she could have been dead already. But let me finish the job. Let me prove myself to you," responds the first figure. The figure's voice quivers in intensity and hints at fear.

"No, not now. You already have proven that you can fail me, this does not make up for *that*. I will do it if I must. You go and await me," replies a harsh, cruel, and unforgiving voice.

"Yes Mistress."

Linum hears the other figure walk away. She attempts to steady her breathing.

The cruel voice yells, "Maintain the breach."

The voice is twisted. It shakes with anger, but it sounds so familiar that Linum winces in trying to make it out. Thus, turning the attention of the figure to her. It perches over her, observing Linum. Linum can not move and silence ensues. She can make out the sound of water dripping from what must be a nearby stream. The air is cold as it stings Linum each time she takes a breath. Then, a screech so shrill and awful sounds. It erupts from the silence and it forces Linum's hair to stand on end. Linum tries to move her arms to cover her ears, but the stem of the rose bush holds her down. She can feel the thorns press harder into her skin and the warmth of fresh blood rush over her.

Linum's body shoots up into the air then drops to the ground. She is cushioned by the same rose stem that has engulfed her. She is higher up now and balanced on a small damp rock. Linum remains still for if she moves, she is sure that she will plunge to her death. Another blood curdling screech sounds, but this time it is followed by a gentle songlike voice. The gentle voice echoes from the walls, suggesting that Linum must be in a cavern. It repeats, "To the Mountains of the Sun Blessed Everglades."

Linum begins to ponder the words of the song. It sounds too familiar to her; she knows that she has heard of it before. Then, the song is disrupted by the cruel voice of the figure. Linum feels immense pain shoot through her body as the repetition of the song fades.

The figure's voice turns sweet with an underlying growl, "Do you remember me?"

The sweet voice stings Linum. It hurts her more than the screech.

The figure calls her name lyrically, "Linum." It continues to taunt her, "Linum, it's time to get up."

The voice pauses as if waiting for Linum to respond. Moisture settles above her brow as a dark realization creeps upon her. She identifies the voice, but her heart begs to differ. She is speechless, not because of the rose bush covering her, but out of the fear of the silence that ensues. Linum is afraid of the response if she does speak. She trembles at the thought of giving the figure a name, to acknowledge that she *knows* the figure's name. The voice grows bored of waiting for a response. It loosens the stem around Linum's mouth to make sure that she can speak.

It waits for a moment, but is obviously unpleased by her silence. Thus, it cries out mockingly, "Do you have no words for me? Do you not know who I am? Do you hold your silence over your life?"

Linum responds to the figure, her voice is strong and patient, despite her fear, "I do not wish to name you."

"Then you will die clueless as to who I am."

Linum winces as the thorns press further into her skin, prying for an answer. "End me now so I will no longer crave the world around me," replies Linum with impudence.

"Very well." The figure's voice, being unsatisfied with Linum's response, presses on for a reaction. It taunts, "Did *she* not imprison you? I know that Penelope made you suffer. You were tormented for a crime that you did not commit. Did she make you pay and were you in fact sorry for *me*? Yet, you gave me what I wanted. You whittled the key to my plot! How could a servant be a sorceress so great and powerful as I, and yet use no magic to get you to do what I ask?"

Linum's heart drops as she refuses to accept the identity of the figure before her. She prevails in silence.

"Possession, it appears the weak mortals long for it." The shrill voice howls with laughter.

Linum trembles with hatred.

Then, with death's voice, the figure names itself, "You are correct in your assumptions, Linum. I controlled her and I became her. I am Judith. But I am also—"

A great cackle arises, but it is shortly disturbed by the yelling of the other figure from before. It shouts with a deep voice, "Mistress, I cannot maintain the breach any longer!"

The following words are muddled by the onslaught of the sweet heavenly song coming from the walls, "To the Mountains of the Sun Blessed Everglades." With a great flash of light the rose bush snaps, dries, and crumbles around Linum, freeing her. The deceitful Judith figure screams. Linum rubs her eyes and searches through the darkness to spot her oppressors. However, Judith's features are unrecognizable since she is shielded by the flashing lights. Linum scrambles to her feet. She balances herself upon the edge and peers at her surroundings. She is in a cavern. Linum takes a trembling step forward. The icy air no longer pains her, instead it refreshes her. She hurries towards the Judith figure, yelling wildly in hatred. As she runs, she hears pebbles tumbling down. She was resting on the edge of a cliff in the cavern. Linum charges at Judith. Her head pounds. She begins to feel faint. The Judith figure turns slowly to face Linum. However, Linum is only able to make out the figure's maroon dress as a result of the flashing light. Linum's vision fades as the world appears to spin. She stumbles backwards and then falls off the edge. Her heart races. Her breath shakes. Her head is dizzy. Then, she hears a loud bang. A comforting warm feeling travels through her body. Her skin glows and she draws in a steady breath. Her surroundings grow dark and she closes her eyes.

Linum awakes in her bed, covered with sweat. She looks around her room, frantically throwing off her tattered covers. Her arm is no longer cut, it is only marked with a faint scar, and there are no signs of bruises or any scratches.

The guards rush in with spears pointed, one of them yells, "What in the Sun's name is going on in here!"

Linum turns away from them. Then, she catches sight of a single dried red rose lying limp in the corner of her room. It is embellished with the watching dust. She collapses.

Chapter 6
Destiny in the Dark

The great glorious Sun glows a furious shade of orange and begins to set behind the distant dark mountains of Crystal Common Grounds. The Sun lingers there. Its radiant glow twists, turns, and paints the sky a magnificent dark purple and appraises the dismal faint lights from the faroff. The satin burgundy curtains twist and churn with violent apprehension, crackling with the apprehending wind. The sound of the wind and the flapping of the curtains, awakens Linum. She jolts upright. Her brown eyes twinkle as she yawns and stretches. She takes in her surroundings carefully. The bed she lies on is soft and well cushioned, the sheet is a luxurious burgundy that matches the flapping curtains. She has been undressed, and thus pulls forward the sheets, while observing her body and notices that it lacks the wounds she once bore. For a moment she sighs a breath of relief and affords herself a quick conscious laugh. Such comfort is unknown to Linum for never has she felt a bed so soft, but in recalling the rose, the beast, and the monstrous Judith she turns to face the corners of the room, breaking away from her momentary bliss.

A young man sits in the far corner of the room. He is tall and quite handsome with a strong face, and he has gentle blue eyes contrasting with his dark brown hair. He appears to be around eighteen years of age to twenty. The man wears a dark black vest over a surcoat cut short at his waist with puffy sleeves and rough knightly pants with black boots. He looks down with no apparent desire to speak to the inquisitive Linum, who observes him from the bed as he stares at the floor. The golden light of the Sun enlightens the room, filling it with a warm glow as the light attempts to cling to the walls. The golden light streams through Linum's hair and falls lifeless on the man's vigorous face. She eyes the man while running her fingers along the bed cover. Linum examines the entirety of the room as if seeing it for the first time in her life. It is a huge room with grand windows and columns, with a balcony view of the entire Kingdom of Dalium, and a delicate harp besides a crooked wooden desk, mahogany drawers, and multiple mirrors. The man stirs slightly, his soft ocean blue eyes catch Linum's dark eyes and he turns away, his face reddening.

Linum stares at him. She knows that she has not met him before. He is not one of the knights that guard her. However, she decides that she will question him. She hesitantly asks, "Why have I been moved here? Who are you?"

The man remains silent. He stands and cocks his head upright, turning away from her.

She tries again more earnestly in a futile attempt at communication, "I remember I was wounded, did you attend to my wounds?"

At this he responds with a sigh and snidefully mutters, "Was it only a nightmare, princess?"

With great offense taken, Linum glares at him. He jeers at her with a false smile and given awareness of

Linum's anger he continues coolly, "You had a bad dream and woke half the
castle! Gave myself and the other guards quite a start though. Your mother is disappointed and the king frowns upon your actions. I am your appointed knight, a caretaker for a seventeen year old, what a *shame*."

He emphasizes "shame" prudently with mocking eyes as the blue twists and churns like the violent sea, delighted at having ensnared Linum in frustration. Her fists curl as she glances daggers towards the young man, who abruptly turns to face Queen Penelope. Penelope enters with a prudent stride, deliberate and cautious in her movements. With obedience and a slight frown of disappointment, the appointed knight retreats to his corner.

She takes in Linum's furious appearance before remarking casually, "Awake are you not?"

Linum nods grudgingly, her eyes are locked onto Penelope with hatred.

Queen Penelope continues her stride to the window, she stares with little interest at the violet sky. "Well you have quite a day ahead of you, Linum. You shall retreat to your room and attend dinner. That is all I will have to hear of you, at dinner and only at dinner. Enough dreaming, it is time for you to remain in your room and learn how to be a lady. And to be sure you do not have a nighttime catastrophe again, Zoren will be your appointed knight." She gestures to the young man in the corner, who bows his head towards Linum.

Linum begins to protest, but Penelope cuts her off with a stern and cruel look, "You caused chaos throughout the castle which sent your guards into a panic. Zoren was the only knight who had any sense! He revived you. Your heart stopped beating you wretched girl! You should be on your knees thanking him rather than protesting his very being. You did not just faint, you were in the grave."

Linum glances at him, sizing him up, but her eyes fall short of recognition. He is not one of the guards that beat her; they were taller and more muscular. Zoren lacks an overbearing muscular build, he is rather lean but still strong in appearance.

Linum faces Penelope, shaking with rage, "You told the guards to beat me, and you locked me away." Linum's voice drops, she pleads, "Why won't you tell me what's going on?"

Penelope's eyes are full of despair, she dares Linum to make another sound. In silence they both exchange hateful glances until Zoren speaks up, "Your Majesty, I believe she still suffers from delusions as a result of the nightmare. With your approval I can escort her back to her room to ensure she makes a full recovery. Also, if you would like, I may report any abnormalities in her behavior."

Penelope jumps, startled by the sound of his voice, as if she forgot he is there. She nods, her expression grim. She speaks with a quivering voice, whispering, "Just a nightmare." Penelope turns away from Linum, clenching the pillar in front of her and leaning her aged body against it.

Linum glides out of the bed, wrapping herself in the burgundy sheets. She takes a confused and solemn glance back at Penelope and scans the room. The satin curtains fall restlessly against the curtain pane. However, Penelope remains slouched against the pillar, Linum can see her trembling. The queen coughs. Linum's voice turns cold and she whispers loud enough for Penelope to hear, "And you lied. Judith still lives."

Penelope stares wildly at Linum. Her mouth gapes open and her face is that of true fear. Her body trembles and she shakes her head in disbelief. Linum begins to walk away. She hobbles at first and Zoren rushes forward to help her. Linum slaps away Zoren's extended hand, expressing her ability to walk. She hears Penelope sob and let out a pitiful wail. However, Linum does not stop. She walks quickly out of Penelope's room. Zoren trails behind, allowing Linum to lead the way to her room.

Zoren diligently waits outside as Linum pulls on an olive chiffon dress and combs her hair. She examines her appearance in the mirror and tries to see if she is able to inspect the corner of her room. She twirls and the green dress spins with her, appearing like the bud of a blossoming flower. Linum draws in her courage. She looks at the corner of her room and notices that the rose is no longer present; rather, there is a pile of crumbled petals. She takes a step forward and the petals ignite into a vibrant blue flame, turning to ash as she draws closer. Linum draws in a shaking breath. She scoops up the ash in her hands and observes its glittering remains, then lets it seep through her fingers and fall to the hard floor. Her head pounds. *Judith, the beast, the song, and now a new knight.* Her head begins to spin and she groans, leaning on her bed for support. She sighs at the sound of Zoren knocking on her door.

Knowing that she may not avoid the inevitable, Linum opens her door to face Zoren. Zoren, who once appeared sour and callous, smiles with his oceanic eyes and bows his head. He steps in and Linum moves aside, watching carefully with mistrustful eyes as he examines her quarters.

He places a cold hand onto the bleak wall, his oceanic eyes stare at the dusty corner, "It is quite dreary in here. I can see why you hate being locked up." Zoren swiftly turns to face her, and with a pleasant and triumphant smile inquires, "So are we going to search for your brother, princess?"

Linum's eyes widen as she tries to search for a sign of malicious sarcasm, but she only spies sincerity in his beaming face.

He moves closer to the window, his hand restlessly toys with his empty scabbard. Zoren reassures her speculation, "We have a lot of land to cover if we are to hunt down the Midnight Persecutor."

"Who are you?" she whispers in disbelief at his sudden change.

He pauses for a moment, his eyes dart to the window and he appears to feel the words he says with great caution, "I am Zoren, eighteen years of age. I made a name for myself by joining the royal guard." He faces Linum, "And as your appointed knight I may grant this search for the benefit of the entire Kingdom of Dalium," he takes a step towards her and adds, "I apologize for my adverse speech earlier, but I did not want to be looked upon as sympathetic."

Linum nods, her mind wanders off to the distant fields and the great clouds. She imagines the ocean surrounding her, splashing at her feet and the Great Sun tenderly kissing her rosy cheeks.

She lets out a pleasant sigh, turning her attention back to the young attentive Zoren standing before her. She says, "Let us slay the Midnight Persecutor."

Zoren leads the way, pushing open the stale door to the luminous hall glowing dim in comparison to the bursting light of the moon settled in the night sky. Linum touches the door, pressing her fingers into the ridges and tracing the familiar scratches. She glares at the keyhole, despising whatever plot she contributed to and how she had been deceived by Judith. Zoren senses her uneasiness. "Adventure awaits, princess," he urges her forward.

Linum sighs at yet another chance of freedom. Her eyes glisten and she laughs, closing the door with great satisfaction, she strides beside Zoren. They pass through the many halls in silence, waving to empty corridors and flashing quick glances around corners. When they walk by the dining room, full of candle light and eager faces of maids and servants, cleaning the tables, setting fresh metal plates in neat stacks on carved wooden trays, and placing fresh roses into empty vases, they pause. Linum observes the maids and servants, she notices how dutifully they work. She frowns at the thought that they will not even notice her absence since so few actually know of her existence. She has lived a shadowed life in the castle. Zoren peers ahead, twisting and turning his head, cocking an ear in anticipation of some kind of sound, but finding none, he turns to Linum with a satisfied gleam of approval and carries forward. He turns into the ominous hall leading to the forsaken door where death had lingered in the recent days.

Linum frowns and shudders as a cold dry wind blows through the hall and cracks open the door, Zoren signals for her to follow. Linum remains still. Impatient, he flashes a quick annoyed glance at Linum, raises his brow and beckons for her to follow with a tinge of aggression in his rapid movements. She takes a step forward, grasping onto the barren wall for support. Her hand lingers in the air to reach for the grim knob of the ghastly door, before she turns back, retreating to the farside of the hall. Linum looks straight ahead at the heavy garden door with a silver crested latch and detailed windows beaming due to the moonlight.

In a harsh whisper Zoren calls, "Linum, this way."

She turns frightened by the sound of his voice, coming from the hall. The door to her right appears to darken further into a growing spread of hatred and demise.

She shakes her head and calls back, "I cannot. The door to the garden is before us, but that door will lead us nowhere... except to an empty storage room."

She knows that she is lying to herself, for the door where she witnessed death firsthand, could never be *just* an empty storage room.

"Linum, it is just a room so we can gather supplies. I already scoped out what is in there, I believe it will be useful."

She walks up to him, meeting his bluish grey eyes that churn and twist and change like the sea, and gathering her composure she reaches for his arm. She slides her hand delicately down into his and holds it, still eyeing him with intense concentration. Pulling in she reaches out with her other arm, sliding her hand behind his neck. With a sudden change in expression Linum shoves him against the wall, pins his arm behind his back, and presses down on his head with her left hand.

"Who are you?" she demands. "What do you really want?"

Confused and startled he responds, stammering, "I am Zoren, your appointed knight!"

"I've never seen you before in my life! Until this morning, after the strange event last night occurred with the roses and the creatures and–"

"Linum, I honestly am not here to harm you," he pleads. His eyes widen and his hands fight to push hers away. "I just got appointed."

Still unsatisfied with his response, she pulls in close, whispering fast, "If you're a knight, then why are you dodging corners and avoiding being seen? And what do *you* desire with this particular room?"

"Please, I can explain, but we need to act fast."

She pulls back, relinquishing her grip on him, daring him to move with her steady dark eyes. He stays against the wall, panting in relief, clutching his empty scabbard. Like prey becoming aware of a predator, he scurries behind Linum, drawing her closer to the door as she inquires more of him.

"Why did you appear after Judith died?" She corrects herself, "Well, after I thought she died."

He creeps back, keeping distance between himself and her, lowering his voice, "I don't know who Judith is, sorry."

She presses on, "Did you really find me after a so-called nightmare occurred, and do you believe it was more than that?"

Desperately he chimes, "You fainted and there was no sign of an attack, so we brought you to the queen. That's all I know, but I'll believe you if you claim there is something more." Zoren glares at Linum and with urgency he commands, "All I need you to do right now is listen to me."

Linum freezes and Zoren's face flushes as footsteps sound from the other hallway and the doors of the dining room open further. He grabs ahold of Linum's hand and pulls her to him, opening the barren door muttering, "Get in, now."

She obeys, grudgingly. Linum flashes a daring glance at the hall in anticipation of being seen, but both of them manage to get behind the door and pull it shut before the footsteps can be heard turning the corner to go down the dismal hall. The room is dark and the air is thick with a foreboding presence of despair. Zoren consoles Linum by placing a reassuring hand on her shoulder and an apathetic smile upon his credulous face. He gestures at the grave emptiness of the room. She stares forward, resigned to the circumstances, but solemn in a firm state of fear. She no longer mourns over the memory of Judith, but recalls the hopelessness of seeing the dejected body and the feeling of the warm blood spread upon her arms.

A great rustling sound stirs Linum to life with a renewed consciousness of the present moment, in seeing Zoren shove and push the empty chests around, flipping over barrels, and tossing aside blank parchment.

He shakes his head frantically, appearing wild and disgruntled with his surroundings. He declares to himself, rather than to Linum, "It's not here!"

"What's not here?" she inquires with furious haste. Linum skeptically observes him. She questions, "I thought you scoped this room out?"

He spins around, facing her with immense exasperation and haughtily replies, "I did."

The room is empty and desolate, lacking color and light as it dismally soaks in dust.
Linum narrows her gaze at the numerous shelves. "I do not understand why Judith had me carve the key to unlock this room. There had to have been something quite special in here."

Zoren nods his head, hardly paying any attention to her at all. He scans the room, impatiently touching his empty scabbard tapping against his waist. Linum's attention is drawn to it, she stares riddled with concern at the man of mystery standing before her.

She sighs, "Why do you carry an empty scabbard?"

"I was instructed to remove my sword so you would not attempt to disarm me," he replies half conscious of her presence and with a tiresome heave of a huge box of scrolls he cries out with pitiful excitement, "Aha. For you."

Linum reaches out to grab the small wrapped item, it glistens in her hand and stands out within the dismal display of the small brooding room. She unsheaths it letting the cloth drop to her feet and she blows away the dust to reveal a small dagger, the blade only as long as her hand. A miniscule flicker of appreciation appears only momentarily in her eyes, but with a quick blink and shaking of her head, she complacently examines Zoren. His misty ocean eyes are filled with exuberant determination as he reaches further into the shelf and pulls forward another wrapped object. Like her, he unsheaths it. He lets the dry cloth drop at his feet and examines the large blade, while sliding it into his scabbard with regard and a triumphant wink at Linum.

He presses his ear against the door and determining it is safe to leave he pushes it open, letting it collide with a great bang against the stubborn wall. Linum steps out, quickening her pace as Zoren begins to run towards the glorious garden door with heavy silver latches. She chases after his side, exclaiming in hurried breaths, "Why did you do that?"

"Give you the dagger or slam the door?"

"Both."

"If we encounter the Midnight Persecutor we must be armed. Not to mention, we are leaving this blasted castle, so we might as well make it quite an exit!"

He exclaims this with facetious excitement as he dashes against the garden door, pressing his face against its silver crested latch, and pulls forward a key. It flies open and he lets the key fall from his hand, reaching out for Linum to follow. She runs through the open doorway looking at the beautiful night sky and the twinkling diamond stars enshrining the crescent moon. Gentle wisps of dark fog settles across the stone city resting beyond the large walls. She takes in her surroundings and smiles at the beautiful display of roses creeping up upon the castle. Zoren nudges her forward, taps her shoulder, and bows with a benevolent gesture to the garden path and the stone walls surrounding them.

He whispers to her, "Beyond the garden gate, I promise you adventure awaits."

"Why would you trust me to the arms of freedom? No knight has ever offered me this chance to explore Dalium," she whispers back to him.

Zoren smiles. "I believe in justice, princess." He motions to the garden gates, "I believe that you deserve freedom."

The two rush forward at the sound of the clinking of knightly metal approaching from inside the castle walls. They run to the heavy wooden gate, where a bored gatekeeper sits, lounging against the metal lever that is used to haul open the gate in times of great danger.

Zoren yells at the man, bellowing, "Open the gate by the official command of Princess Linum's appointed knight!"

Surprised, the gatekeeper lifts his beige cloth coif and trembles at the sound of another human voice. Slowly he peers over the edge and calls back, "Identification."

Zoren looks down critically, searching himself for some kind of seal, while Linum steps forward echoing, "I am Linum, the princess, and he is my appointed knight. It is urgent that we are let out immediately."

The gatekeeper shuffles toiling with the metal lever and sheepishly calls back, "Your highness, I cannot let you out."

"You must, for it is Queen Penelope's order," chimes in Zoren, revealing a small glistening object in his palm that glitters under the reflection of the night sky.

The man peers at Zoren from above. He lifts his hand above his eyes and scratches his rough chin before tossing aside his coif and exclaiming, "Right away sir!"

The gate rattles to life, lifting ever so slightly inch by inch upwards. It clings reluctantly to the stone wall and screeches in action. The guards tumble outside the grand garden door and Linum stares impatiently at the rising gate, that is barely above their thighs.

The knights bellow in unison, "Shut the gate," to the poor old gatekeeper who scratches his head with mild confusion before pulling down on the rising lever.

Sir Brandwyn, who stands ahead of the guards, holding a blazing torch, glares at Linum, beckoning her to come to him. His voice quivers with fear as he pleads,

"Linum, come back here peacefully and get away from *him* and that gate."

Linum exchanges a quick glance with Zoren. She nods her head and smiles. Linum stands back and dives underneath the gate to escape. Zoren follows, scraping against the rough metal lining, the hilt of his sword gets caught in the metal.

"Damn! This is why I don't carry swords," he exclaims exasperated, not in the least intimidated by Brandwyn, who approaches triumphantly.

Linum exchanges a frightened glance between Sir Brandwyn and the trapped Zoren. The gate slowly presses itself downwards onto Zoren's back.

Linum reaches into the folds of her dress pulling out the miniature dagger begging, "Please! Sir Brandwyn, it's going to crush him!"

Brandwyn looks at her in earnest disbelief over whom she has sided with. He approaches the gate and bangs on it with his curled fist, glaring at Linum.

"Linum, put down the dagger. No one needs to get hurt, trust me." Sir Brandwyn urges her.

She shakes her head and cries out, "Open the gate now!" The old gatekeeper turns away and faces the night stars.

Zoren groans and Sir Brandwyn calls out to Linum again. He harshly yells, "I said stand down."

She bites her lip and reassures her mind, transfixed in ambivalence, she throws the dagger at the old innocent gatekeeper. It pierces his hand and he tumbles downwards cursing at the cold ominous air. The gate pulls upward, relieving Zoren to move and wiggle the hilt of his sword free from the grasp of the metal gate that screeches in anguish as he jolts forward into the open arms of freedom.

Sir Brandwyn roars out in anger, "Linum, do not dare betray the Kingdom of Dalium!"

Linum and Zoren run down the grassy hills bathed in brilliant moonlight. The glow from the midnight sky makes the hills appear silver. Brandwyn and the guards create a fierce fiery trail behind the two runaways. They hold their torches up to the Heavens and chase after Linum and Zoren. Linum looks behind her. *I'm finally free*, she thinks to herself. Then, she trips on her dress forcing Zoren to collapse down the hill as well. When they stand they are surrounded by Brandwyn and the rest of the stone-hearted guards with swords drawn and pointed at their throats. Linum turns with bold ferocity, stepping closer to the impeding blades positioned at her neck.

Zoren closes his eyes and informs the guards, "I am armed." He inquires, "May I remove my weapon?"

Brandwyn nods at another guard in gleaming copper, who lowers his weapon, giving enough room for Zoren to unsheath the blade from his scabbard and drop it at his feet.

"Linum, drop your weapons as well," hisses Brandwyn.

Looking past the guards with a plain uninterested smile, she replies coolly, "I have none to drop."

Threatening her with his blade, Brandwyn pulls closer and spits in her face, "I said drop your weapons!"

"And I said that I have none!" She declares with impudence, "None other than the weapon that currently remains in the gatekeeper's hand."

Brandwyn whips his metal coated hand out and strikes Linum across her face. She reaches up, touching her reddened cheek in pain. Yet, she continues to taunt Brandwyn with the intention of quarreling in hand to hand combat.

Passive and fed up with the tedious display before him, Zoren yawns and remarks casually, "Had enough yet?"

"How dare you abduct Princess Linum!" Brandwyn booms at Zoren, his eyes are as cold and dismissive of the young man as the grave is welcoming.

Brandwyn launches on him and Zoren takes a fist to the nose, but to Brandwyn's dismay it does not break nor appear marked; rather, Brandwyn's metal gauntlet cracks before his very eyes revealing his tender bruised skin underneath. In disbelief he moves to strike Zoren again, this time with his blade, but he finds himself unable to lift his arm. Linum gasps in astonishment at the fanciful feats that had just occurred. The other guards take a step back, weary of the abilities possessed by the young man before them.

Sir Brandwyn murmurs, "This is impossible." He strikes again with his blade. This time his blade bounces off Zoren. It falls to the ground and melts.

The sword resting at Zoren's feet begins to churn and bubble, bursting forward like a lion stalking its prey. The sword pounces onto Brandwyn, demolishing his exposed flesh and striking at him with increased intensity. The silver crested guards shout in disbelief, but like Brandwyn they find themselves unable to move as their armor encases them, bringing them to their knees, choking them with their own hands.

Zoren turns away, reveling in success and leaving the others to their demise, he sweetly calls for Linum to follow, praising her rash bravery out loud.

She too is overwhelmed by the events that unfolded and as she resigns to follow after Zoren, she hears Brandwyn whisper into the night sky, "She is dead. Linum, the queen is dead."

And with the horrified exchange of glances between Brandwyn and Linum, her heart sinks. Her face glows a ghostly white, she clutches her stomach in pain, and her face scrunches and strains as she looks at the rough soil. Linum bellows out in hopelessness, a pitiful moan, and she races to Brandwyn's rescue. She attempts to pry loose the suffocating armor clinging to him, he manages to grab a hold of her arm and pleads, "Go."

She turns to watch the grave faces of the guards resting dejectedly on the ground, she is caught between leaving and the somber attempt to help. Her feet shuffle back and forth as she shakes Sir Brandwyn's armor, which sticks to his skin and lashes at him while ignoring her pitiful attempts to save him.

"Go save yourself," cries Brandwyn desperately.

"Zoren, save them!" Begs Linum, her voice straining with guilt.

Yet, Zoren keeps walking forward as if he did not hear her plea. At the sound of her voice rising up and down with desperation, she heaves in deep breaths of air and gasps while tears stream down her face, he pauses, shifting from side to side.

"Help them please..." Her voice trails off.

He faces her with frivolous attention and pronounces loudly, "It won't save them," and with a great sigh the metal freezes its attack and reforms the shape of the knight's armor and their swords. The swords fall, crashing down to the ground beside them. "It won't save them," he reiterates with greater authority and continues to walk towards the many buildings.

"Sir Brandwyn!" exclaims Linum as she presses up against him, trying to gather her composure and make out a pulse, "Brandwyn?"

"It is too late to turn back now, for it has begun. You must find *him*, Linum," Brandwyn says hoarsely to the dimming light enshrouding his eyes as he reaches out to touch Linum's cheek. Brandwyn smiles softly, resigning himself to death's hollow grasp.

In melancholy horror surrounded by the gloomy oppression of death at her hands, she remorsefully stands shaking with rage, leaving Brandwyn and the others to face the night stars and await the Sun's blessing on their own. Zoren is already past the flourishing group of trees and turning the corner to enter behind a slick alleyway into the calm city. Linum runs to catch up, her hair flapping in the wild uncontrolled wind. Her hands are dotted with blood that smears as she wipes at her wet cheeks. She passes the group of four trees with dead flowers hanging from lush leaves, she dodges behind the same corner, and enters the slick alleyway.

Linum lingers several feet away, watching Zoren's freshly cut dark hair press against his head and cling to his neck, as he cautiously sneaks around the side of a bakery and avoids the dim light from candles within. In anger, she picks up a small pebble and launches it at him, aiming for his head. However, Zoren ducks and it crashes against the bakery wall causing a stir inside and the shuffling of feet. He glowers at her briskly and carries on picking up his pace. Zoren dodges behind the tavern, while three drunks stroll out laughing and stumbling around, waving their hands in the air, and taking wobbly steps around the empty street. Their faces are dark and sinister with the glow of the dismal torchlights, stretching monstrous shadows across their dizzy faces.

Linum follows after Zoren, shivering from the cold wind that sweeps at her hair blocking her vision as she attempts to keep track of his swift movements. He races from side to side of the rough buildings, leaps over fences, and ducks below signposts. He does not pause to see if she is still following, rather, continues on masked by the shadows. Finally, when he reaches a vacant shop full of cobwebs and dust, he pauses momentarily to glance around. Seeing Linum close behind he jumps onto a wooden crate and lifts himself inside through a shattered window. She watches bitterly, examining the grave sign swinging against its post. The sign hangs limp and grasps onto the hollow and bare metal pole for support. The words have been scratched out by time and its color has faded making it appear like a skeleton with its hollow frame jetting ghastly shadows across the bleak pavement. Linum pulls herself up onto the dreary crate. She peers inside the building, trying to see if she can identify Zoren in the darkness. However, no light penetrates the vacant building, except a small glow from a single lantern in the far empty corner. She hears no noise of movement nor any signs of life, but being alone in the alley, cold from the blowing wind, and not knowing where Charles can be found, she decides to enter.

The single room of the building reeks of mold. As she lands onto the hard wooden floor a loud creak sounds and the scurrying of rats makes her quiver. The tiny scratches of their claws on the wood magnifies and screeches into the open air of the night while a forlorn gust of wind blows through the single cracked window. A plume of dust rises and blinds her in the darkness as she rubs her eyes frantically to see again. Once clear of the dust she listens to hear nothing but alarming silence. Linum steps forward to approach the unwelcoming light hanging against the dreary wall while taking guarded steps. The oppressing silence appears to soften as she hears the slight shuffling of feet each time she moves. The closer she gets to the torch, the louder the shuffling sounds and every once and a while she hears a quick breath being taken and released. She dares herself to take another step, entering the small circle of light from the lantern, but she is not close enough to use it to illuminate the room. Quick thuds sound rapidly from behind her and she swipes at the air. Yet, she hits nothing and the sound stops.

"Zoren, you filthy liar get out here and fight me!"

In return only silence answers. She steps back inching towards the wall while eyeing the darkness.

"Come out and" –the footsteps are loud and pronounced closing in on her, but her eyes see nothing– "show yourself!"

She takes a huge step backwards, crashing into the cold leather and stinging icelike metal of his vest, she feels his warm breath clash against her neck, and she whips herself around to see Zoren, standing behind her. He raises the lantern upwards. Linum yanks away, falling back into the darkness, he remains gravely still, watching solemnly with his piercing bluish grey eyes. The shadows fall across his face and stretch into sinister forms dancing before his skin in monstrous waves. He reaches out and Linum crawls away. Yet, he does not reach nor signal to her at all, he merely hangs the lantern on a glaring hook and slumps down to face the floor. His black boots clink together and the empty scabbard falls from his side. He pulls out a simple small tattered brown notebook and flips through the pages lost in thought. Linum stands, wearily taking glimpses around at her surroundings while watching Zoren, who casually ignores her.

"You may help yourself to some cold stew or bread," he suggests without looking up.

She does not move. "You killed Sir Brandwyn."

"And the others," he responds with apathy.

"You monster!"

He sets aside the book with distaste, peering at her gravely from the hollow corner, "I did what I had to do."

"You fiend," she snarls.

He shrugs his shoulders brushing off the comment with indifference and leans back against the wall.

"If you possess such great powers, why didn't you just prevent them from following us?"

He stares at her, "And why exactly did you toss the dagger into that innocent man's hand?"

She stamps her foot and replies coolly, "That's different."

"It is the same thing, really."

"You're not a knight, you're a scoundrel, a–"

"A beast, a murderer. No I'm not any of these titles." He pauses looking at Linum with a cunning smile, "I was appointed by Queen Penelope with an operation to remove you from the castle in secret."

"Then you are a liar."

Zoren digs his hand in his pocket, pulling out a small glistening pink crystal. He extends his hand out for Linum to grab it.

She does so, snatching it and walking over to the lantern to better examine it before turning back to him, stating, "And what does this prove? It's only a crystal."

"No, it is one of *the* crystals."

She laughs, "You mean from the legends?"

He nods gravely with a foreboding morose frown at the crystal in her hand before shuffling uncomfortably to a stance. He reaches for it, but she evades him.

"So how did *you* come across it," she states looking him over with disapproval.

"A symbol from the queen to gain your trust," he interjects mildly, reaching for the crystal, but still Linum perseveres, stepping away and avoiding his reaching hands.

"How can I tell if it's real? I hear there are plenty of counterfeits." She juggles the crystal from one hand to another with a facetious grin.

"For one, you shouldn't be tossing it around so light-heartedly."

She pauses, examining the gentle glow of the pink crystal. After a moment's examination of the glittering stars carved into the translucent edge she drops it into the miniature fire of the lantern.

"No!" He roars, stretching his hand into the lantern to pluck the crystal away from the fire, he drops it onto the floor and smoulders the flames emblazing the gentle pink of the crystal with his hands.

Linum watches with eager anticipation as the crystal erupts in light – despite Zoren's attempt to put out the fire – and the entire room glows. The walls appear to be composed of a bland red paint peeling in certain areas and wrapped in spider webs. The floor is old and broken at some parts, revealing the dry earth underneath. The only window they entered from is completely shattered with fragments of glass spread across the dark wooden floor. In the far corner of the room sits a pot with a foul green liquid inside and two floating rotten potatoes, and to the left of that sits one measly loaf of stale bread on a broken miniature crate. A long hooded cloak lies restless on the floor. It is stuffed crudely into the dim corner closest to the heavy wooden door. It is a dark blue cloak with silver scales lining the rims, but it is covered with holes from prior use and roughly patched with a mix of fabric. Her attention returns to the crystal, that simmers at her feet unscathed by the fire, and shimmers like the night sky.

Zoren bends down and touches the small fire circling the pink crystal letting it ride up his hand and engulf his arm. Carefully he traces his steps to the lantern and dips his fingers into the embers. The orange flame slides down his arm and leaves his skin without a mark.

Awestricken by the crystal, Linum remarks, "It radiates like the Sun!"

He nods without satisfaction and retains grave watchful eyes over the glittering crystal between them, before ushering her to retrieve his cloak.

Linum does not move, rather she stares intensely at the singed floor and the pink Sun Crystal. She exclaims, "This is the signature crystal representing the Kingdom of Dalium."

"Yes, and the whole damn world will be searching for it!" he whispers with a gruff voice, and commands Linum, "Get my cloak."

She walks with swift successive movements to the corner of the room, retrieving the tattered cloak. Linum freezes holding the blue fabric against her chest while she hears voices sound from outside as startled citizens press against the vacant building.

"I hear movement inside," the people whisper among each other.

Another person chimes in, "It could be the Midnight Persecutor!"

She hurries over to Zoren tossing him the cloak and uttering, "The people of Dalium must have seen the light from the crystal!"

"Of course they did." He mutters indiscreetly with a sour tone. He bangs his fist into the wall and repeats, "Of course!"

Zoren gathers the burning crystal and places it into the pocket of his black leather vest, but instead of pulling the cloak over himself, he orders Linum to put it on.

She protests, but he claims, "So they won't recognize you," with the utmost sincerity and remorse. He simultaneously reaches out and places his other hand onto her shoulder for a brief moment, looking into her eyes as if to reassure her. The ocean grey of his eyes are calm and still and Linum detects some fear amid the relaxed expression. She pulls the cloak over her dark hair, and fixes the hood to fall just above her eyes so she may see. She follows Zoren to the window. Spying torchlight from outside, Zoren shakes his head and walks over to the corner where the lantern hangs and reaches for the flame. Cradling it between his hands he throws it out the window. A heavy shriek erupts from outside as the citizens scurry while the orange flame erupts with violent intensity over the dry walls of the vacant building. Disbelieving Zoren's abilities, Linum follows close behind him as he rushes over to the door to press his ear against it.

He listens and gruffly mumbles, "There's a lot of them and the ridiculous peasants won't listen to reason." He curses under his breath as he spins around and his foot crashes into the pot of foul soup, which spills across the ground and splashes up onto him and Linum.

"Great!" he booms. "Just great!"

Zoren bends over, picking up the bread from the broken crate. He places it in his mouth. The clamor grows from outside as the door rattles and shakes from the might of the citizens slamming against it. Zoren races to the empty lantern that no longer gives off any light. The lantern is sizzling hot from the prior fire. He sets it on the floor and pushes Linum aside. The metal whips to life leaving the glass to fall and crash against the floor. It twists and churns acting like the tentacles of an octopus swiping at the air and creating a barrier between them and the door. He runs over to grab his small book, and he slides it into his vest pocket.

Zoren shudders and pulls the loaf out of his mouth, taking one bite and then spits it out, disgusted. He looks at Linum miserably stating, "By chance do you have a weapon?"

She shakes her head in despair, watching the metal beast expand across the room.

He sighs, his breath shaking as the door collapses with a heap of dust splattering up into the air. One by one the citizens file into the building. They gasp at the sight of seeing the metal stretch across the walls, creating a net between themselves and Linum and Zoren.

"Get back," Zoren yells.

The people step forward, and one of them, that yields a pitchfork, dares to shove the metal net. The metal coils around his arm; the citizens gasp in horror as the metal twists and churns before them and lashes at them.

The man with the pitchfork screams, "The Midnight Persecutor is attacking."

Zoren nudges Linum and tilts his head back. "Get behind me and cover your face so they don't recognize you."

She pulls behind him, fearful of the onslaught of citizens. She is sure that they will penetrate the thin metal net from the lantern in a matter of minutes. Then, the crowd hushes in hearing the sound of trumpets blaring and horses galloping. Zoren turns to Linum, his expression is gloomy and filled with terror. More horses are heard approaching and neighing anxiously as their riders dismount. The citizens file out in a hurry to see what has approached from outside. One elderly woman with a lilac purple shawl hunched over her prominent shoulder bows to a man standing before her. Through the dust Linum is able to make out the old woman's piercing deep wrinkles and permanent frown stapled across her face as she points a gnarled finger at Zoren. The steel armored figure, with a large helmet, clutches a huge metal sword that appears too big for the knight. He nods and the woman scurries away.

Linum begins to tremble. She whispers to Zoren, "My father's knights."

He nods grimly in response. Linum thinks about the punishment she would receive for running away, the fatal chamber she would be chained to, and how hostile her father would become when he hears that the queen has passed away. *Yet, how did she die?* Linum's breathing becomes heavy, she looks to Zoren and whispers, "The Midnight Persecutor, it must have struck the castle. Is that why Penelope ordered you to—"

Zoren scowls at her, "Do not speak."

Another figure bearing more armor and many more showy torn medals, approaches the first. Its face is shielded by heavy dust. It has an even larger helmet embedded with plumes of bright purple feathers. The two figures enter with swords drawn while many more silver crested men wait outside, calming the angry mob of citizens.

The man, who attempted to break the net, squeals at the knights, "Avoid the metal, it's the Midnight Persecutor's trap!"

Zoren lifts his hand and the metal net snaps to life again, tossing the trapped man aside. The metal presses down on the armored man with the feathers. The other knight takes the opportunity to approach, while the feathered knight remains helpless upon the floor. He slashes with his sword, missing Zoren by a longshot. He swipes again, this time nailing the edge of Linum's cloak into the wall. Tugging at his sword in desperation, Linum unties the cloak to free herself. She pulls away towards the feathered knight. Linum wrestles his sword away from him as Zoren concentrates on crushing him down into the floor, using the thin metal tentacles.

With sword in hand, Linum swipes at the other knight, who barely pulls his own sword from the wall. She draws in on him hitting his armor and he falls back against the floor. He clutches his sword loose before him and she catapults it out of his hand with one slice from her sword. Shivering, he calls with a squeak for backup to the other knights standing outside. They rush in with weapons drawn making a barricade with their shields. The feathered man prys himself loose from the floor by clutching the thin metal arms from the lantern and bending them back. Zoren's face drips with sweat, his face flushes at the sight of the oncoming silver men bursting through the door. The feathered man takes the opportunity, he knocks Zoren out by striking him on the head with his fist. Linum stands alone, pressing the sword closer to the exposed portion of the pinned man's neck. She kicks his sword further away.

"Take one step closer and he's dead," she calls out with an admonishing force.

The knights linger, agitated. They await their orders from the feathered man. He holds his blade against his side, with his hands stretched wide open. Linum is encased in dust, grime, and dried blood, her hair is a mess falling loose across her eyes. None of the knights appear familiar to her. Although she recognizes the silver seal upon each of their shields, being the carving of the eight-pointed star, an emblem of Dalium and the prosperity of Solenium, she knows that the knights will not identify her as the princess.

Yet, she addresses the knights sternly and does flinch as they unsheath their swords, "Stop, in the name of the princess." She adds with a firm voice, "Drop your weapons."

A few laugh, condemning Linum's revelation as a fool's act. They press on closer with their swords clashing against the steaming wall, where the fire continues to burn brilliantly. The flames appear to only burn the single wall, where the one broken window remains like a looking glass into the chilling night. The fire's orange flames watch eagerly with anticipation like a child witnessing something unlawful occur before them, a disaster that they can't keep their eyes off of.

The feathered knight with a helmet so large and overbearing that his head appears like a shadow, since Linumm cannot see his eyes through the holes, strides towards Zoren. He wears torn medals on his chest. He presses his sword against the exposed neck of the unconscious Zoren. Zoren's head is limp, his nose bleeds onto the cracked floor. Linum eyes Zoren wearily, she spots his chest slowly rising up and then falling back down, softly and slower each time.

"I'll kill him." The feathered knight growls with a heartless voice, "Drop your weapon, imposter." The huge knight with purple feathers sheaths his sword and from his back he pulls a heavy cleaver that shines with fresh blood. "I will do it."

Linum rebukes the comment, but her eyes are hopeless as she does not recognize the knights surrounding her to be one of her guards. She believes that she has not interacted with any of them, for her father's elite knights were only commanded into battle in dire situations. They bear the symbol of Dalium but her father's knights would be the least likely to know of her existence. Besides if some of them were in fact aware that there is a princess of Dalium, Linum is unrecognizable at the moment and despite that, an apparent fugitive.

Although Zoren has the legendary crystal, bestowed upon him by the queen to free Linum as proof of the secret mission, she does not trust him entirely. Linum feels uneasy in his presence and weary of his powers. His demeanor frightens her, for he appears as unpredictable as the sea. Yet, his courage, kindness, and powers intrigue her. Consequently, she knows none of the knights before her and is concerned about what they would do if they found the crystal resting in Zoren's pocket. Linum does not trust Zoren, however, she notes that he has made no attempts to kill her thus far. Also, in identifying the crystal to be real, she feels that it is her duty to not let it be given to the unknown knights; rather, she recognizes that she must ensure its safe return to the castle.

The belligerent feathered knight lowers his cleaver upon Zoren's neck. Linum acts just as hostile, she presses her sword closer to the knight's body beneath her foot.

The knight squirms trying to look at her; however, his body rests in an uncomfortable position and his helmet remains immobile despite his struggle.

Linum kicks at him with her foot, "Be still or I will finish you."

Yet, the trapped knight still flaps his arms helplessly, trying to pry loose of her grasp without severing his neck. With diligence he commands in desperation, "You are under arrest for intervening with the royal troops!" His voice is strained and trembles as he speaks, leaving an uneasy hum in his throat as he opens and closes his mouth like a gaping fish.

With an irritated glance at the pitiful prisoner, Linum bends down to pull off his helmet, but the feathered man booms, "Step back at once!"

She freezes. Linum hears the bang of the feathered knight's cleaver clash against the ground as a warning. Zoren groans and Linum gulps down the cold air. She ignores the warning of the feathered knight and with a quick movement of her hand slides off the trapped knight's helmet. Linum blinks in optimistic disbelief in seeing a pair of startled hazel eyes staring up at her.

"Charles?"

He grunts as she releases him from the pressure of her foot and sword. Disgruntled, he takes a step back against the wall, holding his head and barely able to keep steady footing to remain upright. The testy large feathered man intrudes, shoving Linum back and rushing over to help Prince Charles Noapten stand.

"Your Highness, are you alright," he inquires with a guttural croak.

Charles nods, pushing aside the false pretence of his feathered companion. He faces Linum with heartache. Charles squints at her, examining her face with teary eyes and a pitiful frown. The sight of her poor brother causes a cold chill to run down Linum's spine. Linum notices the sorrow on Charles's face: his red swollen eyelids, his bruised nose, and cut lip. Linum has no words for him, she stares solemnly at him. Then, Charles rests his hand upon her shoulder. He faces her and with a whimper he cries out, "He's dead!" Linum's sword crashes against the floor.

Chapter 7
The Fountain

Linum kneels over Zoren, pulling the blue cloak up and wraps it around his neck. She heaves his body upright against the wall so she may better examine his wound. His nose is bleeding and appears broken. She leans onto him, pressing her face against his, concealing him with her hair. Her long hair creates a midnight black shrine over Zoren. She peers into his chest pocket, where the pink crystal sparkles as if it is excited to be seen. Linum looks over her shoulder. No knights are watching her while she tugs at the cloak to uselessly cover Zoren's side. Linum removes the Sun Crystal and drops it in her concealed pocket hidden in the delicate folds of her dress.

Charles approaches her again, after she pushed him aside and ignored his statement. Linum hears his light footsteps. She grabs the corner of her dress and takes the sword, cutting out a piece of the fabric. Charles kneels down beside her and looks at Zoren. Linum ignores him. She presses the piece of her dress against Zoren's face, dabbing at the blood.

"How did you escape from your guards?" Charles stares at her wearily.

Linum's body tenses. She continues to press the fabric against Zoren's face.

Charles sighs. His eyes are heavy. He gets up and leaves Linum next to Zoren. Then, he addresses her from the farside of the room, "We will have to inform Queen Penelope of our father's death."

She ignores Charles's previous comment and calls out to all watching, "He needs help."

The knights do not stir, instead they face Charles. Charles bows his head, giving his consent, and the knights push past Linum. They carry Zoren outside.

Charles yells at them, "He's not the Midnight Persecutor," as if to reassure himself.

Charles approaches Linum with compassion. "Shall we try again. Let me know if you need anything." He forces a smile, "I am here to help you Linum." He offers his hand with benevolence. However, she picks herself up and follows after the knights. Charles moves as if to follow her, but the feathered man blocks him, pulling him aside. He whispers into Charles's ear with confidentiality. Charles's face turns grave and serious.

Zoren is placed onto a horse with a knight in flashing silver armor and a single medal of honor. The knight looks to Linum and reassures her, though she is quite uninterested, "We have a physician at our camp, past the great gate of Dalium." She nods, passively watching the gravel fly up into the air as the knight pulls away with Zoren and heads toward the gate. The knight calls back, "I will see to it that he is taken care of." Linum smiles when she can no longer see Zoren and the knight fades from sight.

The rest of the knights occupy themselves by taming the citizens, who in rage and furious outcry toss stones at Linum. They shout shrewdly, "Hang the Midnight Persecutor!"

Linum glares at them. She begins to search for her brother among the covered faces of the knights. She spots Charles and sighs at the sight of his forlorn face. The feathered man is still whispering to him, he gestures at the burnt building and back to Charles. Linum turns away, she dodges the stones being tossed at her, and she feels the crystal securely placed in her pocket. With the knights distracted, she weaves her way through the clump of knightly horses, who snicker, snort, and neigh.

Dodging the swishing tails of the horses, she crosses the path of a knight. The knight calls out, "You're not supposed to be here," in surprise, assuming her to be one of the commoners. She runs, smacking the haunches of a large brown horse, who already appeared frightened with a nervous twitch at every noise. The horse rears, bumping into its neighboring companion, who in turn frightens another horse, thus, busying the knight, who yells for assistance.

Backing away from the horses, she runs behind a building. Linum has barely made her way into the city. She is by the buildings closest to the castle grounds. The wall of Dalium towers over herself, quite a distance away, but she is able to makeout three horses running near the entrance. She knows Zoren is on one of the horses, being taken away to the camp beyond Dalium's gate. Linum touches her side, where the pink crystal is sealed. She takes it out, and rubs it in her hand. It is smooth. She notices that there are star carvings on the side of the crystal, mimicking the night sky. As Linum lifts it close to her ear, she can hear a soft beating like a heartbeat, coming from within the crystal. However, her fascination with the crystal is pushed aside with a hurried glance over her shoulder as the wind tugs at her hair, pulling her away from the knights and from Charles. She lets the crystal slip back into her pocket, but she keeps her hand there, touching its smooth surface as she sprints behind buildings. Linum heads deeper into the Kingdom of Dalium.

She spies the church on the hill where she had spent her days looking out at distant places she was forbidden from reaching. The shadows stretch across the solemn silver slopes under the moon's attentive gaze. The church appears lonesome in the night. She releases a thoughtful sigh in remembrance of the melancholy days she spent overlooking the Kingdom of Dalium from the balcony. She remembers the green fields, imagines the dark mountains and the endless forests, and now she embraces the thought of freedom. She walks past the church, grinning at the thought of traveling to those faraway forbidden lands.

The Sun begins to rise as dawn breaks out against the night, and Linum wearily glances at the golden beams of light pulling itself above the wall. The sky turns into a fusion of soft pinks, purples, yellows, and blues as if an artist splattered paint against an empty canvas. Linum's thoughts turn to her brother as she draws closer and closer to the walls of Dalium. She trusts Charles but not the knights surrounding him. She thinks to herself, *How could he just expect me to accept what I cannot,* and looks to the breaking sky bringing forth a new day. Linum vows in silence to never accept the title she now carries, letting go of her burden.

The fountain glints at the center of the Kingdom of Dalium. The surrounding streets are empty, golden, and stained by the dried flowers resting in clumps on the smooth path. Water trickles into the fountain's cracked basin, while the outer stone remains lined with golden vines and stone star carvings. King Russelton's plaque gleams and twinkles in the light. Linum stares at it from the shadow of a building. She notices the street is empty, there are no lights within the surrounding houses nor in the small shops. She spies burnt out candles resting on window sills. Linum leans forward in an attempt to read the words carved into the plaque. She is able to make out King Russelton's name but the inscription below is too small for her. She squints at the words with her dark eyes and takes a step forward. Linum cannot believe her eyes, the words appear to be moving. The wind blows steadily, pushing against her back. She shivers and feels drawn out of the shadows. Linum walks forward with swift movements, carefully examining her surroundings. She stands in front of the fountain, being satisfied with the pleasant silence, and she takes a moment to read the words below King Russelton's name aloud. It says, "I have been waiting for you." She blinks and rubs her eyes, the words appear to be dancing before her. She feels an ache in her chest and her head pounds. Linum presses her eyes shut, then she refocuses on the words, bewildered. She reads the inscription again, "In honor of the brave saviour of Dalium, our hero of legend." Linum stares at the metal inscription in utter confusion. She thinks to herself, *How could she have misread that?*

The fountain flashes a brilliant bright blue and Linum's attention is drawn from the inscription. She stares at her reflection in the clear water and sighs. Her hair glows a dark brown with the Sun rising behind her. Her eyes are tired and heavy, her face is covered in dirt and dried blood, and her hands are bruised and cut. Having nowhere to go and no place to return to, she pauses, resting her arm against the rim of the fountain. Linum admires the delicate glow of the crystalline base glimmering in the depths of the water. Although it is broken, the water spills out with ease and shines, drawing Linum closer. Linum yawns and her dark hair falls over her face. She takes another look at her hands and her dirtied face in the water; Linum reaches into the fountain and rubs her hands below the water's perfectly clean and clear surface, to free herself of the dirt and blood. Then, she scoops up a generous amount of water and lets it splash against her face, wiping clear the grime. She wets her dark hair.

Dripping wet she leans over the fountain to look at her reflection, but as the drops fall from her face she notices a slight glow omitting from her once dark eyes. They turn a sparkling sapphire blue as her skin radiates a soft cyan. In shock she pulls away, touching her face with her hands, only to realize her hands are a soft whimsical blue. Her hair flies upwards with the wind, she tries to fight against it, but the wind pushes her back to the fountain. In the water she witnesses a face, not belonging to herself, looking back at her. It is not human and resembles a horse, but its eyes are a distant galaxy and the midnight black coat moves like mist settling over a mountain, swaying with the water. The face rears to life, jumping out of the water. It soars above Linum on celestial wings that twinkle in the black void of translucent feathers. The wings glow like the midnight stars, and the creature neighs as its transparent body lands – like a deep fog setting over a lake – beside Linum. She tries to get a better glimpse at its gentle dreamlike face, but she is stuck to the fountain, her dress pocket clings to the rim like a magnet.

The misty winged horse creature bows to Linum. Its calm eyes stare into hers, and with a sweet nudge of its head, Linum pulls out the pink crystal from her pocket. The horse creature makes a vibrant roar that shakes the water and breaks the crystalline basin within, turning the water into a pool of shimmering debri. Linum relaxes her grip on the pink crystal as it begins to burn in her hands, she drops it into the fountain and feels the misty winged horse creature take off from behind her; it rises into the air and balances at the tip of the fountain, spreading its wings outwards. She looks back and forth between the creature and the fountain, witnessing the same star-like pattern on the wings and in the debri. The fountain and the creature both mimic the transforming sky. The pink crystal makes the water bubble as Linum backs away, but finds herself unable to leave as curiosity compels her to linger.

The water turns from a dark glimmering blue to a gentle pink. She steps forward with shaking feet and trembling hands. Linum looks down at the bubbling water and dips her hands in. The blue glow of her skin shrinks away, draining into the water. Her eyes return to a dark brown and her hair falls down against her back, but in her right hand buried beneath the murky bubbling surface, she feels something tapping against her fingers. She pulls with little force and draws out a sword, sheathed in a brilliant scabbard. The detailed crossguard, lined with engravings of stars, has eight holes that are small in diameter. One of the holes contains the pink crystal she had dropped into the fountain. Raising her left hand out of the water, she sees a necklace with a small charm, an eight-pointed star, hanging with little weight from her arm. The creature stares from above and with a satisfied grunt, shoots into the air, and flies away into the breaking of the dawn sky towards the Sun.

The water follows the creature, dancing and twirling before her eyes, leaving only one clear drop in the basin of the fountain. Linum, amazed and surprised, faces it and freezes, seeing a streak of her hair stained a deep sapphire blue. She tries to drop the necklace and the sword, but they cling to her hand. She tries to walk away from the fountain, but she fails, finding herself unable to make any distance between the fountain and herself, no matter how hard she tries. It is as if the fountain radiates with its own gravitational pull bringing her back to the rim. She had once longed to touch its water out of childish ignorance but now she is playing with fate.

Irritated and scared she attempts to yell for help but her voice fails her and her lips press firmly against one another. Her hand that holds the necklace begins to burn and her neck aches. Yet, she feels that she must wear the necklace. She raises it above her head and the burning feeling in her hand subsides. The star slides down her neck falling above her heaving chest. The wind picks up its speed and spirals around Linum in response. It begins to lift her upwards and turns her to face the intimidating Sun. In her right hand she clings onto the sword, hovering like a hummingbird. Her body is as light as a petal and as frail as a rosebud at the mercy of life, as the wind tosses her into the air. She floats humbly and limply, her head falling back facing the Heavens, her dress clings to her skin, and her feet dangle. Nothing but the wind holds her up. She is a petal afloat on the breeze. A beautiful petal of a rose. Her cheeks are brilliant red, her lips seal together, and she closes her eyes letting her dark lashes press against her face.

A sweet voice rises and swells like the wind. It comes from all directions and sings with beautiful charm, "To the Mountains of the Sun Blessed Everglades."

Linum spins delicately as the wind wisps around her, hoisting her upwards. She tumbles towards the Sun and closer to the Heavens.

The necklace glows a furious sapphire blue as a lyrical voice calls out to her from all directions, carrying a pleasant gentle tune on the wind whispering, "Linum, you have returned to this fountain, without desire, what others would cling to. It is your birthright to hold the crystals and use them to return what has been stolen from the room you witnessed death firsthand," it pauses taking a light breath and holds Linum still with the pulsing rhythmic glow, "The mark of the crystals remain within you. It will give you bravery when you have none and content when you are desolate."

"Is this the fate I am destined for?"

The Sun shimmers a reverent orange and the voice replies, "Life is like a vast ocean, you travel upon unexpected voyages day by day. It is beautiful and graceful but the seas are dangerous as well. The journey itself is one of amazing challenges and wonders. You are but a simple voyager on these strange magnificent tides of fate."

Linum nods, her eyes proud and hopeful and for once, happy. She blinks as a shadowed woman emerges from the beams of the light. She has long hair that spreads loose behind her like wings, her light blue dress drapes down like a waterfall. She reaches outwards, with celestial hands toward Linum, and speaks with the power of the Heavens and the Sun, "I will guide you, but I cannot protect you."

Her face is masked by the blinding light of the radiant Sun, but the pleasant sound of her voice and the charm of the Sun's blessing reassures Linum, who listens to the instructions willingly.

The Sun appears to echo the woman's words as if in a trance, "For the confinement of the sorceress of darkness, trials will be held within the Crystal Caverns in the Crystal Common Grounds. The key to liberty will be offered if a young hero claims her place in the line of long lived Sun Champions. Then shall the evil be released and justice may be delivered among those who are innocent and those who rest guilty and broken. The futile attempts of shedding the blood of the shadows is in vain, for a greater evil awaits. However, you, hero of the Sun, shall mend that which is broken and fight with the greatest honor of releasing the revenge of the past and providing prosperity for the present. If *she*, who is lost and torn, finds the ancient weapon then she may wreck or provide the foundation for the future, but be warned for you are contorted in action and deed, for noble tasks may ascend you or break you and everything you hold dear."

The voice of the Sun breaks off, leaving just the woman's sweet and encouraging singsong voice. "Linum, you must gather the remaining seven Sun Crystals. Medaia has unleashed her forces into the world and is desperately searching for the crystals at whatever cost it may be to the providence of the entire land." She glances at Linum and a consoling beam of light trickles through her hand, "Medaia never died; rather, she has been kept alive by the black crystal of the Crystal Common Grounds. Medaia is a ruthless snake, she is sealed deep within the caves in the Crystal Common Grounds, however, her strength is returning."

The Lady of the Sun pauses. Linum feels a cold chill run down her spine. "How could Medaia be alive?" she asks.

The woman's light flickers and the air grows increasingly cold. The warmth of the Sun appears to vanish and Linum trembles as the woman's voice becomes solemn, "The blood of the Sun is a gift not to be abused and if consumed it will corrupt any individual. The creation of shadow beasts is Medaia's doing, but it is also the creation of an inner monster being released among the desperate innocent. The crystals have great power as you will learn, but they *change* the user. The crystals have a will of their own, for they are alive when put together."

"Alive?" Linum's eyes widen as she examines the pink crystal.

"Have you heard of the true origin of the Sun Crystals? It is an ancient tale, before Medaia and before Solenium. Very few know of the truth and history of the crystals, most only regard the power they contain."

Linum shakes her head, her eyes glow with keen interest.

"It is said there once was a being of the Sun, who roamed freely in Solenium, bringing light to the land. The being had a body that was carved in the Sun's reflection, it was a pure Crystal Being. With the creature of the crystals came hope and prosperous life. Solenium flourished and there was a balance to all of the Sun's creations. However, the Sun was abhorred in seeing the creations of the world turned violent. The balance of nature featured life and death, yet chaos was present. This darkness was brought upon the world through the light that the Sun had harbored. Thus, the Sun feared that nature would corrupt the perfect being, and so it was said that the crystal creature's body was broken apart. Therefore, Solenium was given eight crystals to divide the land and separate the creature's remains. The crystals maintained power through bringing prosperity to each region, separating the children of the Sun from the temptation of war." She points a glowing hand at Linum. "You contain one of the crystal creature's fragments in your right hand. For now it will obey you as long as you wear the necklace and believe in the Sun's guidance. The blood of the Sun flows through each crystal. Beware of its power and the temptations that you will face."

Linum raises the sword into the air. The pink crystal gleams in the light of the Sun. However, her smile falters as she thinks about Zoren. She whispers, "I am uncertain of this birthright you mentioned, since I took the crystal from a young man. It was never mine."

The Lady of the Sun laughs, "Linum, you have been chosen for this by the Sun itself. Destiny is in your hands. No mortal can own the crystals, please understand that."

"I understand." Linum feels the warmth of the Sun press against her, it radiates all around her. "Lady of the Sun, may I ask you a question?" The woman nods. Linum continues, "I had these visions," her head pounds at the thought of them, "it felt too real. I know that it cannot be simply a nightmare. I had dreams of fire, monsters, darkness, and a cave of lights. I saw Solenium in peril. What does this mean, is it an omen?" The sky darkens and Linum hears the distant pound of thunder.

"I apologize for your suffering Linum. You have met with Medaia beforehand and fell for her shameful trick, but rest assured that Judith does not exist, never existed, there is only evil in Medaia. The nightmares you have been having are of little importance, if you believe in the Sun. The disaster you witnessed in your sleep is not the future or the past. It is merely a possibility if Medaia's plot unfolds in its entirety. Her preservation is a result of the black crystal. Her powers have increased as she becomes increasingly reliant on the Sun's crystal, consuming it for darkness. She longs for power and is fueled by revenge. Immortality is her goal as well as to control the entirety of Solenium. She is a great sorceress and although she is imprisoned, she is not trapped. While her body remains imprisoned, she has the innocent do her bidding. Shadow beasts are only shadows of the people they once were and may never be again. Medaia manipulates the weak minded, she tempts the innocent and desperate by plaguing their mind with doubt and desire. The weakness of all creatures is her strength, for when hopelessness settles in she pounces on the innocent victim and scavenges their life. Medaia makes an exchange of hope by offering them a chance to achieve their desires; however, her price is masked in a shadow of deceit. The hopeless make the exchange and she only takes. Medaia steals their soul without any reward or warning. She leaves their body alive and aching, their breaths as hollow and cold as ice, their eyes forever lost, and their ears always listening to the cries and moans surrounding their corpse. These victims become shadow beasts. Shadow beasts are a true evil released from humanity in vain and greed to harness the power of the Sun. Judith was one such creature, a good-hearted woman once, who gave into the darkness and became a servant of Medaia. Once the blood of the Sun is sipped, once that deal is made, they become a servant to whoever controls the crystal they drank from. This is the chaos the Sun fears, the darkness within its own blood. Beware Linum, heed this warning," again she pauses to examine Linum, who appears bold and firm in complacence, "Trust your voice and your strength."

Linum nods, her eyes glow with a bitter realization, "I have seen shadow beasts in the castle. The deaths within the Kingdom of Dalium, the murders in the middle of the night, the Midnight Persecutor, are those all related to Medaia?"

"Yes. Medaia is desperate to achieve her goals, and the reemergence of the Sun Crystals have caused her to act. Her beasts and monsters will increase in strength and number until she achieves her goal. She needs all the crystals to fully free herself from the Crystal Common Grounds."

Linum wearily nods her head, "I understand; however, I am unsure of the role that I will play in stopping Medaia."

The Sun glows a warm and vibrant orange, the woman and the Sun speak as one, "Your destiny is yours to make. Your choices are of your own decisions. The fate you receive will be given to you through your choices. Linum, our warning is one that must be heeded, for while your future is unclear, you must remember to live in the light of this world." The Sun's voice fades again, leaving only the Lady of the Sun to continue, "The Sun has chosen you to gather all the crystals and enter Medaia's realm. Yet, the choices you make along the way will make your role clear to you alone. Remember there are many roles to be played in this quest, not all of which will be your burden. However, if you succeed in gathering the six other crystals, then you must enter the Crystal Common Grounds, gain control over the black Sun Crystal, and slay Medaia, for if she is left to live in that cave her shadows will never cease to spread. Yet, should you fail..."

The woman's voice drops and Linum feels herself slowly sinking as the wind loses its strength. Linum boldly remarks, "I will not fail."

The Lady of the Sun speaks with warm satisfaction, "For the glory of the Mountains of the Sun Blessed Everglades, the future of Solenium, and your fate, I wish you success. You have been selected by the Sun, and I am sure that you will live up to your full potential. I will do what I can to protect and guide you." The necklace echoes her last words before she fades into the Sun, "Trust Asterian, he will follow you and protect you." The loving voice of the Lady of the Sun fades. Linum feels the eight-pointed star necklace vibrate and she looks up at the glorious Sun. The Sun appears to blink and Linum begins to descend towards the fountain.

The fountain refills with clear playful water as the mysterious horse creature, Asterian, reappears from the sky and neighs. With a flash of energy he bursts around

Linum, glowing joyfully, before disappearing into thin air. She lands gracefully standing on the rim of the fountain, her lashes tickling her cheek. When she opens her eyes, she realizes her attire has changed. She is no longer wearing the olive green dress, rather a copper chestplate armor lined with silver and underneath a flowing azure dress that falls loose at her knees. Her dark shoes have changed into a pair of leather caligae, and the sword has moved from her right hand to a silver scabbard detailed with the Sun's rays. A leather sword belt hugs her waist in which she sheaths the sword triumphantly.

Linum looks up at the beaming Sun. She clutches the eight-pointed star necklace, and whispers with confidence and an eager smile to the jovial wind, "I will do what I must."

Chapter 8
Monsters Within

The fountain stands alone in the middle of the street encased in the Sun's warm glow. The morning birds chirp, restless, and banter among each other. The sky begins to enlighten, opening up to an enchanted blue. Linum strolls through the empty streets covered by shadows, following the wind's push and pull as it drives her further from the castle and to the surrounding wall. Torches splutter out and homes begin to erupt in noise as pots clink and clang against one another and children laugh. Still she pushes on, walking with the wind as a companion and carrying the Sun's blessing against her neck. She has a mission now, for she was chosen by the Sun and given a fate to follow to the bitter end or sweet success.

Her thoughts wander to Zoren, who might be waiting for her at the camp, condemning her for swiping the crystal and cursing her name bitterly, but she feels no allegiance towards him. It is her brother that concerns her as she leaves her burden of ruling over the Kingdom of Dalium on his shoulders with the undertaking of her quest. However, she cannot return for him as he would be followed by the ill-natured company of the knights, thus endangering her mission.

The Sun only awards quests to those with benevolent intentions and those that possess the desired traits of a hero in the making, it is exceedingly rare.

Centuries may pass before a Sun Champion is chosen to ride upon a particular fate; however, those who are chosen seldom return alive.

She reaches the wall and places her hand against it, feeling the coolness of the grey stones and moisture from the night. Linum looks up to the sky and is lifted by the winds into the air and above the gate of Dalium. The guards' mouths gape as she floats gracefully by, hands swaying by her side; however, her face remains serious. She lands with a gentle thud against the soft grass and the wind swirls around her, abandoning her.

Linum takes off, as the trumpets sound from behind the wall. She hears the bewildered guards shout. One of them yells, "Witch" and the other screams, "The Midnight Persecutor!" Linum laughs.

She bolts into the dense woods, preparing herself for a long journey. She is finally free and has been given a purpose by the Sun. She cannot help but to feel excited by the news, her face glows from her pleasure. Linum begins to push past the heavy branches and into the maze of trees. She hears more trumpets sound and curiosity draws her to peek out of the treeline to see the gates open wide. Armored horses yielding knights scurry into the kingdom. The knights are armed with spears, shields, and swords. The knights each appear frantic as they rush their horses along. Linum ponders over the cause of their panic. She knows that the rush of the knights surely could not be because of her. She had just Dalium. It was not possible that they could have been drawn from camp in such a rush due to her absence.

Linum recognizes one of the hurrying knights to be the kind silver knight with a single medal, who carried Zoren to the physician at the camp. His grey destrier gallops on the outskirts of the ranks. Linum stares at the campsite and notices that it is abandoned. The tents are flattened and only a few straggling knights can be seen patrolling. Peering from behind the trees, she looks up at the castle and to her horror spies a dark smoke rising. Linum can hear the clash of metal and the bang of an explosion.

"Charles," she exclaims as she runs for the open gate to reenter with the knights. Her quest fades from her mind at the thought that her brother's life could be in jeopardy. She hears yells and screams coming from within the gate. She hears the clash of metal.

When she reaches the passage between the wall, just as it is near closing, the wind holds her back. It pulls at her, whispering furiously, "The Sun has given you a fate." The wind prevents her from reentering the City of Dalium.

"Let go of me, I'll continue the quest after I see my brother is fine!"

The wind moans in response, pushing her back against her will. No matter how she tries to get through, she cannot move forward. Linum yanks out her sword. She slashes at the air but it does nothing to stop the will of the Sun.

Linum feels something clash against the backside of her chestplate. She is knocked onto the cold ground. Linum lifts herself up and braces herself with her sword as she turns to face the cold condemning face of Zoren. His oceanic eyes are a dark grey. He flashes a condescending glare at her.

"Hand me that crystal," he bellows, eyeing the sword with wrathful grey eyes.

"I protected you," she responds with haste.

"I was fine." He shrugs accusingly, his eyes still watch the sword. Zoren roars, "You stole the crystal from me!"

With a moment's hesitation and glance at the closed gate, Linum mutters, "The Sun gave me a fate."

Reproachful, Zoren shakes his head, "Then, you best give it up."

She stares at him, insulted by the cruel words and disappointment in his eyes. Yet, deeming him as harmless, she turns back to face the wind. It roars to life, shoving her against Zoren, who disinterestedly stands passive against the blow. Zoren roughly lifts her up. He grabs her hand and takes a step towards the large wooden gate, pulling her with him. The wind shrieks in outrage and hisses as he approaches the gate with Linum. The wind is unable to touch them which results in a desperate creation of a vortex that expands around them.

"Why is it when you hold onto me, I may move closer to the kingdom?"

Sourly, he replies in a deep sharp voice, "I reject the Sun."

At first she smiles, believing it to be a bitter joke of his, but finding no humor in his eyes she scorns him. Zoren cuts her off stating, "The Sun has done nothing good for me" and before she can reply he grabs a hold of a metal rope that extends from his chest pocket. Holding onto Linum with one hand, they rise up, the metal pulling them upwards to the top of the wall. They land next to the two unconscious bodies of the guards. The metal rope retracts into the compact pocket of Zoren's leather vest and hardens within.

Linum shoves away from him, finding a ladder laid to her side. She looks downwards inspecting the kingdom she had just left. The castle has erupted in flames, and the citizens are in panic while knights fall to the ground. The ground shakes violently as the fountain cracks in half. Dark beasts emerge from the shadows twisting and turning to life, attacking whatever is in their path. They mirror the beast she encountered in her room. Linum drops to the floor and lets go of the ladder, she takes a moment to stare at Zoren, but he does not budge from the top of the wall.

One of the beasts stalks her with its orange flaming eyes and after a mangled lick of its jagged teeth, the green tongue retracts. The monster hisses at her and it pounces. The creature's blood red saliva drips from its jaw as it snaps at the air, howling in rage. Linum pulls out her sword and swipes at the beast. It dodges, jumping backwards, and swings its spiked tail, agitated. With a quick flick of its tail it makes contact with her blade and yelps. The orange flame flickers and flashes a quick blue, before changing back to the malicious violent orange.

She backs up and charges at the beast. She hits its back, locking the sword in its deep skin. Pleased, the beast's head turns to face her and it licks its empty eye sockets, the flame seeps out, scorching its tongue, and just as it was about to bite her, Asterian appears from behind. The mist confounds the beast as it tumbles back in fear, dragging Linum with it. She yanks the sword free from its thick hide, and raises it above its head, and with a furious smile slams it down into the beast's throat. It oozes a dark liquid, before crumbling into dust. Its remains are carried away by the wind.

Asterian roars. He leans against Linum and stretches his wings above her head. Asterian nudges her along, signaling towards the gate.

"I can't leave Charles," she whispers and darts away.

Asterian follows after her. He flies above Linum as she slashes at the oncoming beasts. Zoren still sits on the wall, observing as the beasts devour the knights and chase innocent citizens. He glares at Linum and shivers each time Asterian roars. With a wave of his hand the metal rope zips to life. Zoren grips the end, leaping off the tip of the wall. The rope wraps itself around a nearby shadow beast, tightening itself around its neck. Zoren lands fiercely on the creature's rough back, holding onto the rope like a horse's reins. With a bitter whip of his hand, the beast takes off following Linum from behind. He stalks Linum in the shadows, keeping a steady distance between himself and Asterian. He does not care who gets in his way or who the beast attacks as long as he focuses on Linum's sword and the pink crystal within.

Linum hacks at the horrendous beasts, gags at their horrible odors, and rushes at them with fury. Her arms are steady as she swings the sword with ease and grace, like a violent dance against the raging creatures with caustic breaths and venomous claws. Asterian runs steady at her side, kicking at the beasts when they approach. Together they are forcing their way to the center of the Kingdom of Dalium, where she last saw Charles.

An older woman of about fifty years crumbles onto the floor, tripping on the broken golden path near the fountain. A shadow beast creeps up onto her, while she clutches the lifeless hand of a dead man to her chest. He has a gashing wound across his body where one of the beasts tore clean his shirt and skin. The monster lowers itself ready to pounce with a vicious roar, but Linum intervenes. She charges at the foul creature just as the beast opens its bloody jaws. Linum slashes its mouth with her sword. The jaw hangs limp, oozing the beast's dark blood. The beast is still alive. Its spiked scorpion-like tail cuts through the air and aims at the innocent woman lying over her lover. Linum looks towards her and smiles reassuringly. She whistles and Asterian materializes to the beast's side. He bucks the shadow beast towards Linum, who aims her sword at its chest. The blade pierces the creature's dark hide, breaking through the thick skin and cutting its insides. It moans and fades away to dust that encases the gasping and hyperventilating woman. The woman prays to the Sun and whispers a solemn "thank you" over and over again while hunching over her loved one's corpse with narrow bony hands that tremble. Linum turns away, yanks free her sword, and runs along searching for her brother with a fierce burning ambition lingering in her eyes. She stares at the fountain as she runs by it, recalling the perfect rims and golden light and the heavenly waters, from moments before the bombardment of Medaia's evil shadow beasts. All that is left now of the fountain now is dust, dirt, and the holy water spilling out onto the golden cracked pavement, like the tears of the Sun. King Russelton's plaque is tangled within an eerie rose bush.

The smoke is thick and creates a heavy cloud of ash over the area, allowing easy camouflage for the shadow beasts to travel in. It distorts Linum's vision. She is deafened by the sound of children screaming. She swings mercilessly at the monstrous figures before her, drowning in smoke. She begins to cough while moisture settles heavily above her brow. Her mouth is parched as the dry air fills her throat and engulfs her lungs. Dizzy, she begins to lose her balance, her feet stepping over one another in a daze and her sword swings, aimless. She crumbles down and Asterian appears. He kneels next to her, urging her to leave. There is a silent defiance burning in her eyes and a determination to save her brother. Linum stands her ground, trembling. She takes shaking steps forward, blinded by the smoke. Asterian remains kneeling, looking between the desperate Linum and the far off dim glow of the Sun, shining a ferocious red behind the billows of grey smoke. He neighs with despair, drags his head low, and tucks in his tail, pressing on after her shadow.

The light narrows as they reach the dark building with the shattered window. The orange flame that was once content with scorching a single wall, has overtaken the entirety of the building. It leaps from side to side in furious passion, engulfing multiple buildings with its tiny sparks.

Linum offers a prayer to the Sun that she will find her brother alive. She calls out, "Charles" in desperation while staring at the dark building. Yet, she does not hear a response besides the sizzling of the fire's scorching flames and the crackling of wood. She looks up at the ashes that are falling and stretching across the sky.

Asterian spies the anguish in Linum's dark eyes as she coughs. She slumps against the ground. Asterian lifts Linum up onto his back and spreads his wings, determined to take her away. Linum does not fight him, rather she protests in silence, looking up at the Sun with unease. Her hands tremble and glide up the blade of her sword, she looks keenly into the reflection, to see only herself encased in the darkness. The star necklace, that hangs loose around her neck, aims towards the ground, pulling her attention there. It appears to point to a man covered in darkness amid an opening in the smoke. Zoren stands alone surrounded by the beasts. He backs up towards the furious frightful building but keeps away from the flames. His face stretches and changes in the shadows, appearing sinister and solemn as the flames stretch out to grasp him, and the beasts charge. His metal whip drips with the black blood of the monsters as he slashes at their thick hides to keep them at bay. Zoren meets Linum's watchful eyes from above. He shakes his head in disappointment, returning to the battle before him.

Irritated, she clutches onto Asterian's long mane and pleads, "Take me back. I still have strength. Please let me fight."

Asterian shakes his head and with sympathetic eyes, he brings her lower but not nearly close enough to the ground for her to get off near Zoren. He makes a hard jerk left and lands with an excited neigh. Linum slides off his back. She holds onto the building walls for support as she scans her environment for signs of the shadow beasts. She can see nothing except the plain stone of the building before her. Linum hears nothing except the screams of citizens. She is not away from the battle, but she is not directly in it as she was beforehand.

"Asterian, where did–"

But she pauses as her eyes catch sight of a heap of glimmering silver armor laying hunched against the wall. She approaches with hope and despair in seeing the figure of a young boy with bright hazel eyes and dirty blonde hair, bleeding from the right side of his face.

"Linum?" he questions.

She nods with excitement and rushes forward to grasp his warm bruised hand.

"Leave me now!" he exclaims with sudden passion and fear.

Taken back, she pleads, "I can help you."

"No, leave to help our mother."

Linum sighs. She looks deep into his hazel eyes and solemnly states, "Charles, she is dead. It happened the night I left."

Tears brim his eyes as he brushes his red cheeks with rough hands declaring, "He might be near and it is your duty as—"

"I have no other duty as of now, than rescuing you."

"Linum, with our parent's death you are now queen."

Her eyes drop and she turns to look at the prying Asterian, kicking nervously at the ground.

"No, I'm not," she states with defiance. Linum's brow is perched into a high arch and her eyes narrow as the fog thickens onto an approaching figure.

"But—"

"I refuse."

"Linum, the people need you."

"Shh!" She commands him, in the darkness of the fog. Asterian backs up towards her, his tail flicking from side to side while his ears strain to listen for footsteps. She readies herself for combat by placing herself in front of the limp Charles, who relies on the dull wall for support. The figure steps forward. His dark black leather boots appear from the smoke followed by a furious glowing light held by his gloved hand. Finally his blue cloak emerges from the darkness of the smoke.

His rough voice calls out, "We must get out now!"

Linum turns to him, still holding her sword, keeping distance between him and her brother.

"How did you get the crystal, Zoren?" She presses forward, letting the blade touch his leather vest, "Don't tell me the queen gave it to you."

"I told you how."

Charles raises his head and peers through the thick smoke, he looks at Linum and back to Zoren, then interrupts, "Linum, who is this?"

"An acquaintance," she mutters stubbornly.

Asterian nudges her side, flashing quick glances around. His galaxy eyes appear frightened. She touches his muzzle with a light tap of her hand, then faces Zoren with distrust and distaste.

"Have I done anything for you to distrust me?" he inquires. His eyes glare into hers.

She tilts her head to the side and with an indignant sigh, she orders for Zoren to lift Charles onto Asterian.

"Leave the lantern," she commands, "or they will see us take off."

His oceanic eyes twist with fury and rage, his hands tremble, and the flame glows brighter. He responds, "I cannot leave without Pyro, that is why I had to go back."

"Pyro?" Linum's eyes widen. She takes a confused glance at the lantern and at Zoren's face to see if he is serious.

"Pyro." He states, his eyes serious and brows firm, "He has helped us once before, or have you forgotten?"

"We cannot take the lantern."

"Then, only Pyro," he bends down, setting the lantern aside and reaches into the burning hot glass, brushing off the embers, he pulls out a single vibrant orange flame, "He will remain with me."

It dances from his fingertips, glowing with confidence and contempt as it stretches out to increase in size, bowing to Linum before jumping into his breast pocket. She stares in awe and amazement. Yet, in hearing the voices of knights heighten from all around her, she shakes her head and pulls herself onto Asterian. Like a wolf, Asterian growls as Zoren approaches. He snaps at Zoren's hand with razor sharp teeth, when Zoren reaches out to pet his wild astronomical mane.

"You cannot leave me," Zoren calls out, "besides I saved you!"

"And I saved you too," she looks out at the smoke and with a hesitant pause, she turns to Zoren, "but you are right, for I cannot leave you to this fate."

Charles moans, his voice hoarse, "Linum, behind you! He is here."

She turns, but too slow as the giant figure of the feathered man approaches. His armor is dripping with blood as he raises his cleaver upwards to strike at Linum. Zoren unleashes his metal whip from his breast pocket while Pyro, the small vibrant flame, rides the metal like a knight on a horse dashing into a battle to clash against evil and goodness. Pyro tackles the man's bright feather by setting it on fire, before scurrying up Zoren's shoulder and into his pocket. Zoren pulls the whip tight, holding the monstrous man in place. Linum takes the opportunity to slash with her sword, meeting the cleaver with force.

"Linum, he killed Father! He is the Midnight Persecutor, he ambushed myself and the knights after you left. He has been in disguise the entire time as one of us!"

"A knight in disguise," She yells in anguish, slashing at the feathered man, piercing his helmet and penetrating the impenetrable darkness, "Impossible!"

Instead of collapsing dead, the Midnight Persecutor breaks free of the metal whip and spreads its arms down to its sides, leaking the same dark ooze as the beasts. It drops its feathered helmet, and lets out a terrible screech, shattering the silence of Asterian, who roars in rage. The Midnight Persecutor's eyes are a pair of bright red flames. Its horrendous tongue is the same sick green as the shadow beasts, encased in swelling boils leaking yellow puss as its teeth emerge one by one from its purple gums. Pyro trembles in Zoren's pocket and Zoren whistles for the retreat of his whip.

Zoren grabs Linum's hand and hurries her along, "We got to go, now!"

Zoren lifts himself onto Asterian's back, despite the stubborn reluctance of Asterian, who stirs with unease as Zoren adjusts himself. Zoren reaches out to Linum. TheMidnight Persecutor stands still, letting the dark blood continue to drip. She takes one concerned look at Charles, who sits slumped over on Asterian. Linum draws in a deep breath. With a determined nod of her head, she runs at the monster with her sword drawn. It screeches, extending its armored claws and it swipes with the cleaver. She dodges with scurrying feet that move as swift as a flowing creek. Her eyes are full of hatred and disgust as she swipes from side to side in anguish.

Her cheeks are red and her breath is shallow as she yells out in rage, "For Queen Penelope and King Charles XVII!" With a furious charge, she raises her sword and strikes the beast, penetrating the Midnight Persecutor's demonic throat. Her sword glows a raging brilliant blue, causing flames to erupt from the pink crystal and spread throughout the blade as the creature howls in pain. The beast collapses, dead, its entire body clashes against the hard pavement and the metal of its armor collides with its skin. The flaming eye extinguishes with a harsh hiss, and Linum falls back. Her hands tremble as she meets the cold road beneath her and her body shakes. Her mouth gapes open as she lets the sword drop to the floor, her dark eyes scan her blurred surroundings. She sees Charles force himself into a sitting position as his mouth moves, but no words reach her screaming ears. Zoren leaps off of Asterian, his hands outstretched towards her, but something pulls him away and forces him against the wall. His oceanic eyes are curious and dance before her while the world begins to darken.

The pink crystal pulses a threatening blue. Linum feels the pulse sync with her own heartbeat and with each thud of blue light she scrunches up tighter into herself and strains her eyes to see, but the world appears to close in on her. Everything is dark, she only hears the thud of the crystal pounding like her chest. The screams, her brother's voice, Asterian's roars, all disappear into the void before her. Everything is dark, except the Sun Crystal. Linum stands in the dark world and walks forward, her feet trudging through black sludge as she sinks. Her arms stretch up to reach for the crystal while her head plunges underneath the sludge. Her hand meets its smooth surface and she clutches onto the crystal which yanks her upwards. She finds herself able to stand again on a smooth black marble floor. Her reflection is of the girl she saw in the fountain. Her eyes are sapphire blue and her skin a light cyan, but when she looks closer into her reflection it winks and points to a single streak of hair that colors midnight blue.

Taken back, she grabs her own hair to examine it and spies the same streak of color and gasps with interest and fear. Her reflection waves to her and fades away. She turns to look around at the condemning void of darkness, taking a step backwards. Linum falls and the sludge engulfs her, she tries to yell out for help, but she chokes on its thickness and continues to sink.

Charles shakes and yells wildly for Linum, but she lays unresponsive on the cold floor. Zoren approaches with disappointment strewn across his condemning face as he places his hand onto hers. He feels her cold gentle skin and presses down slightly feeling for a pulse, but shakes his head somberly. Picking up her sword, he examines it and spies the glowing crystal. He instructs Charles to clutch Asterian's mane while he holds onto the sword, and suggests they wait. Asterian bows his head, whimpering like a dog who lost his master, but in hearing the approaching sounds of snarling beasts, he begins to growl like a wolf.

Linum bolts upright with sudden force surprising Zoren, who shudders and Charles who yelps. With a blinding flash of light she no longer resembles her prior form, rather, she changes into the form of a beast. Her skin is riddled with cracks as deep and dark as the beast she had just slain, her nails turn to furious blue talons, her back stretches and molds into the form of bat wings, protruding skeleton-like and hollow. Her once dark eyes flash like the galaxy of Asterian's eyes, but Linum's eyes are slitted. Her face molds into that of a creature with jagged teeth. With a stroke of her wings, what was once Linum, is carried into the air with a deafening screech. Anxiously, with his tail flicking from side to side, Asterian begins to run, his wings stretch out and flap and he lets out a warning neigh. Zoren jumps onto his back as Asterian lifts off from the ground, pursuing the beast.

Pyro pokes out from Zoren's breast pocket and on seeing the beast, he squeaks and faints. Pyro's light begins to flicker. Zoren clutches the sword and yanks free his cloak, wrapping the searing blade in it as he grips Asterian's side. The air is cold, cruel, and merciless, stinging their eyes amid the pursuit. The bat-winged beast dives towards the surface, licking its horrible teeth and strikes without thought, tearing at the flesh of whatever appears closest. Asterian dives following from behind, and with a fanciful stroke of his hoof against the beast's winged back, it collapses and screeches. Charles quivers from fear and moans to frozen air.

Zoren squints at the beast with harsh eyes and pauses before commanding, "Asterian, hold her down."

Zoren walks forward, his legs shake, but his eyes are steady as he lifts the sword above Linum's beastlike head. He plucks the crystal from the crossguard, and taps the pink Sun Crystal against her neck. The beast shivers, screeches, and moans, then it fights off the weight of Asterian's hooves, and bites at Zoren with flashing teeth. He steps closer, pressing his hands against Linum's head and lets the crystal tap with greater force. She screeches, but the screech transforms into a scream as the wings collapse into the shape of her back once more, and her body is once again covered by human skin, and she bears her armor and her dress. Her pupils widen and her eyes change back into their ritual darkness, while the talons retreat into nails. Linum glances with a passive smile and feels the weight of her head knock against the rough floor, while the blue streak of her hair falls across her eyes.

Chapter 9
The Burden of Fate

Warm embers embrace the night sky giving off a fierce inviting light and warm glow surrounding the dying wood of the campfire. Zoren crouches over her warm body, glowing under the heated light of the fire. Linum's neck glistens with moisture. Charles sits slumped against a log, stretching his hands out then retracting them just as fast. Then, he rubs the palms of his hands together and prays. His face is calm, but his dark swollen eyelids, hollow cheeks, and nervous twitch, suggest otherwise. Zoren stretches and yawns. He watches the twinkling stars shimmer above him and he extends his hands. He lets Pyro jump from the flames of the campfire into his palm. He looks up in peace at the night sky. Then, Zoren flashes a nervous glance at the sword with the pink crystal resting in Linum's scabbard beside Charles.

"Do you think she is" –Charles looks at her exhausted face and pauses, witnessing a drop of blood trickle down from her scalp– "going to be alright?"

Zoren nods with mild concern lingering in his bluish-grey eyes.

"How did you meet her?"

Zoren glances at Charles and then transfixes his eyes on Linum's rising and falling chest before replying, "I was appointed by the queen."

Her breath is shallow, he notes. The necklace on her chest glows a soft blue. Zoren stares at her face, examining her. She shivers and the light fades. Her lips part slightly like a crescent moon before recombining to form the full glistening shape of a rose underneath the light of the stars.

"Do you practice magic?"

"No," Zoren replies, his voice harsh.

"But I saw you do something others cannot."

"I am a humble man, striving to achieve honor for my name."

"But you controlled the whip." Charles persists, his eyes wide from astonishment. He points at Zoren's hand, "And the flame! I saw you."

"His name is Pyro," he retorts with a grim expression, extending his arm out to show Charles. Pyro dances from side to side with interest. "I merely command the whip," shrugs Zoren as he retracts his arm and sets Pyro onto his shoulder. Asterian glowers at Zoren from a distance, watching from behind a nearby tree, his wings match the arrangement of the stars above.

Linum coughs and Zoren presses his head close against her chest, "Her heartbeat has grown stronger."

Color seeps back into her ghostlike cheeks as she opens her eyes to see the dirtied face of Zoren staring into hers. Her nose glows from the firelight and as she tries to speak, her voice fails her. It comes out raspy and unintelligible. Her head falls back limp onto Zoren's arms and he lays her back down to rest.

"Still not strong enough," he suggests.

"Do you understand what happened," inquires Charles, his hazel eyes glowing from the fire as he tightens the cloth from Zoren's cloak around his injured arm. Charles's brown shirt falls against his legs, cut and torn. His armor presses against his side, dirtied and bruised.

"No," replies Zoren with hesitation, "but she used *the* crystal."

Charles stares at Zoren blankly. "Do you mean Dalium's Sun Crystal?" He observes Linum's sword from a distance. The pink crystal glows. "The pink crystal in her sword," Charles shakes his head in disbelief, "are you saying that is the crystal from the legends?"

"Indeed it is."

Charles leans forward and his face grows serious. "I have heard the crystals contain immense power."

"The legends say the crystals change you, if used."

The wind blows the ash from the fire, dwindling away the warm glow of the flames and gently scattering the embers. Thus, leaving them in complete darkness with the exception of Pyro's soft light and the twinkling stars.

Linum stirs again and Zoren helps her up to rest against a log. She looks at him with condemning eyes. Yet, she expresses a weak smile as he examines the necklace clinging to her chest. He backs away and tears off another strip of his cloak to wipe at her face and dab the blood. Then, he drops the cloth on top of Pyro. Pryo engulfs it with a wild desire and burning passion. Zoren watches Pyro's flames carefully before turning to grab the cloak and cover Linum with it. Her armor, undented and clean, sits beside her, while her flowing azure dress presses against her body. Her lips shine underneath the moonlight.

A tear slides from her eyes as she mouths in a whisper, "I killed them."

Charles responds, "It was not you."

However, she protests as her face grimaces, "I could see everything, but I couldn't do anything. It was me. I did it."

Zoren snaps, "It was the shadow monsters that killed your people."

Linum whispers, "But I was one of them! I could see them running and screaming. The children were crying and I swiped at them. I killed innocent people. I was a monster. I am a monster." Her voice grows hoarse and dry. Her lips quiver and her face strains as she tries to lift her head to face Zoren and Charles.

Charles shivers from the cold breeze sweeping through and rustling the nearby leaves, "But Linum, you are our queen."

"The people do not know me! No one recognizes me in the entire blasted Kingdom of Dalium, except those who imprisoned me like an animal. Besides, what kind of queen slaughters her people?"

"It was not you," states Zoren solemnly, "now rest."

He pulls away from her and lays down on the moist floor of the woods, adjusting himself and closes his eyes. Pyro follows him and leaps into his pocket. Linum stares, her voice too weak to argue, but she retorts, "We must return to help what's left of the people of Dalium."

"Linum" –Charles pauses, his eyes watch the trembling glow of the pitiful embers scraping the charred wood– "there is not a kingdom to return to."

Her eyes drop as another tear slides down her cheek and rests at her chin.

"The castle is gone. The survivors have fled. The grounds are overrun with beasts."

She shivers as the wind sweeps back her hair to reveal her grave eyes and trembling lips. Goosebumps run along her arms and she turns as pale as a ghost.

Charles bows his head, "There is nothing more we can do."

Linum shakes her head and presses her ears shut. The pink crystal glows and she hears a sinister voice whisper in her head, *You are a beast. Use me and we can cure you of this monster. Touch me and you can be free.* She leans toward the crystal. Her hand stretches to reach it, to touch the crystal. It screams in her mind, *Give into me. Drop the necklace and let us become one. You will be free.* The eight-pointed star necklace becomes unbearably heavy around her neck. Linum tugs at it, attempting to pry it loose. She is standing now, taking trembling steps closer to the crystal. Her hand is nearly touching the pink crystal's smooth surface. Her other hand is sliding off the star necklace. Her head echoes the false promise of the crystal, *You will have the power to save the people of Dalium and become Queen of Dalium. You could rule the entirety of Solenium.*

She stops. Her legs give way and she crumbles down. Charles's arms are around her. He guides her back to the log and helps to lay her down. "Linum," he whispers, "you need to rest. Today the Castle of Dalium may have fallen, but tomorrow the light of the Sun will be with us. The Queen of Dalium still lives and so our kingdom remains strong. There is nothing more we can do tonight, but we will reclaim our home for our people and for the prosperity of Solenium."

Linum's star necklace glows a gentle blue. She feels its warmth travel across her body. She lets her hands fall to her side. She looks earnestly at her brother and replies warmly, "The Sun has given me a fate."

Charles's eyes drop. He forces a smile, "That is exceedingly rare. You must be truly gifted to have been assigned one."

Zoren mutters, "So what is your given deathbed?" He lifts himself up to face Linum. "What great fate did the Sun task you with?"

Linum takes in a light breath, "I must gather all eight Sun Crystals and slay Medaia." Her face grows pale.

Zoren scoffs, "You steal one crystal and now all of us must die along with you in order to collect the rest. Your quest is impossible. It truly is a deathbed."

She glances a pitiful look at Zoren. "I am unworthy of any honorable fate the Sun has offered me. I am a poor choice for a Sun Champion, for I have already failed. I have given into the temptations, I have killed, and I am a beast."

Charles stares at Linum. He expresses genuine happiness and sincerely states, "The Sun could not have chosen a more worthy champion. You are not a beast. You have endured beatings, tortures, survived an army of shadow beasts, and slayed the Midnight Persecutor. You are Queen of Dalium and yet you do not want the power or the title. Linum, you are as fierce as you are honest. However, you must be true to yourself. You have said before that you longed for a quest and now that you have received one, you are shrinking away. I know that you have not given up, but you must realize this," Linum shakes her head and Charles continues with benevolence, "the beast you became was not yourself. I will not deny that the creature killed innocent people but that was not giving in. The Sun Crystal manipulated you but it did not taint your spirit nor did it change you. Linum, this quest may appear impossible but I will be with you no matter what happens. I will stand by your side and one day we will reclaim Dalium."

At his mention of the creature, her body trembles. She sits up and watches the sky. Her necklace glows a comforting blue. Zoren leans back against the ground. She hears Pryo's flames hiss. Charles walks back to his former position, opposite of Linum against another log. He closes his eyes.

"Sleep," whispers Charles, "sleep."

However, she remains upright, trembling from the screams she had heard, the horrific scenes she had witnessed, and the murders she had executed. She lost everything she knew, except Charles. She has a destiny ahead of her. She must not fail. Linum leans against the wood with maddening eyes, her bruised hands form a fist as she quivers throughout the rest of the night, burning with hate.

Chapter 10
The Woods and the Wild

The morning Sun shines a gentle orange and lays a soft beam of light onto her dark eyes. She blinks, her long lashes kiss her cheek tenderly. Linum pulls herself up to a stance, her legs no longer shaking. She bends over to slide her armor on and fixes the sword belt against her waist, carefully stepping over the body of Zoren and Charles to grab her sword and scabbard. She checks tentatively to see if the pink crystal remains in the hole of the crossguard before fixing her sword into position at her side. Asterian's ears perk up and his galaxy eyes gleam with compassion as he springs forward into the air and disappears in a flash of light. Linum's necklace glows, she feels that he is with her, watching over her. She looks around her, puzzling at her location, and sneaks away from their camp. Linum dodges twigs that would alert both Zoren and Charles as she weaves her way around the woods, further from them.

Pyro peers out from Zoren's pocket. He lets out a hushed chirp and hops forward onto the ground, zooming after Linum. She stops and looks behind her startled, only to see the small flame jumping up and down behind her. She crouches with a delicate smile, offering a hand to the cheerful flame. Pyro timidly climbs onto her hand. He glows with a whimsical display of colors and rests against her gentle fingers. He does not feel hot although he is a flame, he does not even give off smoke. He just glows brilliantly.

She marvels at the small flame before whispering, "How did Zoren ever find such a sweet thing as you?"

Pyro appears to shrug as the vibrant orange fades slightly and then brightens up again. He bounces in her hand.

She shakes her head and whispers, "Now scurry on back, before they awake. Do not dare follow me, little flame."

Pyro jumps down from her hand and runs behind her, letting out a slight chirp. She turns to keep an eye on the small flame and follows its path. Pyro stops short of a shadow of a tree and squeals in excitement, his flames grow larger. Linum looks up and realizes Zoren is leaning against the dark brooding trunk of the large tree. His dark gloved hands are crossed and his eyes are stern. There is no delight or compassion in his harsh eyes. His hair is coarse and a mess as Pyro pops up on his head and nestles on top of his wild stack of hair.

"You are not leaving on your own," he states.

"I am not on my own." Linum glares at him. "I have Asterian. Besides the Sun gave me my fate to pursue," she replies, her chin raised, letting the light morning Sun bring a soft radiant glow to her rosy cheeks.

"Damn the Sun," he mutters darkly. Pyro squeaks as if to confirm his statement.

Linum marches forward unaffected by his bitterness. She bites her lip pressing into the soft flesh, thinking to herself about the Sun's duty assigned to her.

However, dark thoughts circulate in her mind, quarrelling with her consciousness. Her mind echoes her fears. *Linum you are a monster. You are one of them, the dark beasts. You will fail the Sun. You have no destiny.* She passively looks around. She sees the same old trees repeating in a sequence clustered together, the thick brown wood with small carvings and natural scratches from animals, all ordinary and natural. The canopy is like the sludge, she notices. It is dark and forbids the light to penetrate its overbearing shade, which creates shadows across the ground and leaves dark marks on the forest critters. A snake slithers past her with a delicate pattern of black diamonds on its tan skin. It slips underneath a pile of moss. A wolf howls from nearby and she hears the pack running, but she does not see them. A loud crunch from behind her sounds and she looks back to see Zoren trudge back to the campsite, where Charles stretches and looks around anxiously towards her from a distance. She hasn't a clue where she is walking nor where the next Kingdom may be found.

"Asterian, take me to the location of the next crystal." She commands this with desperation and flashes quick glances at the blue sky.

He does not appear from the necklace nor soar down from the Heavens. With a sharp glance around her, Linum sits on the moist ground, leaning against a mossy rock. Charles tightens his armor and combs through his dirty blonde hair with his equally dirty hand. Zoren rolls up what is left of his cloak and places it beside a log. They both approach her.

With a smile Charles calls out, "Where to?"

Linum shrugs, "The Sun only told me that I had to find the crystals. I know each crystal resides in each kingdom, if the legend is true, but I haven't a clue where to begin."

"And why do you wish to be the Sun's slave?" Zoren crosses his arms and cocks his head with indifference.

Linum stands, perturbed by his constant disappointing remarks against the entity that protects the land of Dalium and the entirety of Solenium. "The crystals will grant the passage into the Crystal Common Grounds in which I will slay Medaia for what she has done."

Zoren remains silent. He closes his eyes and crosses his arms. Pyro shivers. His flames become a soft yellow.

Charles cries out cheerfully, "The closest Kingdom to Dalium is the Terrace Gardens of Nominia. I read about it on father's map the night before we left to hunt the Midnight Persecutor."

Zoren nods complacently, "I know where that is."

"But do you even know how to get there through these woods?"

He nods, "We are just into the beginning of the wild territory that separates the Kingdom of Dalium from that of the land of the fairies," he pauses, taking in the commodity of time to express what he has left to say, "It will not take us long to walk there. It should only take a day or two. However, the Sun Crystals are relics from legends. We are dealing with ancient sources of power. The crystals won't be easy to find, they have been lost for generations."

Linum touches her star necklace. She feels the smooth silver. She closes her eyes for a moment. *You will know. I will assist you.* Linum's eyes open. "I will know where the crystals are once we get there–"

"And if you don't?" Zoren's cynical eyes shine triumphantly at casting doubt.

"Then we have a long journey ahead. I did not ask for you to accompany me, let's make that clear."

"Crystal clear," he smirks.

Charles chimes in, "Then the three of us will avenge the Kingdom of Dalium and live on in legend. Agreed?"

"Agreed" replies both Linum and Zoren, each staring the other down.

Zoren lifts his hand up and the metal whip follows. He commands it, "Lead us to the Terrace Gardens of Nominia." The whip obeys, springing to life and slithering off into the air like a snake. The trio follow it. Charles with a desire for vengeance, Linum with the goal of fulfilling the Sun's given fate, and Zoren as a reluctant guide.

Chapter 11
The Sun's Lament

They passed over great amounts of terrain from dawn to dusk. The trio has walked by the many ordinary trees in a never ending cycle of hard trunks, stiff leaves, and trembling branches. They have witnessed the squirrel scuttle across the uncut grass and the sparrow cry out to another ordinary bird, the warbler. They took very few breaks throughout their traveling.

When the moon is at its peak they decide to rest. They make their campsite, setting Pyro loose to engulf a stack of dry sticks and leaves. The flames from the burning fire warm their skin as they hurry from side to side, shuffling like ghosts while their shadow's stretch against the woody floor of nature. The night is full of brilliant stars shining with beauty while they toil and work. Linum leaves the campsite alone. Charles feeds Pyro leaves and sticks he has gathered, until they no longer have a meek flame, rather, a burning bonfire before them. The metal serpentlike whip coils around Zoren's arm and hisses deeply.

Linum returns with a rabbit drooping from her hand. She tosses the dead critter to Zoren with disgust and wipes her hands along her dress. She presses her sword into the magnificent fire, letting the metal heat her blade before swiping at the smoke. Linum turns towards the nearest tree to cut at the bark. Charles shuffles uncomfortably, he opens his mouth, determining what to say to her.

"I'm practicing," she remarks.

Charles busies himself with untying his armor and Zoren whistles for his metal whip. It unwraps itself from his arm and the silver melts into a tray. He scoops up the rabbit and the whip skins it, before plunging it into the fire to cook.

The air is sweet and cold. Linum stands hacking at the wood of the tree. She observes the gentle dew moistening on the grass surrounding her and hears the wolves again. She concentrates to hear the soothing sound of water trickling from a nearby creek. Linum smiles. She clutches the necklace and whispers, "Be my guide." It glows as if in response but returns to its normal silver coloration after a second. Her head pounds with the horrendous thoughts flooding her mind. She hears the word *beast* echo. *A monster. You are a monster. You are not innocent. You are no Sun Champion. You are no hero. You are nothing. You are a beast.* Her head floods with these thoughts as she hacks at the wood, trying to create enough noise to break the screams plaguing her mind. She touches her forehead and swings harder. The tree moans and so does she. Yet, she keeps swinging with her sword. Bark flies into the air, leaves crumble, and she is able to see bugs scatter. A grey moth lands on the trunk and she pauses. She reconciles with it, holding her blade steady before her. She takes light breaths, feeling the refreshing air. The moth flaps its wings and takes off into the night sky. She closes her eyes and lets her sword fall by her side. Then, with a single blind sweep of her blade, she slices the moth into two halves that float towards the ground, swaying with the soft breeze. Linum drives her sword into the trunk of the tree with a satisfied sigh and opens her eyes to inspect the moth pieces.

The grey puffy clouds roll in by the time the rabbit is done. Linum rejoins her companions beside the mountainous fire. Momentarily, she relinquishes herself of the weight of her quest. The rabbit steams from the heat, the tender flesh is charred and the scent of the meat is appetizing. Asterian descends from the night sky, he roars and so do the clouds above him, sending rain pattering against the ground. Drip by drip the water falls from the sky. Despite the dreariness of the grey clouds, Linum smiles. She is free, even while the rain lashes out against her face. She cannot feel her hands from the coldness while the fire cries "shhh" to the world. Its light fades and Pyro scurries out. He ducks underneath the protection of Zoren's metal whip, creating a micro tent for the small delicate flame. Linum laughs as nightingales sing and the owls soar and cry out for their freedom. The water drips from her lashes, down the side of her face and twirls to the floor. The clouds roar again, the boom echoing across the trees as lightning strikes in the distance.

While the rain patters across the ground, Asterian poses. He spreads his wings like a shield above the three of them. His wings sparkle like the stars as the rain attempts to penetrate his universe. Linum watches as the lightning strikes grow closer. A stork flies out from behind a tree following the boom of thunder.

"Beautiful," she states.

"And dangerous," reports Charles.

The exuberant winds sends the moist chilly air to them and the three shiver underneath the protection of Asterian. Linum holds up a piece of the rabbit, tender and still warm. Asterian takes it, his head nodding up and down with pleasure.

"I once heard of a man who could control lightning," suggests Charles.

"Hmm," replies Linum.

"A man who could tame it and control it. Father told me about this, the first night we were out in the woods. You know before," he gathers his composure drawing in a long deep breath, "before he heard rustling in the nearby wood and left with two other feathered knights. He told me to stay behind and ready myself for anything. I waited with a shield that was too big and a sword too heavy, informing the others to prepare. He didn't return."

"I'm sorry, Charles." Linum watches her brother as he rubs his eyes and turns away from her to face the splashing rain pounding against the ground.

He stretches his arm, letting the droplets hit his hand. "A knight with armor covering everything except a tiny slit for his eyes and purple feathers on his helmet came out alone. He held Father's sword. He extended it towards me, but I did not have the courage to grab it. I let it fall from his hands onto the soft soil. I buried Father's sword, like I wished I could have been able to bury him. I sent an entire party of knights out to search to make sure that he was not still out there in the woods. Yet, they returned unscathed and informed me against sending any more search parties. I was alone. And I was a fool to trust the feathered knight... to trust any of them."

"It is not your fault." She whispers, her eyes delicate and tranquil.

"You would have disobeyed him and ran into the woods with him. You would have gotten up and searched yourself. You would have fought with valor."

"Charles–" she sighs.

"No! Linum it is my fault. I trusted too easily and was too weak. I am still too weak. My armor does not fit, the sword is too heavy of a weapon, and I am the worst knight in all the lands of Solenium. I am not you and can never be equal to your strength and valor and cou–"

"Charles you should not want to be me! I have killed innocent people and I don't even know how to control myself. Whatever, you say or believe, you are not the cause of Father's death. You possess something more valuable than blind courage. You are more benevolent and amiable than myself, or Zoren, or anyone in Dalium and the entire world!"

Zoren flashes her a warning look, his eyes as gloomy as the surrounding storm.

"Yet, I have no place, Linum."

Linum places a delicate hand onto Charles's shoulder. She presses firmly down and offers a reassuring smile. "Trust in the advice you gave me."

Charles bows his head. Linum's lips form a gentle smile and she begins to sing,

Let fate not be an illusion to the mind
And make us blind
And let us not fool ourselves to blindly trust,
But not let others depict our destiny.
Live on life in hope, despair, treason, and death.
Always for freedom, love, and prosperity,
For the hope that we all have.

To the Mountains of the Sun Blessed Everglades,
Where the light and stars never fade,
And the glow of the Sun penetrates.
Our hearts and minds will grow there,
Our hope and vision expand,
And together we will outlast
All struggles around us
To honor Solenium's past.

Zoren glances at her, watching as her lips move up and down and as her voice rises and falls delicately like the autumn leaves soaring amid the wind's powerful gusts. Her smile is gentle and her lips and her eyes are relaxed and full of hope. The nightingales song silences to hear her sweet jovial voice fall deep and rise from the ashes of a newborn passionate fire stirring in her heart. She continues,

Hope where the land lies,
Hope in the seas,
Hope in the hearts

And minds of mankind,
Hope is in the breeze.

She pauses letting the wind brush her hair back and Asterian to neigh. When she picks up the song again, Zoren joins her with a deep voice echoing the tenderness of the earth,

We feel hope in everything,
And life where things fall.
Hope among all who live,
In the providence of
The Sun Blessed Everglades.

They look into each other's eyes, spying into each other's separate universes. Charles smiles and shouts into the deafening silence, "Where did you learn that song?"

She pulls away from Zoren's gaze and admires the stars glowing vehemently above, "I don't know, it came to me."

"It is an old poem" –Zoren digs his hand into the moist ground– "about the Sun. It was written when the Sun laws were first made. The song itself is ancient and has been passed down from generation to generation. It is a part of the myth of the Providence of the Sun Lands in the Heavens." He looks earnestly at Linum and declares gruffly, "More like a fantasy world if you ask me."

She taps her bare feet together and lies down on the cold surface, using her arms as a pillow, "I thought you hated the Sun."

Zoren scoffs. "I do."

Linum turns away from him and hums the song again. She smiles at Asterian and Charles, and closes her eyes.

Zoren presses on further, "I bet you don't even know what you're doing. The Sun did not give you a purpose."

Linum pushes herself upright and glares at him, "I have told you before that I will slay Medaia."

Zoren laughs, "Do you even know who Medaia is?"

Linum growls, "It doesn't matter who she is. The Sun has given me a fate and–"

"And you are a fool to not question the fate the Sun has provided you. You do not even know who you are to slay or why you must face her."

Linum stares at him blankly. She replies in an irritated fashion, "Medaia was a shadow sorceress trapped in the Crystal Common Grounds."

Zoren smiles, "I believe you mean thriving."

Charles speaks up, "Are we discussing the same legend? The one in which King Russelton died for the glory of Dalium and the whole of Solenium. Then, the shadowed sorceress was locked away. That is the only telling of the legend that I am familiar with."

"Medaia did not perish that day she was sealed away. She remains alive in the Crystal Common Grounds. It is the same legend, only my telling is true. For she has remained in the Crystal Common Grounds for twelve centuries."

Charles glances up at Zoren. His brow wrinkles and his nose twitches. He says, "Impossible! Medaia was a mortal."

Linum nods her head in agreement. "She is a mortal. However, she did not die, the Sun has informed me of that."

Zoren sighs, "Twelve centuries ago, Medaia was sealed away. It is true that she is mortal but–."

"The crystals have preserved her." Linum stares at the pink Sun Crystal in her sword. It pulses and she quickly turns away. "She has been kept alive by using the crystals in the Crystal Caverns."

Zoren nods. "You are correct. She has used the crystals to survive. The Crystal Common Grounds was the first land that the Sun had created. Although it has since been penetrated by dark creatures, it was once the birthplace of the Crystal Being. Thus, all the crystals within the caverns are the kin of the great Sun Crystals."

"How do you know of all this?" Charles peers at Zoren.

Zoren averts his eyes. "Books and scrolls," he states. He then looks towards Linum and gestures to the Sun Crystal in her sword. "For twelve centuries Medaia has been exploiting the crystals in the Crystal Caverns. Although they do not possess the same power of the Sun Crystals, they are still powerful. Also there is no doubt that Medaia possesses the eighth Sun Crystal, for it is said to be found in the Crystal Caverns. It is my fear that her experience yielding the crystals will prove to be too great for you. I worry that you are following this fate to your death and dragging us along with you."

Linum yawns. "I am not afraid of Medaia. I will gather the Sun Crystals and defeat her. I am the Sun Champion and I will not fail." She shivers. Her thoughts turn to how readily she had been deceived by Judith, who was really Medaia.

Asterian neighs and Linum forces herself to smile.

Charles boldly states with a grin, "I believe in the Sun's guidance and I have full trust in you."

Linum and Charles both look towards Zoren.

He grumbles, "You have my crystal, so what choice do I have?" He looks at Linum and sighs. Zoren then whispers, "It is my duty and honor to serve you."

Linum smiles and addresses both Charles and Zoren, "We will not fail on this quest. The Sun has given me a fate, so let us have hope and bring peace to Solenium."

Asterian relaxes his head and lifts his wings up higher. His body shimmers as the rain continues to splash against him. He roars and Linum leans back against the ground. Linum stares at the night sky. She watches as the clouds part just enough for her to see the distant soft light of the stars. Asterian looks up and watches them too.

Linum turns away from Charles and Zoren, so they cannot see the uncertainty in her eyes. Her smile fades. Her mind echoes the foul thoughts again. *You beast. You monster. You wretch.* She takes in a deep breath. She closes her eyes. Linum attempts to picture Medaia. Her heart beats faster. She shivers. Softly she mouths, "I am not afraid. I will not fail." Her mind screams her doubt and her fears. *You're a murderer. Your fate is to die. You will fail.* She feels something warm and soft press against her. Her eyes shoot open. The poisonous thoughts stop flooding her mind. Asterian leans closer against Linum. She smiles up at him. Asterian nods his head and lets his feathery galaxy wings embrace her. Linum whispers, "I will succeed for the Sun."

Chapter 12
The Emerald Dagger

A woman with golden hair leans against the back of a wooden throne. She wears a golden crown twisted with wolfsbane. The room is dark. On the floor, a man crouches. He is draped in a dandelion tunic. The woman smiles, her purple lips maliciously stretch. She has startling blue eyes. She commands with a powerful voice, "Vondur, open the door."

The man raises his callous face and hurries to the greatly detailed wooden door. "Would you like anything else, Queen Aconite." He opens the door with a sour expression, letting a young woman enter the throne room.

"Inform Irene that the Sun Crystal will be moved to my throne room." The queen waves her hand with an exhausted expression. Vondur scurries away.

"Your Majesty, how may I be of service?" asks a young woman with short brown hair. She has eyes the color of an emerald.

The queen claps her hands together. Her icelike eyes glow menacingly. She inquires, "Captain, do you know what the poor man, the rich man, and a kingdom have in common?"

"No, I do not."

Queen Aconite straightens herself on her throne. "A poor man will steal, a rich man will harm, and a kingdom will conquer. They share the same nature. If a rich man beats a poor man, he would do so because he is weak. If a poor man steals from a rich man, he will do so because the man is undefended and therefore weak. If a kingdom claims land that is not their own, that kingdom has taken advantage of another's vulnerability." She looks towards the young captain. "Do you understand?"

The woman shakes her head. She avoids the queen's eyes. "I am afraid that I do not."

Queen Aconite sighs, annoyed. Her fingers tap against the throne. "The predator will kill its prey because it is weak. It takes advantage of any weakness. That is what the poor man, the rich man, and a kingdom all have in common. Each will take advantage of the other's weaknesses. It is in their nature to claim superiority over frailness, need, the defenseless, and any vulnerability." She yawns and draws out an emerald dagger from underneath her wolfsbane dress. "This is what we must do. For the sake of Nominia we must take advantage of our neighboring kingdom's weakness."

The young woman's emerald eyes widen. "We have been at peace with our neighbors. How could we incite war among our allies?"

Queen Aconite smiles maliciously. "I have heard rumors that the Castle of Dalium has fallen. It has been desecrated by shadow beasts. We will face no opposition in conquering the entire Kingdom of Dalium–"

The young woman with emerald eyes interrupts Queen Aconite. She yells in shock, "We cannot invade Dalium! It is our closest ally." Her face glows pink at her realization that she interrupted the queen. She stutters, "I am sorry."

Queen Aconite's blue eyes flash angrily. Her face is a burning red and she screams at the top of her lungs, "How dare you interrupt me! Orelia remember your place." Her voice subsides into an angry whisper, "You know I treated your father well. I gave him respect and I would expect that you would treat me in the same way."

Orelia bows her head, "I apologize Queen Aconite. Please continue."

She glares at Captain Orelia and twirls the emerald dagger in her hand. "Like I said, kingdoms must act on another kingdom's weakness. Dalium was strong and now it is weak. The king is dead. The old queen is dead. The throne is open for us to take. The citizens do not realize this, but they do have a current living Queen of Dalium. In fact, I hear she is on her way, travelling right to us. Orelia, do you remember the girl you met at the Midnight Gala? She had a brother, Prince Charles."

Orelia nods her head, "Linum, was it not?"

"Yes. Well now she is Queen Linum. I have also told you that the girl's royal status was kept a secret from almost everyone in Dalium. This will be the weakness we use. I want her to remain a secret. She is on her way here with her brother. We will strike Dalium for the good of Nominia soon." She smiles viciously at Orelia. The purple of her lips clings to her teeth. "However, I would like you to first get to know both Charles and Linum. Befriend them, question them, but do not let them know of our intentions. You will find them near the creek."

Orelia lowers her head. Her dark skin glows from the Sunlight. Her emerald eyes glimmer. She nods her head. “I understand.” Yet, her wings, which are made of orchids, fall limp to her side.

“Good,” replies Queen Aconite. She shows Orelia the emerald dagger and comments in a bored fashion, “This is beautiful craftsmanship. The blade is poisonous.”

Orelia nods her head. She eyes the weapon wearily.

“One day I will reward it to you, Orelia. It will be yours and you will use it to make Nominia proud.”

“Thank you.” Orelia smiles falsely. She speaks without enthusiasm, “I will look forward to that day.” Orelia bows and begins to head for the door. Queen Aconite yawns. She stops and looks back at the queen, who is slouching on her throne. “My mother wishes to inform you that within the Sacred Sun Temple, she spotted a black rose growing. She fears–”

The queen laughs and cuts off Orelia, exclaiming, “When does Irene not have anything to fear?” Her voice grows stern and cold. Her eyes burn a bright piercing blue. “This is no matter. Nothing can harm our floating island. Tell your mother to burn it. There is nothing to fear.” She takes off her golden crown and watches as the wolfsbane spreads across the shiny metal. She yawns and pronounces loudly to Orelia, “Dalium will be mine.”

Chapter 13
The Green Fields

Linum is on her side. Her hair covers her eyes and her breathing is steady. The light of the morning Sun is gentle and the air is brisk. The storm has left a fresh beckoning breeze in place of the violent lightning and screaming thunder. Zoren sits upright, awake, while Charles snores. Zoren looks towards Asterian. Asterian hovers over Linum's body and peers at the open sky with longing eyes. His mane blows in the gentle gusts of wind. He lets out an affectionate neigh and spreads his wings out to catch more of the breeze.

Zoren calls his whip and Pyro jumps to life, scrambling after it.

"To the Crystal Common Grounds," he mutters in a voice barely audible, more like a muffled breath floating on the wind.

The whip points a jagged line ahead of him and stretches towards his hand, so he may reach out and grasp the end of the silver handle. He extends his hand, his fingers are only centimeters away from making contact with the metal, when he realizes Asterian's watchful eyes are glaring at him. He speaks loud and clear, "To the Terrace Gardens of Nominia" and the whip changes shape and direction. It assumes the form of an arrow, pointing just beyond a shallow group of trees and the flowing creek.

Charles yawns, reaching up to the sky. His hair droops over his eyes that are heavy with little sleep. Linum raises her head with a slight toss of her black hair.

"What?" inquires Charles, who gazes sleepily at Zoren.

Zoren stands impatiently tapping his foot against the ground. He exhales bitterly and yells, "We have wasted precious hours of daylight if you want to get to The Terrace Gardens of Nominia by noon!"

Linum peers past the scolding face of Zoren and his disapproving impatient grey eyes to look at the clear blue skies. She stretches and lifts herself up, fastening her belt by pulling on the strap. She wraps the leather around her waist. Her sword falls by her side with a satisfying clink. Asterian purrs as her gentle hand meets his comforting face, he fades away. She smiles and shuffles towards Charles, who still sits on the floor. His legs stretch out against the ground and his hands dawdle near his feet. He looks like a child throwing a tantrum, but his face is smooth and calm. Charles stands on his own, kindly rejecting Linum's hand. He pulls his armor on above his head with some difficulty. Zoren sets out ahead to follow the metal arrow. Linum watches him. When Zoren dodges behind a tree, Linum begins to follow in pursuit, leaving Charles behind.

She moves through the dense maze of wood and stops short of a creek, where she spies Zoren bending over the water. His face is solemn, it shines from the water's reflection, but his eyes darken and his lips move quickly. He chants inaudibly into the clear blue water that slides onto the bank. His face reddens and his hands roll into fists. Zoren slashes at the water, creating a cascade of ripples that sends the minnows scurrying away. Linum steps forward in silence, but Zoren spots her disfigured reflection in the water and confronts her with a smile.

"Who were you talking to?" she inquires. Her eyes widen and eyebrows rise.

"The minnows."

"And what did these minnows" –she glances at the water– "say to you? It appeared like a difficult conversation." She states this with an innocent pressing smile and shrugs her shoulders casually.

"They scurried away too fast, before I could even ponder what they said," he replies with an unconcerned tone, but his smile falters for a moment.

Linum begins to turn away, she takes a step forward and calls out patronizingly, "If you say so."

He takes a step to mimic her footing. Linum grips her sword and swings it at him. It rests above his neck and she shouts, "Don't ever take me as a fool again."

Zoren raises his hands. Pyro growls from his shoulder. "I do not have to make the mistake of calling you a fool." He touches the top of her blade and slides his hand down the dull part. "You are a fool for having doubt in my guidance and wisdom."

Linum inches closer with her blade. "I want the truth. Who were you talking to?"

Zoren smiles. He lowers her blade with his hand. "The truth?" he asks.

Linum nods her head.

"Beyond the grove of trees I saw something move." He points his hand. Linum glances wearily across the stream. "In the shadows, I saw a creature watching me. It appeared savage with hideous fangs and a flaming eye."

"A shadow beast?"

Zoren nods his head.

"Then why did it not attack?" Linum adds, "Besides I saw you staring at the water."

"I saw the creature beyond this place, hidden in the shadows. The beast only confirms my fears." Zoren kneels by the waters edge. He lets his hand submerge beneath the clear surface. The water becomes murky. He presses his eyes shut and begins to chant.

Linum readies her sword. Pyro's flame glows a vibrant red.

Zoren speaks to her with a strained voice, "Gaze into the water and I will show you what I have foreseen."

The water turns a deep purple. She sees an image of a dark mountain, a cave concealed in shadows, and then crystals. They glow blue, purple, grey, and red. Within the cavern there are numerous ghastly forms stretched across the ceiling and walls. The monsters hang like bats. Their fangs shine violently. One of the beasts crashes to the ground of the cave. The shadow beast is monstrous in size. The beast's flaming eye is a daring shade of red. It growls and Linum can hear it. She leans closer to the water. The beast roars. It sniffs the air and shakes. Linum freezes. She takes in steady breaths as the shadow beast draws nearer. It appears like it is emerging from beneath the water. She can make out the horrible green tongue. Linum extends her hand above it. She feels the ghastly chill of its disgusting breath. Then, its head breaks through the surface of the water. Linum notices that this shadow beast has wings. She stumbles to her feet and swings with her sword. Yet, the beast does not flinch. Her blade cuts straight through the body but the beast is unscathed.

Zoren chants loudly. His eyes are pressed tightly shut. The purple water creates a whirlpool and the shadow beast sinks back below the surface. The water becomes clear once more as Zoren draws his hand out. His body trembles and he coughs. Linum sheaths her sword. She helps him to stand.

He smiles wryly at her, "Believe me now, princess?"

Linum stands in silence. Her body trembles. She finally states with despair, "Medaia has an army of shadow beasts."

Zoren smirks, "Of course she does."

Linum glares at him. "The place that those beasts were located in, was that the Crystal Caverns?"

He nods his head. "I foresaw this army of beasts. They dwell deep within the Crystal Caverns, but unlike Medaia the shadow beasts are not trapped. The images I showed you in the water, those beasts, will be unleashed."

"How long do we have?"

He ignores her question and continues, "I fear that we will be wasting our time traveling to each region. I believe that it is best to take on Medaia now. The Sun Crystal you have already possesses great power. It transforms you into a form that can match the power of any of those shadow beasts. One crystal versus all eight will not matter. You will be even with your foe and allow us a fighting chance. Yet, if we wait we will be killed off before we can even reach the Crystal Common Grounds. The beasts I showed you, those horrendous creatures, are dormant now. Through the vision in the water, they are harmless. Yet, you know that will not be true when the time comes that they will attack. I can make no promise of time, however, it is for our best hope that I urge you to take into consideration my suggestion. You saw what happened to Dalium. We did not stand a chance, but now we can act before the beasts make their move."

"The Sun told me to gather the crystals before I face Medaia. I will not stray from my quest."

Zoren sighs, "You are letting the Sun control your destiny." He scowls, "You are a fool."

Linum turns her back on him. She storms off into the woods to find Charles. From his breast pocket, Pyro releases an indignant huff. Zoren rushes forward to follow after Linum's path. Golden light streams through the trees, brushing away the shadows and illuminating all the jovial sensations of the early morning's light. Hope fills the sky with the sweet soothing smell of the crisp air. Zoren watches as Linum sweeps around a tree trunk. Her face is serious and enlightened with a golden shroud of light beaming down from the Heavens above. Zoren's oceanic eyes tinge with the sadness of the distant shadows while his skin glows in the light of the Sun. He squints to see where she turned. He haughtily strides forward and is on the brink of reaching the clearing. He hears Linum's voice call out to Charles. He is about to push past the trees when he feels a sharp pain scorch the back of his neck. Zoren falls forward flat on the ground. Pyro jumps out and releases a loud hiss and scurries away to find Linum.

Charles's shoulders are slumped back and his hands lounge by his sides. He looks like a traveler passing through the woods. He appears foreign in his armor with his small meek frame barely able to support the weight of his heavy silver chestplate. Although he carries a scabbard, he is unarmed. Linum stands at his opposite, urging him to rush so they may chase after Zoren's silver whip. Her armor fits smoothly around her bodice and her face brightens with a vibrant passionate grin.

"Come on Charles!" she hollers.

He grunts in response as he takes a slow step forward like a turtle shrinking into his oversized shell. He peers at the blue sky and scratches his head. "Where did the whip go?" Charles anxiously looks at Linum.

Linum catches sight of the small but fierce glow of the cold fire sprouting up from the overgrown green grass. Pyro tumbles down in front of her, hissing and squeaking with alarm. She does not understand.

Linum bends down and picks up the small frightened flame and exclaims, "Where is Zoren?"

She cocks her head, staring at the shadowed trees. Linum lifts her sword from the scabbard with caution. Her metal blade catches the light, releasing a beautiful glow as the crystal shimmers in the Sun. A branch snaps from behind. Both Charles and Linum hear the rustling of bushes as something approaches nearby.

"Show yourself!" squeaks Charles in a weak and shaky voice, his eyes straining to identify the source of the noise from behind the trees. The light of the Sun shines on him and reflects off his armor.

"Get behind me," Linum warns. Her eyes scan the trees for movement. She catches a glimpse of a shoulder protruding behind a tree trunk. She dares not to move. Linum hears rustling in the grass. She remains in her position and watches as Zoren's metal whip slithers away into the woods, presumably, after Zoren. Pyro runs after Zoren's whip, which leaves Linum and Charles alone to face the foes in the trees. Charles sinks deeper into his chestplate. His face grows redder at each passing moment, like a tomato ripe for picking. The shades of green appear to melt together as the trees sway in the breeze. Asterian floats down from the Heavens and lands with a peaceful thud. His eyes embrace the surroundings as he lets out a casual roar. Linum pats his head, locking eyes with a young woman standing behind the closest tree. The woman jumps, sending her short light brown hair flying upwards.

Linum is able to make out the creek with the clear water flowing silently beyond the outline of trees. She is aware that she is being watched by countless eyes surrounding herself and Charles.

With a powerful and unshaking voice she demands, "What did you do to Zoren?"

No response is given, but as she lifts her sword, points it at the dense line of trees, and takes a steady step forward, an arrow whizzes down from above the treetops. It lodges into the moist ground right in front of her foot. Linum remains in her position. Another arrow lands next to her. With a tired moan, Asterian takes off into the air. He waves his great wings which shakes the first line of trees, causing the birds to take off into the air. With a satisfied huff, Asterian disappears, soaring towards the Sun.

Linum takes another brash step forward and yells into the crowd of hidden onlookers, "I am here to receive the Sun Crystal of the Terrace Gardens of Nominia."

She hears rustling behind the trees. When she opens her mouth to speak again, someone shouts shrewdly, "Thief!"

"I am Linum, and I have been given a quest from the Sun to collect the crystals of legend. I need to gather the green Sun Crystal for the sake of Solenium."

A gentle voice yells back, "And how do we know that you are not here to steal our crystal and bring about a great darkness to Nominia?"

Linum takes a careful step forward in the direction the last voice called out from. "I am not a thief. I am the heir to the throne of the Kingdom of Dalium and this is my brother, Charles. We have left Dalium due to the attack of the Midnight Persecutor and the unleashing of beasts upon our people."

"Then you are a coward." The gentle voice takes a deep breath to summon its strength, "You left your people to die!"

"I killed the Midnight Persecutor with my own blade. I watched the suffering of others and fought until–"

A harsh voice cuts in, "Take your last breath now and savor the sight of the Sun above you, for this is the last precious moment of life that you will live."

"I am the Queen of Dalium, slayer of the Midnight Persecutor, and I am destined to kill Medaia."

A solemn silence rushes over the entire forest, only the shrill laugh of a crow may be heard echoing through the land.

The young woman with short curly hair approaches. Her emerald green eyes twinkle with the affection of the Sun as she flutters her flowery wings made up of clusters of orchids. Her entire body is coated in the orchids as her exposed Sun-kissed skin gleams underneath the radiance of the light. She wears a dress knit from the stems of the flowers and the orchids themselves.

She clears her throat and speaks with stern apprehension at the confident Linum and shaking Charles. Charles's armor rattles against his body as he looks tentatively at the young woman before him.

"I am the daughter of Priestess Irene and General Cedar, I am Captain Orelia Chlonia Oku."

Charles's jaw drops as he collapses to the ground in a rough bow, but Linum remains standing. More people wearing wreaths of vegetation with their hair laced in flower crowns and braided with herbs approach. Some of them hold spears carved from the surrounding trees while others carry bow and arrows composed of animal bones. But all of them have floral wings made of the stems and buds of the flowers they bear as a centerpiece on their heads. Their faces are painted with different symbols – the moon, trees, shrubs, sunflowers, roses, mushrooms, daisies, geraniums, orchids, lilacs, jasmines, tulips, poppies, lilies – of all kinds of natural arrangements. A few of the fairies have two markings, one on each cheek. Orelia has a mark on the left side of her face, below her eye is a painted orchid. On her right cheek she has a turmeric marking in the shape of the Sun.

Linum speaks up. "You will take us to your Sun Crystal and we will not harm any of you." Her voice is powerful. She is unintimidated by the sharp spears made of wood and the bone bow and arrows aimed at her. She extends a hand to Orelia, "Do we have an accord?"

Orelia smiles and laughs, her pink lips stretch into a grin. She grasps Linums hand and pulls her into a hug. Linum backs up, startled. Orelia blinks with her wild emerald eyes reflecting the wilderness surrounding them. She is disappointed by Linum's startled expression.

She asks peevishly, "Do you not remember me?" Her cheeks redden and her wings flutter with the gentle dismissive breeze. Orelia turns to Charles with a pleading look in her wild eyes, "We talked during the Midnight Gala."

Charles, still on the ground, shakes his head. "I remember that Dalium held a huge dance inviting members from each territory. However that was eleven years ago and I apologize I do not remember you or anyone in particular from that night."

She shrugs, her wings flap together and she is lifted into the air, "I suppose it was many years ago."

The wind blows gentle autumn leaves across the tender earth. The fairies shudder as the air pulls them off the ground and into the air. They hover at a steady pace, flapping their vibrant wings to keep afloat.

Linum whistles and Pyro rushes out of the nearby brush. The fairies watch, taken back in surprise as the small creature jumps onto Linum's extended palm. He slithers up her arm and rests on her shoulder. Pyro releases a soft sigh and Linum asks with a coarse growl, "Where is our guide? His name is Zoren and this is his flame." She gestures towards Pyro with a tilt of her head and waits with a steady composure for a response.

Muffled noise erupts from the crowd surrounding Charles and Linum as the fairies talk amongst one another. Orelia does not join them, she flutters a few feet off the ground and lands before Charles. She offers a hand for him to stand. His face reddens and his hazel eyes drop as he lifts himself up and brushes off the dirt and the grass that clings to his armor.

She laughs and faces Linum with a peaceful smile, "Our people only saw the two of you in these woods."

Another fairy with dandelion markings on his cheek and a bright dandelion tunic steps forward. He confirms what Orelia had said with a callous face. The rest nod in agreement and a few others vocalize their same conclusion.

Charles questions, "So you never saw Zoren?"

"He was right behind me in the woods." Claims Linum, her eyes widen and her hands begin to tremble. She states with a cold defiance, "You are all liars."

The dandelion man spits at her, "You dare call us liars! You have insulted General Cedar's daughter even after she gave you a welcoming introduction." He yanks a spear free from a fairy coated in daisies. The dandelion man throws the spear at Linum from a distance. It spirals through the air. Just before it makes contact with her skin, Linum pulls out her sword and with a mighty stroke of her blade she slices the spear into two perfect halves that fly off into the crowd.

Orelia puts her hands out in earnest before her. She turns to the fairies, "Please don't make this meeting end in violence!"

A fairy cloaked in rosemary chimes in, yelling, "Vondur, show respect. And all of you listen to your captain!" With that the rest of the fairies bow their heads and salute Orelia, who in turn nods her head slightly.

Orelia bows to Charles and Linum. "I assure you that the fairies of Nominia are generally peaceful. However, I apologize, for I have no clue who Zoren is. We were making our general rounds through the forest when we spotted the two of you in the clearing. We have made no arrests today and we are the only scouting group deployed at this hour. Perhaps, he will turn up or the others in the Terrace Garden of Nominia may know of him."

Linum glares with distrust lingering between herself and the overly kind Orelia, but her lips remain tightly sealed and she sheaths her sword.

Charles sighs, "And the green Sun Crystal of the Terrace–"

"I do not have the power to grant you the permission of taking it." Orelia interjects with a stern apprehension. She takes a light breath and continues, "It reappeared just three days ago in our Sacred Sun Temple, but if you want it you must negotiate with Queen Aconite."

Linum snarls, "Take us to her."

Orelia's emerald eyes for a moment turn cold. Yet, she blinks and the green of her eyes becomes gentle once more. She indignantly flutters her wings. Orelia warns, "You must watch the way you talk Linum. I recall from the Midnight Gala you were once a good natured young girl. However, your disagreeable hate and wrathful manor, as of now, will only lead to suffering." Her wings stretch. The flower buds blossom into vibrant whimsical turquoise and pink orchids. They contrast the orange, white, and coral orchids already present, cloaking her body. She smiles and twirls in the air. Orelia states, "Besides why let the shadows take away the best gift the Sun ever gave anyone? Every smile is unique and precious. It is the present of the Sun that fills your soul with light." She gives a large grin at the Sun, and winks at Charles, spreading her hands out to Linum. "Hold on tight!"

Linum reaches out to Orelia. The stems of her orchids spread down Orelia's arms and travels onto Linum's hand. The flowers coil up Linum's arm and knot themselves around her waist like a harness. With a whip of Orelia's hands the stems elongate forming a great chain that spreads and wraps itself around Charles. Pyro squirms underneath the green stems and squeezes out on top. He flashes a violent red and singes the corners of the stem. Orelia yelps and faces Linum in anguish, "Control *that* flame or leave it behind."

Linum scolds Pyro, "Do not burn the orchids and hold on if you would like to accompany us" –she adds hesitantly– "otherwise you will not find Zoren."

Pyro hisses and submerges himself underneath the tangle of vegetation engulfing both Charles and Linum. Orelia opens her wings. She signals to her fellow fairies, who each take a hold of the stems. Simultaneously they flap their wings and Linum and Charles are lifted into the air.

"Linum," exclaims Charles, he groans at seeing the ground shrink away. "Zoren could still be down here!" Charles bellows over the flapping of the fairies' wings.

Linum yells back in response, "We have a quest to complete. I will not give up our chance of entering the Terrace Gardens and finding the crystal. Also, Zoren was not leading us properly. His hateful banter against the Sun would only jeopardize our mission."

The birds sing and the hawks soar. Linum spreads her hands out, feeling as free as the soaring birds. The air whips against her face as the Sun's light grows stronger far above the canopies of trees.

"Where are you taking us," asks Charles with an inquisitive beam as they fly over the rushing creek and out of the woods to a meadow stretching as far as their eyes can see. The green fields melt with the dismal grey of distant mountains.

Orelia smiles and echoes, "You cannot walk to the Terrace Gardens of Nominia."

The Sun streams through her wings, scattering shadows on Linum and Charles as they move through the air with ease. Linum looks at the great puffs of white clouds that begin to twist and meld into the shape of a quartz staircase. Orelia and the other fairies land and hoist Charles and Linum onto the smooth surface. The orchids retract and Orelia bows, "Welcome to our domain."

The twirling form of the clouds clear while they hurry up the quartz steps and brush past curtains of ivy drooping from magnificent pillars embellished with gold lace to reveal a wondrous kingdom before them. The skies are a magnificent gentle blue and the clouds linger upon the freshly watered grass. Dew drops from the petals of the endless cascade of the variety of flowers spread across the land. Fairies coated in different floral arrangements and herbal combinations zip on past them; they flutter their wings that appear to glow in the Sunlight. A young girl dressed in lilac, waves to Charles and he bows in return. She giggles and takes off into the air to follow after her parents dressed in lotus flowers.

The providential air is ripe with the Sun's blessing as life teems in wonderful green fields all around Linum and Charles. The other fairies, from the woods, take off into the air, their wings buzz like honey bees. The sound is harmonious and soothing as they zoom away beyond the fields towards the great wooden buildings, beyond. The dandelion man, Vondur, exchanges a distasteful glance at Linum. He follows after the rest for some time. Then, Linum spies him darting around a corner whereas the others continue straight. The overwhelming peaceful vehemence of the green gardens leaves behind only the sensation of the sublime; thus, she does not ponder this any longer than a green grasshopper remains sitting on a log. The air is crisp and cool and the wind is gentle as it streams through her dark hair. Linum's azure dress flows behind her, pressing against her body. The fabric dances like swaying water. The distant grey mountains appear small and insignificant to the beauty of the floating isle. The island is held up by the power of the Sun, according to Orelia, who floats daintily on the breeze. She waves her hand around and directs Linum and Charles's attention with excitement. She directs them to observe the grandeur of blossoming life within the wonderful Terrace Gardens of Nominia.

"To your right you will find the clover patch." Then, she points to a plot of land with bright red fruit, "That is our tomato garden." Orelia lets the wind lift her into the air. She exclaims cheerfully, "Ahead of us are the sunflower fields. They stretch up to the very edge of our great kingdom."

And she mustn't forget to mention the grove of apple trees, birch trees, mahogany trees, the bamboo forest, and the magnolia trees; nor, the endless list of vegetation growing in the farming fields or the bountiful elaborate gardens that remain behind the castle walls. The land is beautiful, but Linum begins to grow restless as the list increases and keeps increasing. Their destination seems so far off as Orelia continues to talk without pausing. She makes small quips about the different types of fairies and assures both Charles and Linum that they *must* be able to relate to that. However, her continuous and endless speech pulls Linum's attention away from the great grandeur that Orelia earnestly expresses with bountiful words. Linum focuses on the sight of the city before them.

The structures are much smaller and not as grand as the natural aspect of flowing flower beds and growing plants, but the naturalness of the light woods, the riverbed pathways, and the appraisal of ivy clinging to the thatched roofs is appealing. The houses are smaller in size in comparison to those in the Kingdom of Dalium. Most of the dwellings resemble small cottages laced with moss or painted with autumn leaves. Orelia suddenly stops, she places her bare feet onto the warm surface of the riverbed rock path and lets her hands dawdle at her sides. The orchids writhe around her and adjust their composure, clinging tightly to her skin. She grins and softly waves her hand in the air to knock on the redwood door of a small cottage covered in ivy.

"This is where I live," Orelia explains as the door swings open to reveal a small woman dressed in yellow marigolds. The woman holds up her hands to the visitors.

"Mother, this is Charles and Linum." Orelia's face becomes serious. Her emerald eyes flash dangerously but her voice is gentle, "They are from the royal family of the Kingdom of Dalium and I was wondering if we may offer them shelter for the duration they remain in our humble kingdom."

Orelia's mother nods her head, but her faded emerald green eyes gleam with tears. Her mouth quivers, but no words escape. She steps back, welcoming Linum and Charles into her humble home and swiftly closes the door behind Orelia.

The cottage is tiny and decorated with wooden carvings of the Sun. The framework of wooden beams, stretching across the single room to hold up the hay thatchwork, creaks as Linum and Charles step forward. Sunlight streams in through small cracks in the ceiling where the hay has given way and fallen across the floor. The floor is a solid mahogany with a simple grass rug placed in the center of the single room extending into a kitchen and bedroom. The beds are made of straw. Animal hides hang on the walls along with thyme and basil and rosemary. On an altar sits a stone carving of the Sun. Next to the carving is a prayer book and a light birch bowl filled with maroon clay.

Orelia's mother, Irene, hugs Charles and kisses Linum on the cheek. Irene's face is ridden with wrinkles.

Her hair is a deep grey. She stands back with a smile and stretches out her hand, revealing a black rose.

"Mother," squeals Orelia in fear, "I thought that you said you burnt it!"

Irene shakes her head and takes a slow step forward, reaching out to hand the rose to Linum. "Take it," Irene whispers with a strong and resilient voice.

Linum kindly rejects, "No thank you."

"You must take it." She urges with wide eyes and tears sliding down her face, "You must hold this black rose, for it is yours."

"I do not understand." Linum glances at Orelia in desperation.

Orelia steps in, her hand rests on her mother's shoulders. She inquires, "Mother, why are you offering Linum this demonic rose? Burn it and purify the ashes so it may regrow into a pure flower for the Sun."

Irene nudges Orelia aside and steps closer, pressing the rose against Linum's hand, "You have known devastation these last few days. You have seen death and it haunts you. You must hold this rose since it grew three days ago for you."

Linum holds the rose tenderly, the black petals twist and fold into itself. The rose slithers in her hand, but when she attempts to drop it, it clings to her fingers. The stem grows and the thorns latch onto her skin. The deathlike petals begin to glow as a drop of Linum's blood lands on a single thorn. The rose stops moving and lies in deathlike tranquility in her hand. Linum looks up, startled, but Irene reassures her with calm eyes and nods.

Linum touches the soft petals with her other hand and the rose shrivels into a pile of ash.

Irene exclaims, "Death may linger even in the ripeness of life. It feeds on those who are willing to let it claim them and those who are afraid of valediction. However, death may be changed into something beautiful like this blackrose. A dark omen and warning from the Sun may blossom into something passionate, graceful, and kind. Power can bring light or darkness. A rose is not evil nor is it good and neither is a Sun Crystal."

From the dark ashes sprouts a small bud which shoots upright in a spiral of thorns and green leaves. The bud explodes in a fury of light into a vibrant red rose with more sentimental petals and passion than the prior blackrose. Everyone's eyes fall on the rhythmic swaying of the new flower in Linum's hand.

Irene breaks the stunned silence, her voice is gentle, "Rebirth is like the neverending waves of the ocean. Some waves will be violent and powerful and others peaceful and gentle, but all will be beautiful."

Linum looks at the small woman before her, who reaches for the red rose and places it into the bowl of maroon clay.

"I was in a prayer at the Sacred Sun Temple, when the blackrose sprouted in our most holy and pure of gardens. I could not burn it because it is a message of your arrival. The Sun has chosen a champion, one that is strong, powerful, ambitious but also desires peace. Linum, it is up to you to decide what rose you will become. One that gives in to death or one that perseveres above it."

Chapter 14
Split Allegiance

The Sun is low in the sky. Shadows fall across the small cottage. Linum has been sitting in silence beside her brother. Orelia smiles and laughs as Charles and her converse. Yet, Linum ignores Orelia. Her eyes are concentrated on Pyro's small flames and the pink crystal in her sword. It whispers to her and her eyes darken with its poisonous thoughts spilling into her mind.

Irene observes Linum from the opposite end of the room. She watches Linum's black hair fall across her dark eyes. She stares at the pink crystal in Linum's sword with awe. Irene nods her head thoughtfully. She notices Linum's unbreaking gaze and frowns. The wrinkles around her eyes harden as she squints, carefully observing the etchings from a distance. Orelia floats forward and lays a hand on her mother's shoulder. Irene shivers at her touch.

Orelia whispers, "I need to go but I will be back for the festival."

Irene fiercely pulls Orelia to the side as Sunlight pours into their home. She gestures to Linum and Charles, who are resting at the opposite end of the cottage.

Sternly she inquires of her daughter, "How did you know that they would be in the woods?" Irene examines Orelia's face. "Did Aconite tell you to search for them?"

Orelia drops her voice. She glances at Linum and Charles. Then, she speaks in a hushed whisper, "I was told they would be by the creek."

Irene nods. Her eyes are solemn. Orelia shifts from side to side.

"Why have they come?"

"They want the Sun Crystal."

Irene stares into Orelia's emerald eyes. She sighs, "I know Aconite did not send you there to help them with their quest. You can tell me the truth or keep it to yourself, but I wish to advise you to be careful of what Aconite commands. Her intentions are not always for the good of the people. Recall what happened to your father–"

Orelia interrupts her, "Mother, you have no proof of that incident. However, I will heed your warning." Her voice is gentle and kind. "I have been told to get to know them in hope that Nominia will prosper from their parting."

Irene looks at Linum and Charles. She shakes her head and pleads to Orelia, "Trust in the Sun's guidance."

Linum rests her head against the wall of the cottage. She watches Orelia and Irene talk. Orelia's face falls in and out of the shadows. Irene appears impassioned.

Charles taps Linum's shoulder. He says, "When do you think we will meet the queen?"

She shakes her head. Pyo squeaks. Linum observes Charles's new outfit. He now wears a clean beige shirt that Irene had given him shortly after their arrival in the cottage.

Finally, Irene walks away from Orelia. She beckons Linum and says, "You and your brother need to rest. Feel free to make use of anything you find within this cottage."

Orelia shouts from across the room, "I need to attend a meeting with the queen. I will inform her of your situation, Linum." She waves to Charles and adds, "I understand that you would like to meet with her to discuss your quest, so I will attempt to schedule an audience with her on your behalf."

Linum steps forward. She is about to protest, but Irene presses a soft hand onto Linum's shoulder. She whispers to Linum, "An audience with the queen is pointless. However, you will meet her soon, I assure you of that. Yet, for now, you must take the opportunity to rest. Aconite will make an appearance tonight. I suggest you wait until then."

Linum pulls away from Irene. She watches as Orelia opens the redwood door and takes off into the air. Irene shakes her head and lets out a sorrowful sigh.

***

The sky is a magnificent blue. The Sun is a soft orange. The morning clouds have cleared from the green fields and the working fairies are visible below. Children covered in vegetation hoe the soil. Men till the land. Women seed the fresh earth. Colorful fairies decorated in bright tunics and festive hats string ornaments across small buildings. Others haul up tents coated in flowers and build makeshift stands. Orelia smells the warm scent of fresh bread. She lands gracefully by a bakery. She enters the shop and takes in the delectable scents. There are pies lining the shelves, biscuits in numerous baskets, and loaves of all kinds of breads. She approaches the counter. The baker has weary eyes. His face is sunken and his nose is a bright red. His wife sits in the corner of the shop, kneading dough. His two young children play on the floor. They all have different vegetation lining their faces and making up their wings. The baker has a wreath of garlic cloves above his head, his wife is covered in daisies, his daughter wears parsley, and his son has a cloak of cilantro. The baker and his children all appear exhausted.

His son moans, "Father, can I not have one piece of bread?"

The wife looks at her son, apologetically. She whispers, "We bake the bread to sell." In turn, she clutches her round stomach, ripe with another child. Her face winces. She too is hungry.

Orelia places five copper coins onto the counter. The coins are detailed with images of a cherry blossom. She then stacks two silver coins, the image is of a blade crossed with an axe. She draws in a deep breath and sighs pleasantly, slipping her hand beneath her orchids. She feels the smooth lining and cold touch of one last coin. Her hand slips it out from within her single pocket on her white dress. It is now empty. She looks at the rare piece within her hand. The gold coins are worth far more than the silver or copper. Orelia had earned it a year ago. She was sent on a long tiresome mission on Aconite's behalf. Orelia had planned to spend the coin to surprise her mother with a new Sun totem and purchase a metal spear for herself. She smiles and places it next to the other coins. The single gold piece is decorated with an intricate carving of the Sun. The inscription on the gold piece reads, "Have faith in the Heavenly Sun Lands." The baker's eyes light up.

He blurts out in surprise, "Captain Orelia, this is too much." He lets out a hearty laugh, "You could buy our entire bakery."

Orelia smiles. "I will take four loaves of bread, one pumpkin pie, and cookies please."

The wife bows her head. Her eyes glisten with tears. "Thank you."

Orelia curtsies to her and the baker hands her a basket containing the freshly baked goods. He drops a couple biscuits on top.

"Tell your mother that I am grateful."

Orelia waves to them and runs out of the shop. She flies into the air, letting the warm glow of the evening Sun fall against the side of her face. She looks at the distant wooden castle, but heads away from it. She lands in the green fields next to the children hoeing the land, the men tilling the soil, and the women seeding it. She sets the basket on the ground and grabs a biscuit. A young boy dressed in oregano, sheepishly backs away from her. She extends her hand and the boy flinches. She can see the purple bruises on his legs, the red welts on his arms, and the scars marking his face. She offers the bread to him. He smiles and snatches it from her hand, taking a large bite. Orelia whispers, "Just to make sure to bring some bread to your mother, Agape." He nods his head, dutifully. Orelia laughs and shouts to the entire group, "Please help yourselves. There is plenty for everyone to share." She flutters her wings and the entire group salutes to her and whistles in cheer.

Orelia carries forward, now heading to Acontie's wooden fortress. The structure towers over all the small shops and cottage-like homes. She sighs and looks back at the streets. They are filling up with fairies as they prepare for the festival. Orelia scans the crowd with sad emerald eyes. She bows to a lonely beggar walking past her. She has nothing more that she can give. Irene's words echo through her mind, *Trust in the Sun's guidance.* The Sun now glows a fiery red. Orelia musters her courage.

Orelia rushes into the throne room. She shoves the doors open. Queen Aconite lazily stares at her.

"I apologize that I am late." Orelia speaks loud and clear. She keeps her voice steady. She can feel her blood rushing through her body. Her heart rate quickens.

Aconite adjusts the golden crown on her head and stretches her wolfsbane wings, creating monstrous shadows across the throne room. Aconite signals for her guards to leave. The doors close with a loud bang. Orelia kneels at her feet.

"I assume they have arrived."

Orelia nods her head. "They are here for the crystal."

Aconite presses her nails into the wood of her throne. "My crystal is safe here with me." She points to a glass box that glows a brilliant emerald green in the light.

Orelia stands. She looks at Aconite and draws in a long breath before stating in a bold voice, "I do not think we should move forward with the plan of conquest."

Aconite replies in an uncaring manner. "I thought you were strong, Orelia. I thought you could handle the job. Did I make a mistake in choosing you to be captain?"

"I am strong and I will live up to my title, but I think that it would be best for the people of Solenium if we—"

The queen interjects, "I am glad that you have remembered your place as captain." Her blue eyes are stern as she scowls, "Your strength is your loyalty to Nominia." Queen Aconite draws herself up from the throne. She strides over to the balcony. Orelia follows her. Aconite states with a heartless voice, "Imagine what my kingdom would be like with the land of Dalium under my influence. Nominia would have enough power to rule over everything and anything."

Orelia glances at Queen Aconite. She shivers and Aconite grabs her arm. Orelia yelps in fright.

"For the good of the people we will do this. I want you to continue the illusion of kindness towards our guests. Gather more information on Linum and Charles. I will direct you further when the time comes."

Orelia nods. She presses her eyes shut. "I will await your further directions."

Aconite smiles. "Enjoy the Festival of Blossoms."

Chapter 15
Floral Night

Charles thanks Irene for her hospitality as he rushes after Orelia into the bountiful night, while flower blossoms fall across the sky like rain. Linum sits on the grass in front of the small cottage as Irene makes tea. She looks at the subtle stars that glow with affection above her. Her damp hair presses coolly against her neck as she hums the song she sang a few nights before. Irene emerges from behind the redwood door balancing a tea kettle and two teacups on a tray. Linum stands to help her, brushing off the dirt from her skirt, but Irene shakes her head. The marigold flowers on her dress stretch to life and lift the tray from her hands, placing it tenderly on the ground before Linum.

"Tea?" Irene asks with gentle eyes and a caring presence.

"Yes please."

Irene pours a cup of warm clear tea made from boiled mint leaves and a dash of honey. Her wrinkled hands shakily grasp the cup. She passes it to Linum, who holds it firmly between both of her clasped hands.

"Thank you."

Irene smiles. "No, thank you for coming to the Terrace Gardens of Nominia and thank you for accepting the quest."

Linum takes a sip of the warm liquid from the rough cup. She coughs, "I never told you of the quest."

"No, but you told Orelia of your goal of gathering the green crystal. Besides if you're after one of them I would assume you must collect all the other crystals from each region." Irene fumbles with her teacup, examining the steam escaping into the night sky, she adds, "To stop Medaia."

Linum sets her cup aside, "I never told you that."

Irene smiles and nods, "I am the Priestess of the Sun. I meditate in the fields of flowers underneath the glass roof of the Sacred Sun Temple each and every day. I pray for the peace and prosperity of Solenium. Yet, I have taken notice of a darkness spreading throughout the land. I know it must be Medaia's presence. Our flowers have begun wilting, the new buds are not as they once were. Our soils are drying and our floating island becomes heavier everyday." Irene draws in a deep breath. "However, we are still trying to expand what we have," she remarks grudgingly and sets aside her teacup.

"Surely you have informed your queen?"

Irene scowls and her hand shakes with quivering pain. "Yes, I have and so have others. The Poppy Fairy Troupe have predicted future violence in our land as evil seeps into our plantations and into their visions. The Sunflower Bards have not been able to recite their songs of cheer and goodness as they find no words to express in the Sun's favor. The Lotus Society's pond has been drying out" –she looks earnestly at Linum, her faded emerald eyes are brimming with tears, as her wispy grey hair blows in the light breeze– "and my husband, General Cedar, had been training his troops in preparation for war. He was taking action because he realized all of this. He went against Queen Aconite's wishes. I do not support war, because it is unnaturally waged by creatures of the same binding blood and origin of the Sun against one another; however, I do not believe that we should sit idly until disaster strikes. Yet, now that Cedar has passed, it would seem my word means nothing to the queen. My daughter, Orelia, has been meeting with the queen on my behalf almost daily to persuade her of my fear. I fear that Medaia will strike at any moment. Death is natural and known among my people, but Chlonia's suffering will not be forgotten as her blood is mine, and my parents, and my grandparents, and their parents before them, and so on."

Linum's eyes light up with excitement. She exclaims, "You are related to the daughter of the king and queen, who fought in the great war against Medaia."

"Yes I am, but no war is great that does not preserve what is right and true in our hearts and minds. The real war cannot be fought with weapons, for no blade can truly pierce the heart of a person, except a skilled blow from the mind and soul. Remember this Linum."

Linum nods, her eyes are solemn as the blossoms fall gracefully around them.

Irene stands, her strength is gone as she takes light delicate steps up to the door. "You should find both Orelia and Charles" –her eyes flash from the glow of lights omitting from the distant fields– "You would not want to miss the Festival of Blossoms." She catches a cherry blossom and examines it in her hands.

"This petal here foretells quite a lot about your future, the Festival of Blossoms will be spectacular this year and–"

Linum interjects, "But I must speak to Queen Aconite."

Irene gives a light chuckle. "You will speak to her and *you* will make her listen to reason." Irene disappears behind the redwood door and with a light clink, Linum knows it is locked. She has not removed her armor, unlike Charles who readily threw off his silver chestplate and slumped it against the cottage walls. Her hand rests on the hilt of her sword, but she does not unsheath it. She whistles the tune of the Everglades and Pyro pops up from underneath the folds of her dress. She offers a hand to the small flame, who eagerly jumps onto her tender palm and parades up her arm.

"Are you ready to storm a festival?"

Pyro squeals with excitement. His tiny orange flame turns a violent red. Linum grips her sword. She takes off in the direction of the sound of laughter and the glowing lights of string lanterns and bonfires. Irene peeks through the window, her sunken cheeks are laced with fresh tears as she waves a silent goodbye to Linum.

The Festival of Blossoms is vibrant and full of color as the sky glows full of fireflies and sweeping tangles of lanterns. Winged children run from place to place. Laughter fills the air as every face has new marks and new paintings of flowers and herbs doodled all over their naked skin. Flowers sprout from all corners, but Linum keeps her eyes scanning for Charles. The flower fields all sway to the sounds of crickets chirping and harps strumming out glorious sounds while a young woman wearing a sweet pea shawl sings a song about the flowers. Her voice rises and falls with her swaying body. The flowers tremble as a result of the sweet sound, stretching over the fields and sinking into the ears of her listeners. The fairies all clap in rhythm as she finishes her first cheery and upbeat song. She signals with the nod of her head to the orchestra of fairies residing in the air above her, and her voice picks up again, singing a rendition of "Floral Night."

Linum pauses to listen. She takes notice of the fairy's words as she sings,

Floral Night
With flowers
Dancing
And twirling
And
Spinning

Floral Night
With laughing
Cries
And singing
Howls

Floral Night
Under the veil
Of a thousand stars

Under the moon
And beyond bountiful tides

It's a beautiful Floral Night
Of spectators
Of sounds
Of music
Of solemn sentimentality
Lingering in the breeze
On the gentle moonlight haze
Of tender waves
With a sealing kiss
As the poets continue to play
On this Floral Night.

Linum watches as the fairies rise from the soil and begin to dance. Their colorful floral wear mix together as the women spin and the men catch and twirl. They all match the fast paced beat of her singing voice and tempo of the orchestra. Linum smiles at the celebration and turns her head away. She moves away from the dancing group of fairies to continue her search. Blossoms from all kinds of flowering trees fall like rain against the ground. She reaches out with her hand and catches a hold of one of the swaying blossoms before her. Pyro growls at the tender petals and Linum tosses it aside. More blossoms continue to dance and sway, falling with grace as she moves deeper into the fields. Linum's hands knot together, her knuckles crack, and the sound makes her hair stand on end. She shivers feeling a cold sensation travel down her spine, and out of habit she clutches her sword. She pulls on the hilt and hears the reassuring clink of metal.

Pyro trembles in anger as a young boy, no older than ten, approaches them. He bows his head and offers a small yellow rose. She removes her hand from the hilt of her sword and spins around to face the young boy. Linum smiles and accepts the flower, watching as he scurries away to chase after the other children, who are running wild and offering flowers to everyone around them. As soon as he is out of sight she lifts the tender rose and places it on her shoulder for Pyro to engulf. He sniffs it and licks it with his small vibrant flames, feasting on the gentle petals. Her shoulder glows brightly during the duration that Pyro spends consuming the flower. Passersby stare at her in trepidation and horror, others merely gesture to one another, but all regard the small flame on her shoulder with fear.

Linum begins to think of Zoren. Her eyes trace the ash that falls off her shoulder, while she strolls through the green fields and swipes with her hand at the flower rain. Like a swarm of gnats the flowers persist to follow her. She notices a small boy brandishing a grapevine and courteously offering the remaining grapes to all who stop and talk to him, she does not stop. However, after an old man plucks the remaining grape off the stem, the boy squeals with delight and he begins to crack the vine in the air like a whip. *Like Zoren's whip*, she notices. Pyro seems to sense this as well, for the petal he is munching on slips from his flames and crumbles onto the floor, but he pays no attention to it, rather, Pyro is locked onto the young boy with the grapevine. He lets out a tiny burst of sparks and a shrill moan. Linum pats his gentle and ravishing flames.

She whispers, "As soon as I get the green crystal, I will search for him." Pyro only whimpers in response.

She continues her journey, entering a large pathway full of many stands with small vendors, who offer little wooden figures to children and hand out free samples of delectable cuisine to the adults. Linum scans the faces of the fairies in vain. Not one of them possesses the emerald eyes of Orelia nor the hazel eyes of Charles. All the fairies before her are consumed by the meager objects on display at the stands. However, Linum knows her brother is not fond of such trivial goods. She knows that if he is anywhere at this festival, it would be where he can stare at the stars and dream. She passes through the vendors, keeping her head up high and ignores the coos and chants of the fairy merchants, "Madam, try some homemade kale tomato juice" and "Miss, brighten your day with these pearls" and "Hey you! Yes you, I have just what you need right here. Consider your life made easy with the use of my very own invention." Yet, she does not stop and passes them by without a second thought, raising her chin higher and higher at each shrill screech begging for her to buy from them. Linum spots the exit from the street vendors' menacing aisle and she rushes for it, pushing past consumed fairies, who convince themselves readily that this new product will work miracles for them! Absolute miracles.

She is just at the corner of freedom from the materialistic hounds, when a man in a dark cloak catches her eye. She only catches a glimpse of him, his face is covered by the hood of a dark blue cloak with silver scales around the trim.

"Zoren!" She cries out in relief. However, the man dodges behind the crowd and through a narrow space between an old booth with sagging satin curtains and another stand. She rushes after him and Pyro clings to her shoulder to stay on, as she shoves her way through the material fairies, and squeezes through the narrow space. She tumbles forward into a dark landscape. The man stands before her in complete darkness. He crouches down and offers a hand. She accepts it with caution, staring into the deep and sullen eyes of the foreign man.

"Linum." He whispers and strokes her hair. She pulls away searching with desperation through the darkness, but there is no trace of light except Pyro, who yelps, causing his flames to grow larger. The man growls, "You may not leave until you have listened to me!"

"Who are you?" She yells back, pulls out her sword, and charges forward to slash at him.

He simply reaches out and grabs the tip of the blade in between his fingers. His deep sullen eyes glow a brilliant white and Linum falls back. Her blade shatters. Pyro freezes mid air. He comments with pride, "I am just a servant."

The man stares her down. He does not offer a hand to help her up. Instead Linum lifts herself up and stares hopelessly at the ground before her. She rummages through the air, feeling for something, anything in the emptiness. The man lifts his hand and a cherry blossom explodes into light, like a candle it flickers.

"Quick follow me, Linum. She must talk to you and you only have until the light fades before I must return you." The man grumbles, he casts the cloak aside which stretches into a doorway and swings open to reveal a room that glows a brilliant green.

Linum stares at him. He does not look like Zoren at all. He has long silver hair that glows green from the reflection of the doorway which darkens his sullen eyes below his bushy grey eyebrows. With the nod of his head, he commands, "Do not waste the little time you have." He directs her with an ominous pointing of his hand.

Linum enters through the makeshift doorway into a bright land full of colorful vegetation. The sky is a welcoming blue with no clouds in sight. The sky is full of flying beasts that maneuver through the welcoming light. The beasts are all covered in miraculous colors with wings as large as the entire kingdom of Dalium. Instead of shadows falling across the ground, light streams from underneath their ruffling and dazzling display of feathers. The tender blue soil beneath her feet sparkles and sways at each and every step as if she is standing in a pool of water. Every kind of plant surrounds her in a vast landscape of greenery and freshness.

"How have you liked the Terrace Gardens of Nominia?" sounds a voice with youthful and resilient freshness.

Linum twirls around, her dress stretches and shrinks and her eyes catch sight of a fairy with the wings of a blue butterfly landing before her. She smiles radiantly and the Sun appears to beam through her pearly white teeth. Her eyes sparkle and she laughs, offering a hand to Linum. Linum shakes her hand cautiously. She follows the fairy as she moves from side to side, waiting for Linum to respond.

"Are you the queen?" Linum responds with a contemptuous frown.

"I was queen, I am no longer." Answers the fairy with a gentle smile and shining emerald eyes.

"Who are you and what do you want with me!"

The fairy with butterfly wings laughs. She rises into the air. After stretching her wings wide, she lands back to the ground and positions herself comfortably on a throne of green shrubbery.

"I am the divine guardian of this portion of the Heavenly Sun Lands. I want simply what *we* all hope that you are able to do. However, I must be quick in informing you, Linum, for I do not have much time. Your candle will fade and I must inform you of what I know, for a mortal may not spend much time here. It would not be wise for you to take in too much of the Everglades."

Linum's eyes grow wide and immediately she looks around in awe, exclaiming, "This is the Heavenly Sun Lands."

"This is only a portion of the Everglades. It is where I have chosen to reside. You will learn more of the Heavenly Sun Lands in time, but that is not why I have brought you here." She speaks swiftly, "I am Chlonia. I am sure you are aware of me from the legends. After my parents both died at Medaia's hands I was given the throne. I was young and strove for the best that I could manage with my powers. I was an extremely gifted fairy, I learned from my mother some enchantments that would be powerful in times where protection would be necessary. I was a very cautious queen out of fear that Medaia would strike again, for the poppies kept murmuring of it on the night she was sealed away. That was when I made a plea to the Sun to raise the Terrace Gardens of Nominia into the sky. This way we would be untouchable from the land."

Chlonia smiles at Linum. She continues, "The Sun is kind and merciful, but it has costs as do all things. Since I asked the Sun for a favor, I had to give up something in return. I gave up my powers. My powers of foresight, which were a blessing bestowed upon me by the Sun itself." Chlonia looks to Linum, making sure she is following her story. "I only mention this, because as of late my powers returned to me. I saw you and another young man with my kin, but I saw darkness in the air. At first I did not understand, for the Terrace Gardens are untouchable in the skies; however, with the return of my powers it would seem something has caused the Sun to go back on its old deal of protection. Immediately, I requested an audience with the Sun itself and was informed war is on the horizon. The Sun has agreed to keep the island in the sky, but it no longer contains its sacredness from the darkness. This is a warning, Linum.

With the return of the blackroses, Medaia is inching her way to Nominia and across the entirety of Solenium. I fear for the sake of this world if she is not stopped."

Chlonia looks past Linum and gasps as the man with silver hair appears. He holds the cherry blossom with a dim flickering light. She speaks quickly, "Linum, you do not have much time here, but I wanted to warn you of this. You hold darkness in your hands. I am also supposed to inform you on behalf of the Lady of the Sun that–"

The man interrupts her with a gruff voice, "Your Highness, she must leave before the light fades from this cherry blossom or else the quest will never be complete and she will be cast out into the darkness of the beyond."

Chlonia nods and smiles at Linum, "Heed my warning. Medaia is close, she is watching you. However, you must know that *we* all believe in you and that you are loved."

She beats her wings and Linum is flung backwards. Yet, Linum clings onto the doorway, fighting against the strength of Chlonia's mighty and immortal wings.

Linum yells, "Wait! Who is the Lady of the Sun?"

Chlonia beats her wings faster and Linum's hands slip from the doorway. She flies backwards into the complete darkness as the doorway disappears underneath the folds of the cloak. The gruff man appears and holds out the dimly lit cherry blossom. The smoke catches Linum and she slides down into a stance amid the darkness. The man tosses to Linum her sword, which she catches in amazement, for it is now intact without a scratch. He urges her to sheath it with his sullen dark eyes and furrowed grey brows. Pyro pounces onto her shoulder and burns brightly. The man crumbles the cherry blossom and it crashes to the ground. He mumbles, "The Festival of Blossoms is a time of visions. It is lucky you joined in on the festivities. I may now envision your mortal world and send you back to Nominia. Good luck Linum, for you must not fail. You are the Sun Champion and you must not fail." He fades from her vision as the darkness disappears rapidly around her, leaving her in a world of bright colors and flashing lights. Pyro squirms on her shoulder. Linum focuses her eyesight on the object ahead of her and finds herself staring at the satin curtains sagging over the old booth. She squints and spots, through a miniscule hole in the curtains, a blackrose, resting on the back shelf.

An elderly man pops up from behind the counter and asks critically, "Anything catch your eye, lady?" Linum shudders and backs away from the booth without saying a word. She brushes off the flower blossoms crashing against her, as she makes her way out of the aisle of vendors.

Her eyes dart through the many colorful painted faces of the crowd. By the time she has reached the center of the fair, where many fairies have gathered around a raised podium and others float in the air around it, she has accumulated a bouquet of roses. Yet, Charles and Orelia are not to be found. Surrounded by so many fairies, all in different arrangements of flower clothing and in such a massive quantity, it would be like shooting the distant stars and expecting to make contact with their fiery pits to locate them. Linum sighs and Pyro hisses.

Trumpets blare and a woman with golden flowing hair and icelike eyes appears from behind the podium. There are no guards surrounding her, but her frozen eyes give the appearance of someone strong, powerful, and not to be trifled with. Her long draping dress and huge wolfsbane wings fall to the floor and rest at her heeled feet. Her face is made heavily up of thick powder and her cheeks are a ruthless pink, while her lips maintain an unnatural bright purple. An ornate golden crown rests on the top of her golden locks as she addresses the crowd with a reproachful voice. "I have heard we have visitors among us" –she scans the crowd with condemning eyes– "but let us not be rude to deny them our hearts and welcome them into our Terrace Gardens. They have come all the way from our trusted ally, the Kingdom of Dalium. It would be my honor as your queen to introduce you to Prince Charles Noapten."

The crowd claps and cheers vigorously and Linum glances at him with disgust. He stands waving and bowing in return upon the quartz stage and Orelia hovers beside him.

"Unfortunately, the other visitor refused to attend our important ceremony, but she will be welcomed nonetheless into our kingdom," continues Queen Aconite with an exhausted smile.

Linum shrinks into the crowd as the fairies float upwards; she holds the bouquet of roses close to her chest and beckons for Pyro to diminish his flame slightly.

"Now onto ceremony procedures. The falling of these blossoms are a blessing to future generations. The flowers mark our strength and purity as a powerful nation. Now, for the ceremonial promotions. With the fall of the blossoms it is time to promote those who have proven themselves. Orelia Chlonia Oku has shown great strength and promise within these last few days. She will make an excellent general. I urge that everyone gives her a well deserved welcome as she steps forward to address you all."

The crowd claps with wild appreciation as the young general steps forward.

"It is with great honor that I address each and every one of you noble warriors and peacemakers. Tonight is the night we remember my father and the rest of the fallen heroes that have died for us to see a bright future. My father's death was a recent tragedy, but it is his memory and others like him that drives us to train harder. We need to hold onto our hope for a better future no matter our struggles. The Festival of Blossoms offers light to all our troubles. The guidance of the flowers will comfort those who have suffered. This festival is particularly special for I have seen a few cherry blossoms fall, which is a rare symbol at this time of year. I consider it a blessing from our most honored past queen, Chlonia. All of us need to have courage. We cannot let ourselves slip away. We need to stay true to one another and trust each other. Let us praise the Sun and let the Sun be our guide."

The crowd claps and cheers.

Orelia concludes her speech, "It is a great honor to receive this promotion tonight from captain to general. I will serve you with a loving heart, kindness, and a cheery smile. I will work daily to protect the people of Nominia, for the sake of prosperity for all. Thank you."

Her cheeks redden as she backs away from the roaring and praising crowd to stand next to Charles. Queen Aconite clears her throat, "I will happily accept General Orelia into the royal court. However, it would appear we now need a captain. Therefore, to maintain our tradition I must ask if anyone wants to fight Orelia and prove their worth to be accepted as captain of our fairy guard. Who has the courage to battle, our greatest warrior?"

Linum raises her hand and yells with a fierce voice, "I will!"

Queen Aconite squints through the crowd, "State your chosen flower and name yourself. Also step forward onto the quartz stage, challenger."

As Linum pushes through the crowd she declares, "I am Linum, Queen of Dalium. I choose my sword."

"You must have a flower to compete," scolds Queen Aconite, "and must have wings."

Linum stamps onto the stage, her sword drawn, "I choose the blackrose and I have wings." She yells out into the midnight sky and Asterian lands behind her stretching out his galaxy wings and roars. She tosses the bouquet of roses aside, but holds onto one blackrose and shows it to the crowd, who all gasp in horror.

"Kill it," screams a young girl.

"Smash it," hollers an old man.

"Crush it," chants the crowd, but Linum still clutches the blackrose. She tightens her grip around the eerie thorns.

After the chants rise and a few fairies begin to edge towards the stage, Linum tosses the rose at Queen Aconite's feet. She yells, "I challenge Orelia, but I am not interested in the title of captain. If I win I get the green crystal of Nominia."

The crowd hushes in silence.

"And if you lose?" hollers Queen Aconite in hatred.

"Then, you may receive my pink crystal of Dalium."

"Deal. Orelia has not failed me." Aconite smiles viciously. "Clear the square," she bellows with a deep commanding voice. All the fairies float upwards, creating an arena net with their flower garments. The flowers stretch and knot until Linum and Orelia are surrounded by flowers.

Aconite declares, "They will fight until one of them withdraws from the battle. The winner will retain both crystals and the loser will leave the grounds immediately. Is that clear?"

"Yes!" Spits Linum, her eyes flaring red as Pyro brightens viciously with flames illuminating the arena. She climbs onto Asterian's able back and raises her sword into the air, the pink crystal begins to glow.

Orelia hollers from across the arena, "I let you into my home and brought you to this city. But if it is a fight you want, then you will have one. My honor will not be questioned and the tradition may not be ignored." She drops her voice to a mere whisper and adds, "Please note Linum I gave you no reason for this lunacy."

Orelia raises her hands into the air and her orchids come to life, sprouting from the earth and breaking through the stone pathways. They wreathe around Linum as the crowd chants in a bleak murmur. Linum raises her sword and Asterian takes off into the air, dodging the piercing stems and twisting orchids. From a nearby fairy, Orelia grabs a wooden spear and charges towards Linum. The wood makes contact with her sword and the orchids grasp a hold of Asterian's legs, binding his feet together. Linum jumps off of Asterian. She begins to fall to the ground from the highest point of the arena. Orelia follows after her, the spear pointed and ready to be thrown. Linum grabs a hold of the vine and swings down to the floor. Pyro leaps off of Linum's shoulders and sets her orchids on fire.

"Ouch!" Hollars Orelia as she pats at her dress trying to extinguish the flame. Pyro squirms and hisses. His flames bite at her orchids with vicious power.

Queen Aconite narrows her cold eyes and signals to the nearby fairy dressed in dandelions, Vondur. He nods his head and leaves only momentarily, returning with a bucket full of water. Linum is busy slashing with her sword at Orelia, who dodges and wacks with her spear. Vondur takes advantage of the moment. He approaches Pyro. Pyro is distracted, spreading his flames across the vines to free Asterian. The orchids are singed as Pyro sears their lush green stems and burns the flowers to weaken their grasp on Asterian. Asterian roars and kicks but Pyro is focused on the flames that scorch the pursuing orchids. Vondur holds the fatal bucket above his head. The red from the flames makes his eyes appear sinister. He floats behind the small and brave flame. Vondur pours the water over Pyro. He rushes back into the crowd.

"Pyro!" Screams Linum as she turns to witness his pitiful angry squeaks of pain. Orelia's spear makes contact with her arm, ripping off flesh. Linum runs towards the meek flame, who falls like a shooting star down to the rough surface of the rock path. She lets go of her sword. She reaches out to touch his dimming light, while Asterian lands beside her and spreads his wings, protecting her from the ravaging orchids.

Orelia pauses holding her spear limp at her side. "I'm sorry Linum, is there anything I can do?"

Pyro's flame pulses like a heartbeat; he shivers and dims as a cold wind blows through, carrying his ashes away into the night sky. With stubby short wisps of smoke Pyro's flames point to the stars.

"I will find him," she promises as his vibrant red flame turns to an elegant orange, then a faded yellow, and melts down to a mere spark. With one last heartbeat pulse of his light, Linum's teardrop falls and surrenders forth the last hiss and puff of smoke. The ashes blow away as Pyro seeps from her fingers. His remains ride the breeze and float away, beyond.

Orelia stands behind Linum, "I'm sorry," she whispers.

Linum's hands roll into a fist as her nails press into her palms. Her face reddens. Her breathing is heavy as she takes in quick breaths and narrows her eyes. Queen Aconite watches intensely from the sidelines, interested and pleased with the outcome as her cruel purple lips stretch into a wicked smile. Linum stands and Asterian fades away, chasing after the cold breeze. Orelia stretches out a hand, offering to help her up. Linum grabs her hand and with a hard yank she throws Orelia to the ground. Linum seizes the spear. She aims it at Orelia's body. Linum's chest heaves. Her hair sticks to the side of her face while blood trickles from her fresh wound.

"Why are you doing this, Linum?" Bellows Charles from the side of the arena, his hazel eyes startled.

Linum raises the spear and throws it. The spear shoots through the air. It does not hit Orelia but targets the dandelion fairy with the bucket, who floats eagerly beside the queen. The spear is about to pierce his heart, when Orelia lifts her hand and the orchids extend and grab a hold of the blunt end of the spear. Orelia lifts herself up with a violent flutter of her wings and pulls. She lets the spear drop with a rough tug of her orchids. Linum runs for her sword and picks it up. She turns to face Orelia, who raises her hands in surrender.

Linum begins to shiver. The pulsing of the pink crystal in her sword matches the beating of her heart. Linum blinks and the world goes dark before her. She is surrounded by darkness. Linum watches her reflection. It is the same image she saw in the fountain. She stares at her reflection in the black granite wall. The black sludge rises and she willfully succumbs to it. She sinks beneath the dark murky liquid, closing her eyes to surrender to the monster within.

Orelia backs up against the wall of onlooking fairies. "Linum?" she questions, her voice trembling.

Linum's eyes shoot open, and the pink crystal glows violently. The sword drops from her hand as her form changes. Her eyes slit and her teeth extend into dagger-like points. Her hands stretch and conform into blue talons like the head of a spear sharpened to kill. Her back twists and molds into skeleton-like wings and her skin cracks. She screeches and runs forward on all fours appearing like a beast. The fairies gasp and fly away, but the beast pursues after them. She raises the bat wings and stretches across the sky to catch the fairies. Like a bat chasing after moths, she snaps at a few barely missing their wings or catching the edges of their flower skirts and tunics.

Orelia calls out to the beast, "Linum?"

It turns and howls at the moon, swooping down at Orelia. Charles runs forward and tackles Orelia to the floor.

He yells, "Get down!"

The other fairies scatter, but now the beast has her prey in her grasp. Like a spider trapping flies she finds Orelia and Charles to be a perfect meal and an easy target. She licks her jagged teeth with a green oozing tongue. With a ruthless snarl she pounces, floating into the air with talons extended to swipe at Charles, who stands protectively over Orelia. Orelia shoves him off of her and stands to face the monster. She reaches out a hand and the charred orchids from her dress extend and swarm the beast. Linum swipes at the flowers with fury, ripping the stems and snapping the newly formed buds. Orelia winces in pain and Charles crawls over to the dropped sword. He picks it up and swipes at the monster, creating a deep cut on her side. She falls back and whines, turning to observe the deep wound carved into her chest. With malicious eyes she releases a deep growl and runs at the two of them filled with vengeful rage.

Queen Aconite claps her hands together with superficial pleasure. She has arrogant and amused icelike eyes. Aconite exclaims, "What a fight. What power!" She stands from a distance with her poisonous flowers clinging to her side, creating a protective collar around her neck.

Charles stretches out the sword in front of him. Orelia retracts her orchids to bundle the remaining few around herself. The petals of the orchids cover the thin white dress she is wearing underneath her net of flowers. The pink crystal burns violently and scorches Charles's hands as he tries to clutch the hilt of the sword. The handle burns his hand with a wrathful glow.

Irene runs forward from behind the dispersing crowd. The beast rises into the air. It charges directly at the sharpened point of the sword, about to collide with it; however, Irene steps in between Linum and the other two. She stops the beast by touching the petals of a blackrose against the forehead of the creature. The beast plummets backwards, crashing against the stone surface of the floor.

It is knocked unconscious. Queen Aconite turns and flies away with a venomous grin stretched upon her face. Irene kneels over the body of the beast. She beckons for help to lift her up. Charles and Orelia rush forward, each grasping a leg and heaving the creature towards the large outline of the Sacred Sun Temple.

Chapter 16
The Sacred Sun Temple

Linum presses her palms against her aching forehead. Her dark brown eyes blink profusely as the light streams in above her and floods her senses. She is in a pool of clear soothing water. She moves her hands delicately, feeling the miniature waves rebound off the quartz walls and splash against her. Her hair floats on the water's surface. She observes beautiful water lilies drifting around her body. Linum is clothed in a white flowing robe.

Irene hovers beside her. She tosses down a white rose into the water's surface and mutters, "You gave in."

Linum tries to stand. Yet, she is unable to support herself since her feet are tangled by the water reeds. The reeds emerge from the small pool in clumps. The pool is located in the middle of a grand glorious room. The room is full of light streaming through an enormous glass dome that resembles the Sun. Pillars coated in ivy hold up the walls, stretching up towards the Sun. Golden eagles soar and perch upon ledges protruding from the walls. The eagles observe Linum as she struggles in the pool of water.

Linum notices Charles, who stands on a giant lily pad with burnt hands.

"Help me," she pleads as she tosses and turns in the water, splashing it over the sides.

Charles remains still. His brows furrow and he raises his chin. Linum's sword sits beyond her grasp on a small oak stand with the pink crystal still intact in its rightful place. Her blue dress and armor are neatly stacked beside the sword. All of her possessions have been cleaned and polished, except for her eight-pointed star necklace. Her necklace remains protectively around her neck. Orelia pushes open the grand golden doors laced with rose and grape vines. She floats beside Irene in silence.

Irene speaks with a straining voice, "Hear me Sun and purge the darkness from her heart and mind. If she is your champion let the water soak away the evil within and may she learn to control the beast with the strength of her heart. Give me the strength I need to teach her."

A solemn echo vibrates off the temple's walls. A warm breeze passes through with great force. The light in the room flickers and the golden eagles screech. Irene smiles, "I am Priestess of this Sacred Sun Temple. I am a healer of the mind and cleanser of the body. I grow the Sun's blessings, tame malice where it poisons our hearts, and I will cure Linum of this inner monster. I will turn the disease into a blessing of the Sun." Her attention turns to Linum. "Give me your hand."

Linum reaches out, water drips from her arm. The drops fall back into the pool, gently splashing water. Irene pulls Linum up and the reeds give way. Linum stands with caution. She is hugging the robe that sticks to her soaking frame.

Orelia whispers to Irene, "I must not be late on my first day as a general." She looks at Charles and continues,

"I was wondering if you would like to accompany me? There is always room in our formations for one more. Not to mention, our daily practice sessions will train you either with the skills of the bow and arrow or the spear."

Charles faces Linum, his eyes tentative. "I will go with you. You never know when those drills may come in handy. Besides, it will be best for me to train since you never know when your own sister will turn on you."

He turns away scowling and follows Orelia out the door; she pauses and looks back at Linum and offers a forgiving smile that appears to say, "It's alright, I understand."

But how could she? How could she understand? Nobody can understand. Linum's mind echoes these thoughts in her head over and over again, until she begins to choke on the air as if the sludge is pulling her down again. *You are a monster!*

Irene grabs onto Linum's shoulder, pressing a small bud of a blackrose against her cheek. Linum's eyes snap open and the air returns to her lungs.

"The crystal is feeding off of you like a parasite. If you ask it for strength and power, it has a cost. If you give into its temptations, then in return it asks for your life. The crystal wants to overtake you, because you are what keeps its concealed power alive."

"Alive?"

"Alive."

Linum shakes her head. "The legend never mentioned anything about this nor did the Sun."

"The Sun does not have to explain. It just gives and it takes. The power within the crystals is alive; there is blood in each one of these crystals as their centers are hollow. It is the blood of the Sun." Her emerald eyes twinkle and her gaze narrows to the pink crystal resting in Linum's sword. "I have studied these crystals for ages, but never have I seen one up close until our green crystal returned." She pauses to catch her breath and shivers, "No mortal may fully command the blood of the Sun, but you may learn to control it at a price. If you desire to use the power of the crystals you must fight a battle within. You must resist whatever challenge is offered, you must not fall into the blood of the Sun, and you must understand as you acquire more crystals new challenges will arise."

Linum nods.

"Do you accept the trial before you as it is your duty assigned by the Sun to carry out no matter where fate leads you?"

"Yes."

"Will you succumb to the Sun's possessing blood?"

"No!"

"And are you willing to undergo the struggles of learning control," Irene smiles, her eyes shine, "beginning this very moment?"

"I am ready and will do whatever it takes." Linum bows and the light streams over her.

Irene clasps her hands together and commands, "Then remove the robe and let the flowers clothe you for your training."

Linum obeys, she tugs off the white robe. It falls against her feet leaving her tan skin exposed to the Sun's radiant beams of light streaming through the glass. The surrounding flowers stretch up into the air. Lilacs dance, marigolds twirl, sunflowers swing, orchids blossom, bluebells shine, but only a red rose inches forward towards Linum. It twists and turns wrapping itself around her body. The thorns press against her skin, but do not cut it. By the time the rose reaches her neck, she is covered in a dress made out of ruby red petals. Linum twirls. Her cheeks glow and her eyes sparkle. The roses on the dress stretch out around her, extending as she spins. They swish by her side as she slows down.

Irene smiles sternly, "Roses are powerful flowers of both beauty and strength. They will provide life and hope while you undergo this training. After we are done you may shed the roses, put on your clothes and armor, and convince Queen Aconite to give you the next crystal."

"Thank you–"

"Do not thank me yet, for we have not begun." She collects herself and instructs Linum to stand on one of the ginormous lily pads. "Tell the roses to reach for the pink crystal only. The sword is just a means of conducting the energy of the Sun. Yet, this will require direct exposure, so you may grasp the full potential of just one crystal."

Linum nods as she stretches out her hands. The roses come to life, grasping the pink crystal and pulling it free of the sword. They retract around her body leaving the burning hot crystal in her hand. Her heart begins to beat faster and the pink crystal starts to pulse a soft passionate glow.

"Good. Now focus on your own heartbeat. Ignore the glow of the crystal and feel what it is like to be human. How does your heart feel?"

"It's beating really fast, I feel it pounding against my chest."

"But is it still your heart?"

Linum pauses, trying to block the tingling sensation in her hand as the crystal throbs harder. It attempts to pull her in. *Her heart?* She feels her heart struggle in her chest, sometimes skipping a beat to catch up with the crystal and then slowing down to match her own pace. Her chest begins to heave as sweat drips her cheek.

"Linum, is it *your* heart?"

"It is my heart."

"Focus Linum, try to stop the pulse of the crystal. The Sun is in you already; the Sun made your hands, the Sun made your smile, the Sun made your heart and helped to craft your mind. You do not need the Sun's blood, because it already flows within you. You do not need the power of creation, because you have already been blessed by it. Linum, you are most powerful when you are able to accept being you."

"I cannot." She groans, the crystal vibrates in her hand.

"Stop the pulse."

Linum tightens her hand around the crystal, she feels pain shoot through her fingertips and the light slowly fades from her eyes as darkness arises in the shadows of the room. The roses pinch at her skin and the light flutters back to existence. Her ears ring from the searing pain omitting from the crystal. She moans as the world becomes blurry, but the roses pinch at her again, drawing her back to consciousness. *I have the power of the Sun within me already. I am Linum and I will save this world from the shadows of evil.* Her mind repeats these phrases over and over again, but it battles against the lurking thoughts pumping through her veins from the pink crystal. *You monster, you beast, you need me, you want me. I am what you desire.*

"No!" She screams and presses her brave hands against the markings of the stars, carved onto the pink surface. The light of the crystal fades into a pale glow and her eight-pointed star necklace burns a brilliant blue, "I am Linum and I am the Sun's champion!"

The crystal changes to a murky pink color, its brightness is gone and the pulse is barely distinguishable.

"Have you stopped the pulse?"

"I have regained my heart."

"Excellent. Now you must access the power of the pink crystal without the help of the sword. You have only penetrated the fear of death within you. You must now fight the challenge the crystal possesses underneath its surface. Draw in your strength, find power in your breath, and close your eyes. Focus on what matters most to you."

Linum's eyes close softly, her lashes rub against her cheek and her breathing remains steady. She only feels her heartbeat and not the crystals, but sure enough the granite wall emerges from the darkness. She sees herself painted blue in the reflection. Instead of backing away she places her palm against the darkness of the mirror. Linum's blue strand of hair glows and her necklace vibrates against her chest. She is wearing the Sun's azure dress and the bronze chestplate. Her reflection is an exact mirror image of herself with the exception of the complete blue tint of the skin, the eyes, and the hair. It copies her movements as Linum stretches out a hand, tapping the black granite wall. The polished surface shatters.

The dark dismal sludge begins to rise, bursting through the wall. It swallows Linum whole, but she remains calm. She feels her heart in her chest. She feels the ooze of the Sun's blood glide through her crystal, but she does not take in the liquid. She holds her breath as she sinks in deeper, restraining herself from letting it enter her body. Her face reddens and her ears burn as her nose twitches. She is submerged in darkness, her body is cloaked by the midnight fingers of the Sun's blood. Linum hears Irene's voice echo in her mind, *what matters most to you.* She concentrates amid the darkness on the beating of her heart. Her mind floods with images of the roses, Penelope's cold hard stare, the king's tightened fists, Charles reaching for her hand, Zoren cursing at her under his breath, Orelia happily grinning, and Irene's motherly guidance. Her thoughts turn to the poor Pyro whimpering as his flames dim, Asterian as he floats in the clouds, the Sun beaming with jovial pride, and the Lady of the Sun's warm voice. She even thinks of Medaia. She remembers all the people, who have shaped her and made her who she is today. Linum wells with tears at the images of hope flashing through her mind. Her joyful thoughts bring forth the warmth of the Sun and free her of her prison. Linum feels the sludge part from her. She thinks of freedom, of love, and happiness. She believes in the Sun and the prosperity of the land. She desires no one else to suffer what she has suffered. She finds joy in her image, her sword, and in her friends. Linum is the Sun's champion. What it means to be a champion is what she cherishes most, the kindness of those around her and the benevolence of fate's endless game.

A clawed hand locks onto hers and pulls her up above the sludge. Linum smiles at the monstrous form and hugs the beast with cracked skin, skeleton wings, slitted eyes, and blue talons. She admires its hideous form and monstrous appearance. Linum approves of the soft glow in its eyes that replaces the dark universe within. She pats its purple head and whispers to it with confidence and compassion, "I accept you and understand. We have suffered and fought so long to break free, when freedom was inside us all along. We pushed away others and chased them away when they tried to help us, but no longer. We can do this together." The beast whimpers, licking its jagged teeth with its sick green tongue.

She whispers, "We are one. I can do this." Linum reaches forward pulling its face to hers. Their foreheads touch and the beast screeches shooting upwards into the air and disappears behind the blinding glow of the pink crystal. The pink crystal shatters and fragments fall like stars glittering around Linum. She states with a bold expression, "Sanity is a thin line and life is a tightrope. If the tightrope snaps then we fall too and, thus, snap. But not only would our person fall, but the mind too. Therefore, the line between sanity and insanity is thin. We are two sides of the same half and no longer need to be scared. We all take falls, but we pick ourselves up or help each other up. This is when we are at our best, when we are together. Society is great, when at the bottom of a great gorge a friend is there to help pick us up or exist as guidepoints holding our rope together, so we are strong. I will not fall, so long as we keep together in our own personal world. I need you and you need me." Linum calls after the beast, hiding behind the shattered crystal. It lands away from her with an exuberant screech and nuzzle of its head. The beast approaches timidly from the darkness and walks on the shattered fragments.

Linum turns to look at the beast. She bends down and offers a gentle hand with a compassionate smile towards the creature. "We have made mistakes. Fatal mistakes, but we are ready to persevere above death." It stamps its feet and growls at her, but she moves forward, "We are strong. We can pick these pieces up and" –she touches its hurting head gently, stroking its hardened flesh– "pick ourselves up too."

The beast closes its galaxy eyes and reopens them to reveal two sapphire blue pupils staring wide eyed at her. The creature transforms before her eyes, stretching its jaw open and configuring it in a mask of gentle pink light. The fragments of the crystal glimmer in reflection of the changing form before her. When the light fades, it no longer resembles a beast, but a toddler with dark blue hair, a body with a blue tint, and purple coloration on her back. The little girl wears the hide of the beast and reaches forward, wanting to cling to Linum.

Linum takes a light step forward and sees herself in the child's blue eyes. The little girl is her reflection of youth, emerged as a frightened child shivering in the empty cavern of the crystal's heart. Linumm strokes the child's hair and embraces the ice cold skin of her former self. She whispers, "It's okay. It is okay. I am with you and you will always be with me." The quivering lips of the child kiss her cheek and Linum sets her down. The toddler picks up a small fragment of the pink crystal. Linum smiles, "I will help put us back together and I will keep us together this time." She bends down and lifts the matching piece of crystal to the one the child holds. Linum and the child connect their glittering pieces together. Light streams through the empty darkness. The black granite wall reappears. The child walks away through the black granite wall and reappears on the other side as a blue reflection of the teenage Linum. Her reflection waves and Linum bows in response. Everything erupts into a blinding blue light around her as shadows disperse.

Linum's eyes flutter open. She is once again present in the Sacred Sun Temple. The roses, now dried, fall off her body. The wilted petals leave her bare skin to shimmer in the Sun's light and she finds the warmth of the Sun soothing. Irene helps her out of the pool. The pink crystal vibrates gently in her hand and the wind blows through the temple. The blackrose resting by the poolside morphs into a peaceful pink. The room is filled with the sweet sounds of birds singing and crickets chirping. Linum changes into her clothes, pulling on the tender flowing fabric of the azure blue dress and the stiff bronze chestplate. She fastens the crystal to her sword. Linum catches sight of a faint reflection of the blue child in the light of her silver blade, glinting in the Sun. However, with one blink, the toddler disappears. Linum is left alone with Irene.

"I have never witnessed anything like what I have just seen," stammers Irene after a long impassioned moment of reverent silence. Linum faces her with calm, determined, and brave eyes. Irene explains, "You blacked out and crashed downwards into the pool, but the roses lifted you up. Then the entire room darkened around us and the winds howled, shoving open the golden doors. The eagles all screeched in harmony as the Sun itself turned a midnight blue. The holy waters rose up into the air and cascaded around the room like a whirlpool. Then, everything just stopped. The water returned to its resting place, the eagles grew silent, the doors slammed close, and the Sun resumed its normal glow. You shot forward with eyes pressed tightly closed, but you were ice cold to the touch. I pressed a blackrose against your forehead again, but it crumbled into dust. I thought you were lost." Irene laughs and shakes her head in disbelief, "Never in my years as a priestess in this temple have I ever witnessed such fanciful strength and power of the Sun."

Linum's eyes shine with new content and hope. She bows, "Thank you for your teachings."

Irene smiles, "Thank the Sun and remember this moment. Whatever you faced will not be the same the next time you encounter a Sun Crystal and attempt to use it. It will try to break you again and again and it will not rest until you have tamed them all. Do not face Medaia until then."

"Thank you once more, I will remember this." Linum turns away but pauses. She asks, "Priestess Irene, how did you know that I would be able to access the crystal this way?"

Irene chuckles, "Linum, in truth I did not know if it would work." Her emerald eyes twinkle in the light. "I am a disciple of the Sun and after years of swallowing the legends and taking up every word to memorization, I will admit that I was blind in action. Yet, I had a dream that awoke me from my cottage on the night of the Festival of Blossoms. A powerful and sweet voice emerged in the appearance of an eight-pointed star" –she points at Linum's chest– "like the necklace you are wearing. It instructed me that I must make my way to the center of the city. It told me to carry a blackrose with me and that I must become a teacher. However, I had no clue what that would mean or result in. I merely took it as a sign of the Sun."

"Yes, but how did you know that I would be able to control it?"

"I did not know. That part was left up to you." Irene points her hand up at the sky. She continues, "I suppose that you have a guide in the Heavens watching over you."

Linum smiles and clutches her eight-pointed star necklace; she whispers "Thank you" to the gleaming silver and it glows in response.

Irene bows her head, "The Sun is watching over you."

Linum makes to turn away again, but stops, "What do you know of Medaia and of the Lady of the Sun?"

Irene frowns, "Medaia is troublesome but do not let her shadows poison your mind. I have studied her from the legends. When I was younger I thought it was just a fairytale, until I began my work here. She is evil Linum. Medaia is a result of the consumption of power and nothing will quench that thirst. As far as the Lady of the Sun, I apologize, for I know nothing of such a woman or such a thing. If a woman in the light of the Sun gave you this quest, then perhaps it is the Sun's mortal form. However, that is only a mere assumption, for I have no proof or basis for that theory. It just means that you have seen more of the Sun than any other mortal in our time, for a direct quest given by the Sun is as rare and as perilous as fate any could get. I wish you well Linum."

Linum smiles. She shakes Irene's hand.

Irene laughs, "Do you not have somewhere to go, Sun Champion?"

"I need to face the queen and demand the crystal for the sake of Solenium."

"Go now and be swift." Irene watches as Linum runs off and pushes open the golden door of the Sacred

Sun Temple. Irene's face grows serious. Her voice is saddened as she offers a last warning, "Linum. Do not trust *her*. My husband is dead because of her, but I cannot prove it so she remains queen. Aconite is dangerous and I fear that she craves the power that the pink crystal possesses. She will not part with the green crystal willingly." Irene waves, her face cheers up and her emerald eyes glow, "Go and do not take no as an answer!"

Linum nods. Her face is serious and determined with a renewed spark in her eyes of confidence and compassion. She leaps down the quartz steps and lands onto the paved river rock road. She runs forward towards the towering wooden fortress resembling a palace in a mighty treehouse.

Chapter 17
Buried Prisoner

Charles makes a sharp turn around the corner, dodging behind a large wooden fence. His blonde hair sticks to his scalp and his wooden chestplate hangs loose from his shoulder. His knee pads, made from the bark of a tree, are marked with scratches and his hands are bruised.

"Come out, prince." A muscular fairy taunts him, his spear poised and sharpened. He reeks of the smell of fresh growing parsley mixed with blood and sweat.

Charles takes a deep breath in, mutters a silent prayer to the Sun, and raises his spear. The muscular fairy and him clash. Their spears hit one another and shed small scraps of wood.

Orelia calls out, "Remember the goal is only to disarm your opponents as a training exercise." She keeps a keen eye on the muscular fairy. As he moves to jab at Charles she yells, "Not to maim anyone, Brutus."

The muscular fairy, Brutus, chuckles with intensity growing in his eyes. He pushes Charles back and sneers, "Is this the bloodline of the noble Kingdom of Dalium? Pathetic!"

Charles swipes with his spear, ducking below Brutus' large arms. Charles weakly strikes Brutus in the chest with the blunt end of his spear.

"Pitiful. Better call your sister, Charles."

Charles hits him again, this time knocking him back. The parsley-covered fairy throws his spear, but

Charles blocks using the wood from his chest plate as a shield. Brutus is now defenseless. Charles walks forward and presses the sharpened edge of his wooden spear at the muscular fairy's neck, muttering, "I am Prince Charles Noapten of the noble Kingdom of Dalium and I have unarmed you, Brutus." He offers a hand to the fairy, but Brutus swats it away and curses at Charles.

Orelia cheerfully announces, "We have our final winner. Well done everyone that will conclude practice for today. I will see you all tomorrow for drills." She glances at Brutus and the group of fairies covered in herbal arrangements. She announces, "Herbal Squad your team lost, so take five laps around the length of the creek before we meet again, and no flying."

Brutus storms off, kicking at the turf below his feet, before fluttering his sturdy parsley wings to take after the other herbal assorted fairies.

Orelia expresses a proud smile on her face. She watches as the fairies leave the training field. Then, with a lighthearted giddiness of a child she squeals, "That was fun!"

Charles attempts to catch his breath as he sits languid on the ground. His face drips with sweat underneath the midday Sun.

"Quite." Charles manages to grin. He yawns and collapses against the grass of the green fields and stretches on its soft surface, letting the blades glide against his skin. Moisture builds on his chin and dribbles down his hand as he wipes his face with tired hands. "Do you think Linum is doing alright?"

"I would believe so, my mother will cure her." Orelia leans back onto the grass beside him. She looks up at the clouds.

"I just do not understand why she would attack like that. I understand that Pyro was extinguished but it was just a flame. She became a beast once before in Dalium, but that was out of protection. Zoren had snapped her out of it back then." His eyes light up as if he is remembering something. "I hope that Zoren is alright, wherever he is."

Orelia looks him over with curious delicate green eyes. She states, "I can help you search for your friend."

Charles shakes his head. He looks at the clouds and to divert her attention away from him he questions, "Does that cloud look like a Sunflower?"

She stares up at the sky with her glittering calm content eyes. "It does, but it also can look like a flame dancing in the wind and riding the breeze. Look there are its wisps of smoke and over there," she freezes and her cheeks glow red in realization of what she had just said, "I'm truly sorry about Pyro. I hope Linum does not hold it against me. I think she had every right to attack, but I wish we never dueled."

Charles crouches, tearing at the grass before him. "Do not mind Linum. It was not your fault, you had nothing to do with it. Besides, she challenged you to a duel."

"But only to get the queen's attention."

"Orelia, you have done so much for us. Do not trouble yourself over the event, for I am in your debt."

She gazes at Charles, startled by his kind words. Orelia stretches and yawns, her light brown hair falls across her eyes and she smiles.

"The queen must be lucky to rule over a land like this. You do not have to worry about invaders from the surrounding lands, because your people rule the skies."

"I would not call the queen lucky, rather, formidable."

Charles faces her, and brushes his blonde hair from his eyes to see her face grow faint. She appears ill with a nervous expression.

"What is wrong?" He asks with a hint of fear in his quiet speech.

Orelia draws in a breath. She steadies her shaking hands and faces him. She wants to tell him of the plot on Dalium, but she is divided in her actions. She speaks quickly and says, "My mother sends me to the queen on her behalf. I report not only information for the army, rather, in regards to the Sacred Sun Temple as well. She tells me to keep a keen eye on the queen and distrust every word ever spoken."

"Why? This entire kingdom is flourishing. I have never seen so many happy faces and welcoming smiles!"

"But have you noticed the frowns? The hungry? The homeless?" Her face is solemn and her sweet voice is melancholy. She states, "They enter the Sacred Sun Temple seeking guidance from my mother, who preaches nothing but the truth of the Sun. The queen does not favor Priestess Irene, for my mother lectures against

Aconite's power and warns the citizens to make a change in the name of the Sun."

"I do not understand this place is—"

"Look, do you see those kids over there." Orelia points with her hand to an open meadow.

Charles stares off into the distance. He looks beyond the small wooden buildings and at the fields full of farm crops. He spots four children hoeing the ground. "Yes. I see them."

"They come to the Sun Temple every week and ask for the Sun to mend their hands, which are swollen and bruised from constant farm work. I fear for them, especially during this time of year, for they are the ones put to work to clean up after the Festival of Blossoms."

Charles interjects, "Why must they work? Can they not quit?"

Orelia sighs, "They must work in order to provide for their mother, Agape, who is a dear friend of my mother. We do what we can to support them." Charles watches her as she runs her fingers along the small blades of green grass. She sighs and lifts her head up to look at the many buildings, "And look there, just past the marketplace." Charles looks and nods when he sees an old fairy, crouching over a pile of wooden carvings. Orelia continues, "He sells wooden figures that he carves with a small knife. He is ninety-two and without a home or family." Charles listens as the wind picks up the sorrowful pleas of the frail old fairy. The old fairy in a long night gown with only a small patch of iris flowers growing on his head, like a nightcap, stumbles forward. Charles watches as he addresses the passing fairies. The old fairy reaches out to them, rubs the metallic surface of his glasses, and grabs a hold of a detailed carving of a horse. "He suffers daily with hardly anyone buying the figures he makes. The queen does not care, she has said so when I addressed it during a meeting. I suggested we build homes for everyone since we grow most of our materials, but she only shrugged and said that it would be a waste of time." The old fairy kneels down and looks up at the Heavens above. A young woman approaches him and points to the little horse carving. The man's face glows brightly. His eyes well with tears as he bows his head and makes the small exchange of currency. Orelia offers a slight smile. "Henry is his name, he reminds me of my father."

Charles nods.

She continues, "I just do not understand. Queen Aconite always promises to the people that she will help them and secure them with wealth. They take the false premise of her proposals for truth at each ceremonial selection for the next ruler. I suppose it could be due to her venomous flowers since fairies relating to the toxic group normally do not run, however, she is an exception. She talks of expanding, while not everyone here is well. She reaps rewards from their hard work. This is why my mother has me keeping watch. I took over for my father." She taps the turmeric markings on her cheek, and traces the image of the Sun, "I apologize. I shouldn't have said all of this to you. It makes me appear as a traitor since I am her general. You mustn't tell anyone about what I just spoke of, for it is treason."

"I will not speak of this at all. Not at all. I believe that you have a right to be frustrated. I think I understand your confusion. You see in Dalium, we had a strange method of order. Women were not allowed to possess weapons even when circumstances were desperate enough that their lives were in danger. The use of any weapon in a woman's hands was a death warrant. And the people would willingly give into the Midnight Persecutor, one of Medaia's beasts, because it offered a better life simply by false pretences. They were tired of living, and gave into the shadows, becoming one of them. For so long the Midnight Persecutor had corrupted our lands and only of late did we try to stop him. I lost my father then and I was not brave enough to cut down the monster myself."

Orelia grabs a hold of his hand and whispers, "Do not blame yourself. You have valor, because you are here now to liberate your home and bring peace to Solenium. Your father would be proud."

Charles pulls away from her. "Everyone always says that I should not blame myself but they do not understand. I am the one person they should be blaming. I am a failed prince. I have let the Kingdom of Dalium fall."

"My father died too at the hands of a shadow beast. He was on patrol alone, because his partner became terminally ill overnight. My mother prayed for his partner in the Sun's name and the doctors tried everything they could, but he didn't make it through the night. My father, General Cedar, wanted to attend his partner's early morning funeral and the releasing of the ashes. However, Queen Aconite insisted he must go on patrol by that creek we found you by. She warned him that there were sightings of shadow beasts in the area. The only problem was that the other fairy troops were deployed two days before on a long journey across the seas to make amends with the Gardium Kingdom for past brawls over trading. Thus, he went alone. I was only seven when it happened, a part of the Junior Cadets, and I felt helpless when I received the news that he disappeared. The queen reported the following day that he went missing and that became the general report. However, my mother has held his death against Queen Aconite ever since. Therefore, she distrusts her every word she says, suggesting there is a snake behind that wicked smile. Thus, I carry on both my father's duty as general and my mother's duty of reporting the daily commencements occurring within the Sacred Sun Temple."

"I am sorry," consoles Charles.

"What in the Sun's name for? I have not looked back on that day with grief since it happened. Instead, I like to believe he is in a better place and roaming the Everglades, doing his part in the Heavens. Personally, I do not hold his death against anyone, except the beast that did away with his corpse, leaving no trace behind." She glances at the Sun standing high in the sky, "That is why I will do everything I can to assist you and Linum."

She shoots into the air with fluttering wings, "Oh! I almost forgot I have a meeting with Queen Aconite today after practice. Would you mind coming with me?"

"Do you think Linum will mind?"

"She is probably still training with my mother."

They rush off together running through the green fields. Orelia slows down so Charles may catch up as they head towards the large wooden structure at the far end of the city. Orelia grabs a hold of his arm and hauls him up to the open balcony. She leads him into the great throne room. Queen Aconite sits bored on her elaborate wooden throne. Guards with sharpened animal bone spears stand by her side.

Charles notices a small glass box that glows a brilliant emerald green in the light. It rests beside Aconite on a wooden stump next to her throne.

Queen Aconite clears her throat and addresses Orelia with an exasperated tone, "Thank you for coming, General Orelia, but Charles will not be permitted during this meeting due to what we will be discussing." She yawns and waves her hands, the guards step forward, their poison ivy wreaths stretch out towards Charles.

He bows and excuses himself from the room and wanders down the hall. His last glimpse of Orelia is of her kneeling before Queen Aconite as the wooden doors slam shut before him. Charles's head rolls back, as he glances around his surroundings, trying to find his way out. He notices the clean cut walls and the patterned flooring are all made from wood and hand carved to perfection. The walls tell a story of the legend from the fairy perspective. There is an evil witch holding the eight crystals over her head and eight rulers bowing down to her. Beside that picture are two fairies, one holding a spear and the other a young girl with wings. The next photo depicts King Russleton's death and the final image displays Chlonia being crowned as queen. He stares at the incomplete choppy storyline carved into the walls and at the face of the young girl with an oversized crown on her head and small wings. He tries to imagine how Chlonia must have felt in receiving her new title after both of her parents were killed. He decides it must have been similar to what he experienced, except it is more like what Linum is dealing with since she is next in line. He presses his hand against the perfect carving. He traces the crown on Chlonia's head. He notices that the girl's eyes in the carving are sad. *She must have felt guilt. She must have felt unworthy of her position.* Charles becomes consumed by his wandering thoughts, that stretch dark circles underneath his hazel eyes.

Charles hears a scuffle arise from the end of the corridor as guards with sharpened wooden spears rush out from a dark hallway. They charge forward, climbing up numerous stairs. Charles presses himself next to the miniature carving of Chlonia. The guards ignore him and rush off down the hall. He hears grunts and moans echo off the wooden walls. Charles decides to enter the now empty hallway and descend down the numerous stairs to avoid the brawl above. He shivers from the cold as he hurries down the stairs encased in spiderwebs. The steps appear to keep going in an endless spiral illuminated by only a few torchlights. He tumbles forward into a dark room. He hears water drip slowly from the limestone roof above his head. He figures he must be in some kind of underground prison. Charles spies a wooden stool that a guard had toppled over after they rushed upwards due to the pressing sounds of violence. Keys hang from a wooden rack mounted roughly against the stone walls. The air is damp, dreary, and stuffy. He hears shuffling and moans behind the wooden bars. Men curse within the darkness of their cells. Charles takes a shaking step forward. He feels uneasy with the eeriness of the surroundings. However, the loud racket above does not appeal to him no more than the darkness of the prison. The sounds of swords clashing and deep howls of pain from above frightens him. Charles determines it would be unwise to climb up the steps until the mess clears, for he is unarmed and if anyone questioned him he would merely state he was avoiding a scuffle, which in itself appears suspicious.

He presses on, walking deeper into the dark stone chamber. Charles peers behind one of the wooden bars to see an old man with a long grey beard and white whiskers scramble up to the gate. He has been stripped of his clothes except for a small cloth to cover the sensitive parts. His frail back is hunched over his feeble legs. He has deep dark circles under his sagging eyes and his ribs poke out through his skin. His pale ghostly white hands appear like bones attached to his toothpick arms. He gags and begins rocking back and forth mumbling, "I hear you. I hear your breath. I hear you. Do you know the wind, the chimes of the air? Do you know the danger? It surrounds us all. I know you! In fact I hear you. What do you know of me, what do you want from me? What do you..." His voice trails off and the old man begins to cry, rocking himself harder. He then springs to life grabbing at the bars and reaches for Charles.

Charles steps backward and crashes into another set of wooden bars. He tries to pull away, but the prisoner stretches his hands over his neck. Charles's voice falters, he tries to scream, but nothing escapes from his lips except a quivering whisper, "H-h-h-help!"

"Drop your keys" replies a deep, rough, and cold voice.

"I do not have any keys," chokes Charles.

"Drop them!"

"I am not a guard."

The arm retreats back into the cell and Charles pulls away, creating distance between the two separate cages, ensuring that he is out of reach.

The madman howls, "Beware of that man. He is crazy! He seeks out those who dwell peacefully to scorch their hope and plague their lives with misery, so his victims will lay in their beds and awake, starved, and deprived of all nourishment. If you see the man with tomato cheeks, pale blue eyes, and dark hair, stay away. He is savage, insane, a lunatic. He is a raving lunatic!" The man begins to foam at the mouth then harshly spits "raving lunatic" again out into the wild air. "Be aware of his wild eyes and evil stare. He prances around with vicious eyes, and hard looks, and he is mad!" The madman coughs and cackles, his lips twist and turn with violent apprehension. Blood falls as he spits, "I heard that man talk in his sleep, I watch that man as he thinks, I know his thoughts, I see that man is lost, I see that man in my dreams. I know that man, I hear him. I was once *that* man."

"Shut up!" Yells the man who bangs his fist against the wooden bars. He is young and his hair is dark. He has oceanic eyes and a tightly drawn frown. His hands are bruised and bloody and covered in welts. He wears a dark black vest over a surcoat cut short at his waist with puffy sleeves and rough knightly pants with black boots. The old madman cackles and the young man yells, "Did you not hear me?"

"The wind speaks to me again!" hollers the old madman, who howls with raving laughter and rolls on the floor like a poor malnourished dog.

Charles takes a step forward in the direction of the prison cell with the young man. His eyes dare himself to be deceived for he is almost certain of the man's identity. "Zoren?"

"Who is asking?"

"It is me, Charles!"

Zoren's face brightens as he clings to the wooden bars, "Get me out of here."

Charles rushes over to grab the key which he fumbles in his hand. He picks a slender key made stiffly out of birchwood from the wooden rack and plunges it into the wooden door, twisting and turning to release Zoren. It clicks open and he bursts out.

"What about me?" asks the madman with wild and merciful eyes. "What about me?" he whispers to himself and rocks, banging his head against the bars and scratching at the stone floor.

Zoren takes in his surroundings. Fiercely he demands, "Where is Linum?"

Charles looks at him startled by his ferocity and threatening bluish grey eyes, "What happened to you? Orelia said they did not capture anyone on their rounds."

"Charles, where is Linum?" Zoren presses onto Charles's shoulders and shouts, "They are going to kill her. Charles, tell me where she is."

Charles's face grows pale. He shakes his head. "That cannot be. Orelia promised she would help us on our quest."

"It is true," states Orelia who leans against the entrance to the stairway.

Charles turns around with a hurt heart. His jaw hangs open and his brows knit together firmly in disbelief. He yells at her, "Is that what your secret meeting was about? You said you did not know where Zoren was. You acted like you were our friend and then betrayed us." His hazel eyes sting from the cryptic air.

Zoren charges at Orelia. He swings with his bare fists. She dodges and flutters down to the cold surface of the stone floor. Zoren tumbles down. He picks himself up from the floor, grudgingly. He presses his eyes shut and mutters in silence to the damp ceiling. The floor begins to tremble and his body convulses forward. The air tightens around the three of them and the madman coughs and howls from the comfort of his cell. Orelia brushes off the dust from her orchid skirt and runs over to a chest sitting beside the empty stool and below the rack of keys. She fiddles with the lock and opens it. Then, she holds up Zoren's metal whip, offering it to him. His eyes flash open with the bitterness of lightning striking and the air relinquishes its tight grasp. He snatches the whip from her hands and lets the metal flash to life. Zoren's metal whip extends before him. He draws it back and cracks it in the air. It sounds like thunder roaring. He reaches out to whip her.

"Please." She begs with emerald eyes and looks at Charles. "It is true that I have been meeting with the queen to discuss the conquering of Dalium. I have betrayed your trust. Yet, I never knew of Aconite's true intentions. I brought you to the meeting today because I was hoping you could inspire peace among her plans of domination. I did not plan on supporting her any longer. I was ready to resign when she dismissed you because her path is clouded by darkness. I must trust in the Sun's guidance. Yet, I was a coward and still held my tongue. Queen Aconite has sent me to kill you, Charles, with this blade." She pulls out a metal dagger from behind the mass of orchids entangling her body. Orelia continues, "I had no clue your friend was captive here. I was not informed that we took in prisoners on that day we found you by the creek." Orelia reaches out offering the sheathed dagger to him. The hilt is made of emeralds and sparkles even in the dimness of the stone dungeon. "The blade is poisonous and made from her flowers. I was supposed to kill you with it." Her voice trails away and she kneels. Orelia lowers her head. Her light brown curls fall over her face and leave her neck exposed to the bitterness of the stone dungeon. Orelia's voice is sincere. She states, "But I cannot betray the Sun. I have come to warn you of Aconite's intentions towards Linum. She believes that Linum may be used as a weapon to expand our kingdom and her power. I do not support this, for I want only prosperity for our people and Solenium. Therefore, I must act truthfully and no longer fear her. I want to stand up to the darkness of the shadows. However, I understand that you will continue to mistrust me. I was a fool but at least I will die free from her intimidation. I pray to the Sun that I have not jeopardized your mission." Orelia draws in a light breath. Her voice is steady and her emerald eyes tear up. Softly she whispers, "I offer you this emerald dagger."

Charles unsheaths the unnatural blade and raises it above her head. His eyesight is blurry as the world changes and melds into a mass of watery waves before him. He yells in anguish and lowers the dagger. The tip rests above the back of her exposed neck. His hands tremble and he throws the poisoned dagger aside into the empty cell where Zoren emerged from.

"Help us to find Linum." He speaks sternly with nervous eyes.

Orelia looks up at him with dazzling emerald eyes that gleam in the darkness of the cavern. "Thank you for your mercy."

"Get up and take us to her before it is too late!" Zoren condemns her with his unforgiving frown.

They race up the steps of the spiral staircase and free themselves from the despair of the dungeons.

The madman scowls, yelling after them, "The wind is angry. The Sun is mad. I am alone to hear the tidings and voices. I am alone." His voice echoes solemnly off the empty walls, unheard and imprisoned.

Zoren, Charles, and Orelia dash up the many steps, pushing through the darkness and dampness of the stairs. They run past the dreary webs drooping with remorse. Orelia explains further, "After you left the throne room, the queen asked me to end your life. She claimed that you murdered a fairy, but I was with you the entire time so I knew she was lying. I may be her general but I am not a murderer. Although I accepted the dagger I knew that I could not complete the task she had given me. Thus, I set out looking for you." Orelia glances at Charles. She adds, "Aconite is after Linum for her strength, power, and ability to change forms. She wants the pink crystal of Dalium. If Linum reaches her, she will die—"

Zoren intervenes, "Where is Pyro? He possesses great strength although he is just a small flame and he will be of great use to us."

Orelia pauses, nearly causing Charles to lose his footing and smack into the solitary Zoren.

With hesitation Orelia replies, "He is dead."

Zoren howls with the ferocity of an erupting volcano. His moans are of pure agony and his hands bend and fold maniacally with a screaming hiss. He booms with a furious voice, "Dead! The only way to kill Pyro is with water. What idiot poured water on a living flame?"

"I apologize. I was battling Linum in the arena and he was there burning my orchids. He was sprayed with a bucket of water. He was going to burn me up and then I would have died. My life is connected to my orchids." She shows her wings that are full of blooming purple orchids.

Zoren reaches out with condemning hands. His whip flies out of his chest pocket, aiming at her with a vibrant hum as he shakes in rage.

Charles steps in between Zoren and Orelia. "It was not her fault or Linum's fault. Some fairy from the sidelines did it."

"Then I will burn down this entire island with my bare hands." Zoren's hands ignite into blue flames, but he shakes them out as quickly as they were ignited. "We need to reach Linum now."

Orelia flies forward. Her cheeks are stained with tears that wipe away her turmeric markings of the orchid and of the Sun. Charles runs below her and Zoren dashes ahead of them all. He stretches out his arm and the whip coils around it. Guards approach from around the corner as they emerge from the hallway.

The guards ask, "What are you doing here–"

Yet, Zoren does not give them a chance to finish their speech. The whip comes to life and with a single stroke, like a serpent stretching out to bite its prey, they are cut into two separate halves. Orelia gasps and Charles looks away. The walls are marked up with scratches and are dotted with blood.

Zoren stares at the bodies of the two guards. He grumbles to Charles, "How can we trust *her*?"

Orelia begs, "I am telling the truth. I was willing to sacrifice myself to prove that I am being honest. I am willing to die to restore my honor after deceiving Charles. Zoren I am not here as an enemy. I am here as a friend."

Zoren stares her down and callously laughs, "A friend? An ally?" His eyes harden and he whispers with growing animosity, "Your kind imprisoned me. Your kind killed my magic flame that took years to craft, and that magic cannot be performed again to recreate a creature such as Pryo. That flame was a combination of the fires of the Sun and a willing soul that was rebirthed to harness the fires of a heart strung out in malice. I do not possess the strength to give life to such a creature any more, for it takes a sacrifice that is more poisoning than anyone can imagine. I cannot live through such events again."

"Zoren! It is not her fault. Orelia may never be blamed for the faults of others. A civilization must not be scorned for the mistakes of a futile small group, while the majority are innocent, benevolent, and honorable!" Charles smiles at Orelia and nods approvingly. He braces himself for some shrewd remark from Zoren, but Zoren remains silent. Zoren turns his back on Charles.

Orelia pleads, "I am not asking for forgiveness nor for you to uplift your blame. I just hope that you may trust my word that Linum is in grave peril for every second we spend bickering. If Queen Aconite manages to accomplish her goal of overpowering Linum, then our world will become just as gloomy as if Medaia was ruling Solenium."

Zoren averts his attention to the walls, tracing the blood and the scratches. He sighs and looks past the guards he killed. A few feet away rests more guards leaning against the wall in pain. They are alive but maimed with gushing wounds and deathly cuts.

"Linum's passed through here. We better hope that it is not already too late." He points towards the large wooden doors at the end of the corridor. "There. I believe that is where we will find her."

They hurry forward. The three of them are ready for a fight. Orelia's orchids spin around her like the arms of an octopus, Charles picks up one of the guard's wooden spears, and Zoren raises his metal whip above his head. They charge forward, bursting through the grand doors and into the throne room.

Chapter 18
Collision of Fates

Linum pounds on the front door of the fortress, but no one replies. She cocks her head, exasperated. Linum spies a nearby open window. She raises her sword and listens to the beat of her heart pounding against her chest as she gasps for air. She transforms into the creature with batlike wings, but its eyes remain her own. She looks into the air. Linum is proud of her new ability to transform into the tame monstrous beast. She takes off, clutching her sword in her talons. She flies through a window and lands, crashing into a dim hallway.

Guards with spears rush out and declare, "Put your hands up!" and "What is that thing?"

Linum transforms back into her normal self with a blue flash of light. She raises her sword, charging at the fairies. They fall one by one. The guards moan and howl as she swipes, cutting their floral outfits and dicing their herbal wear. She ravages more guards as she fights her way through the corridor. The metal of her sword clashes with the fairies' animal bone and wooden spears. She does not kill the fairies, merely injures their garments and pierces their skin which in turn makes them howl in pain. She forces her way through them towards a grand wooden door. The surrounding walls contain the legend of the Sun Crystals, mapped out before her very eyes. She focuses on the carving of the evil witch, Medaia, as she disarms a man dressed in cotton. The small carved

Medaia appears powerful and grand as she boasts the power of the eight crystals raised above her head. Linum touches the wall with her hands, tracing the carving as it appears familiar. With the touch of her gentle skin against the cold wall, it cracks like glass shattering, creating a small opening to the outdoors. The wind rushes through the hall and roars.

Linum steps backward observing her hands with a foreign regard. She swipes with her sword at more guards. Blood splatters across the wood carvings. She swipes at the wood with her sword, cutting the miniature Medaia in half. Satisfied, she pushes onwards and charges towards the grand wooden doors. They swing open and Linum into the throne room. The room glows warmly with the Sun's light. It is full of guards wielding spears and cloaks of poison ivy. Linum spots the green crystal immediately, since it rests in a glass box beside the queen.

"Looking for this," Queen Aconite waves her bored hand at the glass box, "You may have it."

Linum keeps her sword pointed as she takes careful steps closer to Queen Aconite.

"Just take it, Linum."

Linum steps closer to the box, watching both the poison ivy guards and the queen. She is one step away from being able to reach the crystal. She feels its strange pulse manipulate her heartbeat.

"Now!" Yells Queen Aconite standing up to direct the guards. They run at Linum with drawn spears and swipe at her bare flesh. She dodges their surcoats of poison ivy that stretch and lash out at her. She strikes at their spears with her sword, but is severely outnumbered. Linum backs away, but the guards rush in from behind her.

"Halt!" Queen Aconite stands and approaches Linum, the deep purple of her lips sticks to her teeth as she smiles and applauds. "You gave a decent effort, but the only way you are getting out of here alive is by giving me *that* pink crystal. I will admit I was astonished by your power and crave it. What do you call that creature?" Her wolfsbane dress spreads out towards Linum, swarming around her, but does not touch her. "Hand over the crystal or die. I need it to protect my kingdom."

"You monster," curses Linum with bitterness.

"Just because a snake may be venomous does not mean its heart and mind are poisoned too. I was chosen by this flower, because its toxicity attracts me. I feel untouchable when I surround myself with poison." Aconite's evil smile falters. She continues with a snarl, "Or I should say that I felt untouchable until I witnessed your power. Once I get your crystal I will combine the power of both the green and pink Sun Crystals and feel truly secured. No one will touch the Terrace Gardens of Nominia and I will reign supreme."

"Asterian!" yells Linum with desperation.

"Who is this being you call upon? Your friends are all dead. I ordered the death of that pitiful flame and now I have sent General Orelia to finish off Charles. What a pity, he seemed like a good natured young man. However, it is just a sacrifice necessary for the growth and expansion of the Terrace Gardens of Nominia. After you hand me your crystal, I will claim Dalium."

"I will never surrender to you."

"Then, you will die."

Her flowers zip to life shooting straight at Linum. She chops the flowers of the first wave, but another comes and the poison ivy follows. Linum listens to the pink crystal's slight hum. She turns into the beast. Linum flies into the air, releasing a screech like death. She strikes with her sword in her talons. She races across the sky trying to outrun the growing poisonous plants surrounding her. Linum swoops downward for the green crystal. Her claws hit the box, but she does not pick up the crystal. Instead, Linum causes the glass box to topple to the floor and shatter. The Sun Crystal slides against the wall, opposite of the grand wooden doors. Linum drops from the sky, falling amid the tangle of poison and transforms back to herself. She closes her eyes and moves the hilt of her sword, sheathing it midair. Just as she is moments away from landing on the mass of wolfsbane flowers and poison ivy, situated on the ground like a deathbed, Asterian materializes below her. He roars and flaps his galaxy wings, wilting the flower's surrounding her. They dry and crumble into ash and he swoops upwards to catch Linum. Asterian taps Linum's star necklace and licks her face, then disappears into thin air.

The shadows on the walls darken and stretch. Linum swipes her sword through the horrendous air of the throne room which sends a stream of blue light that knocks the guards unconscious. Linum is left alone with

Queen Aconite. Flowers droop from the wall, watching the battle before them like eager spectators. The flowers lean closer, feeding off the feud over the crystals.

"I command you to stop. I am the queen!" Aconite's golden hair bounces by her side as she struggles to retreat towards the grave walls of the throne room.

"You are not my queen." Linum approaches her, her sword is drawn. She swipes at the wolfsbane flowers embracing Queen Aconite's body. They fall limp to the floor and reveal the queen's violet dress underneath. Queen Aconite screams in pain. She clutches her leftover flowers that cling to her chest. "You are a sick vile snake, and I will dethorn you!" Linum raises her sword to cut off the remaining strand of wolfsbane flowers that hang off of Queen Aconite's shoulder like a shawl. She gets ready to strike just as Charles, Orelia, and Zoren burst through the grand wooden oak doors.

Chapter 19
Refuting Poison

"Linum!" Charles, Orelia, and Zoren shout in unison and dash beside her. Linum whirls around to confront them, lowering her sword as she embraces Charles. She nods at Zoren with delight in her dark eyes and he smiles in return. She rushes forward embracing Zoren in an awkward hug. She holds her sword loosely in her hand. Then, Linum draws her sword and swipes at Orelia, knocking her down to the hard wooden floor.

Charles steps in, "Orelia is with us!"

Linum sheaths her sword and offers a hand to Orelia, who clambers to her feet and flaps her orchid wings.

A noise like the beating of a thousand drums sounds from behind their turned backs. They each look to see Queen Aconite hold up the green crystal.

She hollers with a sinister voice, "I will steal that pink crystal off your corpse!" Aconite waves the green Sun Crystal in the air and closes her eyes. She presses her nails into the designs of ivy leaves stretching across the green crystal. Linum braces herself, she clutches her sword to face Queen Aconite and the rest follow her example: Charles positions his wooden spear, Zoren releases his metal whip, and Orelia's orchids come to life.

"I do not understand!" She declares, staring at the green crystal in disbelief, "Why can I not access your powers?" In agitation, Queen Aconite throws the green crystal aside and forces the remainder of her wolfsbane flowers to rise and leave her body, forming a deadly mass of flowers. "Nevertheless, I will learn how to use the crystal's power in time."

Linum raises her sword up to the light of the Sun that streams through the stained glass windows of the throne room. The fairies carved onto the red, purple, orange, and yellow glass appear like glaring angels looking down at Queen Aconite. The pink crystal reflects off the walls and Linum charges forward to kill Queen Aconite, who stands without her poison and is dressed in a simple violet dress. The toxic mass approaches and stretches towards Linum's companions. Zoren scourges the flowers, Orelia flies overhead combating them at a distance with her graceful orchids, and Charles keeps them at bay from Linum.

Linum lifts her sword to strike at the ice-eyed Queen Aconite, when a large explosion blasts open the doors to the throne room. Shrieks and shrill screams fill the room. Irene stumbles through the door. She limps towards the center of the room and all action freezes, as all eyes turn to watch the hurt Priestess of the Sacred Sun Temple walk forward. Her stomach has a deep wound, for when she lifts her hand, the gash becomes visible and the blood dyes her yellow flowers red.

Irene moans, "Medaia is ambushing us from the skies. No fairy is able to fly out, we are trapped." She groans and collapses to the floor. Her voice is still strong. "Linum, you must not be found here. Take your companions and leave the Terrace Gardens. We have lost, unless the fairies fight back now. But you must not be here, you must continue your quest before Medaia's shadows spread across Solenium."

Linum pulls away from Queen Aconite, who stands cowering under the weight of her golden locks. She walks over to grab the green crystal without opposition. The wolfsbane mass retreats back to its host, leaving the others to approach Irene and support her as she tries to keep her balance. Linum clutches the green crystal in her hand.

"Act quickly, for you must leave now." Irene gasps and tries to swat away Orelia's helping hands. Irene glares at Queen Aconite, who inches away towards the grand wooden doors.

"Mother, I cannot leave you." Orelia grabs a hold of her wrinkled bloodied hands and smooths out the creases in her palm. "I cannot," she whimpers, her cheeks are wet with fresh tears.

They embrace and the faded emerald eyes of Irene stare into Orelia's shining emerald green eyes.

Irene whispers, "My little light, go with your friends. You can help them and do not worry about me. It is not your fault, I did everything I could to stop her. Medaia came to the Sacred Sun Temple in search of the green crystal. I refused to tell her where it is, so she did this to me. She is here, approaching this place at the very moment. She let me go as a warning." Irene looks at all the young faces in the room and smiles reassuringly, turning to bow to each and everyone one of them. She addresses them all, "Do not play her game and you will win. You are the children of the Sun and you will outshine her evil dark center. Now go, I will finish things off here." Irene yells at Queen Aconite, "If you leave out of these doors, Aconite, the beasts will devour you in your entirety."

Linum walks up beside Irene. She bows her head, "Thank you for everything. May we meet again in the Mountains of the Sun Blessed Everglades."

"Linum, remember your true strength and never forget yourself in the process."

Linum nods and fastens the green crystal to her sword with a loud bang as it locks into position. Her blade glows a bright green and she sheaths it in her scabbard.

"Charles, take care of them and never forget that your sister loves you." Irene pats his face and runs her feeble fingers through his blonde hair.

"You have chosen a good side." She waves to Zoren, but he pretends not to hear her or see her, his oceanic eyes twist and churn like the unforgiving sea. Eventually he nods and turns away to follow after Charles and Linum, who stand patiently by the door, blocking Queen Aconite from escaping.

Orelia runs forward and hugs her mother. She plucks a white orchid from her dress and places it in her mother's cupped hands.

"I will miss you," whispers Irene, "Now go be brave and survive. I will see you in the Heavenly Sun Lands when it is your time."

Orelia lets go of her hand and takes one last look into the shining faded eyes of her mother. She finds only peace and courage in her light green pupils. There is no fear in her mother's eyes, so she flutters out of the room with benevolence and grace. Tear drops fall from Orelia's wild eyes, running down her burning red cheeks and splashing onto her melancholy orchids. Orelia winces when she hears the doors slam shut behind her. She follows after Linum, Charles, and Zoren.

Irene turns her back to the door, clutching her stomach in pain. Her feet give way, but she forces her wings to carry her. She glares at Aconite and yells, "It is time for unfinished business to be resolved." She takes weak floating steps towards Queen Aconite. Irene's breath is faint.

"Irene, can we not just talk about this?"

"You murdered my husband. You are a tyrant feeding lies to our people to keep the crown for yourself. No longer will your poison harm our wonderful civilization."

Queen Aconite backs against a wall, pressing her venom laced hands against its rough wooden surface, "I crave power, just the same as you or anyone."

"I do not want power. I believe in the gifts that I already possess. You will never be able to use a Sun Crystal, because you have chosen Medaia's side. I know that you plotted against my husband those years ago. I know that you killed our greatest soldiers in combat because they had the bravery to stand up against you and your tyranny. You helped Medaia spread her influence by welcoming her shadow beasts into Nominia. My husband did not just disappear! You murdered him."

Queen Aconite stretches out her hand to Irene. Her face gloats with the revelation of the truth. She responds with a bitter laugh, "Yes. I did all of this. No kingdom is great that expresses weakness. I crushed opposition for the good of Nominia. I have saved our people by killing those who oppose me." Her frozen eyes observe Irene. Aconite smiles maniacally, "I still remember your husband's face when he died."

Irene launches herself at Aconite with the remainder of her strength, but the poisonous flowers touch her skin and climb up her arms. Aconite's few wolfsbane flowers tear apart the golden marigolds covering Irene's body. Irene is left exposed in a simple cloth dress. Irene places her hands around a small group of marigolds tightly coiled around her stomach. She feels the warmth of the blood from her wound.

Arrogantly, Aconite trembles with power. Her voice taunts Irene. She continues, "Actually, your husband's death face resembles yours right about now. Soon the toxin from my flowers will settle into your skin and bloodstream."

She presses further choking Irene, who winces as the wolfsbane scratches her skin and tears at her flesh. She feels the poisonous flowers tighten around her neck and the world becomes blurry.

"For the Sun." whispers Irene.

The white orchid Orelia had given to her mother bursts to life, wrapping itself around Queen Aconite. The queen collapses suffocating, trying to yank the single flower and its stem from around her neck. However, the orchid begins to multiply and Queen Aconite is soon fully covered by the delicate white flowers that shine in the Sun's light.

Irene smiles. She releases a tired and painful breath as she gradually pulls her hand loose from the wilted wolfsbane flowers that bind her arms. She lets her wrinkled and bruised hands fall on her chest to feel the remainder of her marigold flowers as they begin to lose color and droop. Her face falls to the side, looking towards the light of the open balcony window. Irene smiles seeing the afternoon Sun glow warm and proud in the grey sky. The stained glass fairies above her, smile with glittering eyes of approval. Then, the throne room darkens as if night has fallen. A monstrous demon lands on the balcony carrying a quartz crystal with the image of Medaia inside.

Medaia glares at Irene. "Where is it?" she demands with a cold and harsh voice.

Irene coughs, she places a hand on her stomach. "You should have killed me in the Sacred Sun Temple. I warned them of your arrival and the green crystal has been moved."

Medaia's voice screeches. It sounds like that of a beast yelling wildly. Her eyes savagely stare at Irene. She points her hand at Irene and commands the giant shadow demon. "Kill her," she bellows out in hatred.

The image of Medaia fades from the huge quartz crystal. The monstrous demon licks its twisted teeth and charges at Irene on all fours. It releases a vicious roar.

Irene lifts her hand. The last strand of her marigolds rise from her body. The flowers are faint in color and the stems are dry. Her emerald eyes gleam in the light. She feels the warm blood flow from her gashing wound across her stomach. Her hands are cold to the touch. The beast raises its claws. Irene directs her marigold flowers. The beast cuts through the stems and smashes the petals.

"The Sun will forever live on," whispers Irene as she closes her eyes, accepting her one way ticket to the Heavenly Sun Lands and beyond. The golden glow of her flowers fade as they crumble to the ground, which leaves her body dry and lifeless on the cold floor. However, Irene's benevolent loving smile remains on her face even in death. Her husband appears beside her and grasps a hold of her hand. Together they soar upwards to the Sun.

The monster stops its approach. It sniffs at Irene's body and examines the crushed marigold flowers in disappointment. Media reappears within the reflection of the mirror. The demon screeches, showing its bare teeth and monstrous dragon like wings. It takes off into the dark sky swarmed full of monstrous shadow beasts and it clutches the large quartz mirror displaying Medaia's reflection in its talons. She has dark hair and darker eyes. She wears a tattered maroon dress that clings to her body. Her dark brown eyes overlook the burning floating island, scanning the land for a sign of the crystal.

Linum and the others wait behind a long building, watching monsters stalk the grounds and haunt the air. Linum beckons for her friends to follow her as she jumps a plain ash tree fence and ducks behind the covering of a broken tavern. Her companions follow close behind, each hurriedly shuffling together. A monstrous creature takes a huge whiff of the air and stampedes toward them with flaring nostrils and a hanging green tongue. Linum takes a brave step forward, she rips out the green slimy odorous tongue from its mouth with her sword. The beast yelps in pain, gurgling on the dark shadowy ooze filling its mouth. It watches as its green tongue wiggles away like a lizard's tail. Linum makes the final stroke with her sword and the beast falls silent. However, more shadow beasts approach, each looking for an appetizer to claim for themselves. Zoren flogs a nearby monster that dared to take a step too close to Charles, who grasps his spear with a shaking hand.

Orelia batters the beasts with her orchids. She calls out to Linum, "We must fall back. There are too many shadow beasts."

They are surrounded by the demonic creatures with thick midnight skin and boils. The beast's eyes glint in the demonic grey of the brooding sky as they lick their lips and growl deeply. Their rumbling growls sound like the grumbling of an active volcano preparing for eruption. Linum desperately searches her surroundings, she sees fairies flying and running, trying to avoid being caught by the talons of the beasts. She hears screams of innocent children flooding the dark afternoon sky. Linum witnesses raw flesh exposed all around her and burning in the disheartened fires. The paradise has turned into a site of complete destruction. The fairy kingdom is being brought to ruin.

Linum takes a concerned glance at the shimmering green crystal. It invades her mind as her fingers tap against the Sun Crystal's surface in her sword. It whispers to her, *Use me.* It promises, *Use me and everything will be okay. Use me and you can save your friends at a small cost. Use me!* She begins to close her eyes and feels the pulsing of the green crystal taking over her fast beating heart, thumping against her chest, but Charles brushes against her shoulder and her eyes flit open. The pulsing stops and her head clears, she looks around only to see the beasts press against her body. The monstrous shadow beasts appear to savor her death as they slowly reach upwards with extracted claws and raging fiery eyes. Her friends are caught too. Zoren holds his whip like a barrier between the gnashing teeth of a giant beast and himself. Orelia is cornered against a demolished building wall, her flowers hug her small frame, seeking her warmth against the devastating cold heartedness of the beasts. Charles, who is on the floor, prods with his spear hopelessly. It pokes the monstrous beasts like a splinter in the foot of a giant.

"Wait!" Howls the voice of a small fairy cloaked regally in dandelions.

"Vondur, help us!" pleads Orelia, recognizing the small dandelion man as her lieutenant and the trusted assistant of the queen.

"No." Vondur laughs satisfied with denying her, "I will not. No!" His mouth lingers in the shape of an 'O' as his beady little eyes watch a creeping realization settle onto Orelia's face.

"You monster." She yells, "You little nasty coward!"

He laughs again and leans onto the snout of one of the beasts. The beast simply sits down and breathes steadily, licking its lips with greedy intentions. "You honestly think I would help *you*, the girl from the Junior Cadets who at age seven entered the Flower Patrol. The girl who outshined the older, wiser, and skilled young man, who rested below your father's side for years running back and forth as a servant. Ha! No way am I going to save *you*. I was placed below the two of them, your father and his trusted captain, for so long that I was most pleased to do a way with the old man, so I could move up in rank. And even then you still stood in my way."

"You beast. You killed my father!"

"No, I killed his partner, gave him a serum of mashed wolfsbane to drink at the tavern."

"You really are a monster."

"Not at all. I just did what Queen Aconite had instructed me to do. Queen Aconite killed your father, she knew these glorious beasts were waiting for him. I just had to slip them in for her." Vondur triumphs over his moment of revelation, he stretches his dandelion cape arrogantly over his shoulder. "And for so long I had done Queen Aconite's bidding, and yet she still chose *you* over me! Can you imagine my frustration that night when you rose up in rank from captain to general. You skipped over my rank of lieutenant after all my hard years of work.

Besides you got all the respect no matter what your rank was beforehand. The queen gave you all the credit for everything."

Charles chimes in, "Because unlike you she possesses a kind heart and skill!"

Vondur glares at Charles and continues on, "So I killed that ridiculous flame that night, because Queen Aconite told me to do so. She said it would reveal the true power of the Sun Crystals to us! And it did."

He smiles a crooked smile at Linum who yells at him, "And for killing Pyro, we will kill you!"

"No, you will not!" He walks towards her and breathes in her face, releasing a foul odor. He whispers, "We kept Zoren in good condition just for you." He winks at her and smiles, cocking his head towards Zoren, whose hands stretch outwards and simmer with heat.

"Zoren, how did you like our prison? Was your stay pleasing and will you come again?" He jokes and his dandelion wings lift him into the air. Vondur gloats, "Now that the queen is dead I have found myself in brighter spirits."

"You murdered Pyro." Spits Zoren as his hands burst into blue flames, illuminating his oceanic blue eyes, "You killed the flame I crafted with my bare hands."

The beasts growl as Vondur floats upwards. They inch closer to the four teens pressed against the wall of a destroyed building. A few of the shadow beast's with wings float in the air, circling above them.

Vondur chuckles and a maniacal grin spreads across his face. He boasts, "Not to mention, Medaia has promised me greatness if I am the one to drag all of your corpses back to her." Vondur whistles and the beasts spring to life, their teeth flashing.

Linum transforms into the beast using only the power of the pink crystal. She shoots into the air tackling shadow monsters. Orelia hacks at them with her flowers that lift them off the ground and snare their feet. Charles stabs at the beasts with his spear. Zoren sets his hands down onto the ground; he watches as Vondur floats higher into the sky, directing the monsters with wings to attack. Zoren's whip flies out of his pocket, it zooms to life whacking any beasts that approach him while he crouches onto the soft soil.

Zoren's eyes close. He takes a deep breath in, expelling blue flames from his nose. His hands, pressed firmly to the riverbed road, ignite into blue flames that climb up the length of his body. The flames hover over his dark hair and engulf him. His eyes burn a bright blue. The shadow demons all freeze. Their single flaming eyes turn from a violent red to a soft blue. The creatures all screech in unison and build up their strength. The beasts direct their horrendous power to their throats, which begin to inflate like a frog's vocal sac. The creatures burst open in a massive fiery explosion, leaving nothing but ash surrounding the four teens. Zoren's burning eyes turn towards the frightened Vondur, who attempts to fly away in a futile attempt to escape.

"For Pyro!" He howls in a deep booming voice. His silver whip stretches out towards Vondur, who is flapping his dandelion wings furiously. The deadly sharp edge of the whip wraps around Vondur's foot and yanks him towards the ground. The fairy smacks to the floor with a deafening thud and Zoren bends over his body, "Never in the name of the Sun or the trepid night will you ever enter the realm of the Heavenly Sun Lands and find peace for your crimes." He spits at Vondur with a voice that echoes off the surrounding buildings and travels furiously on the wind.

Vondur whimpers, "Please, have mercy." He reaches out towards Zoren but his eyes glance at Orelia. He screams, "General Orelia, please save me."

The whip hurries back into Zoren's vest pocket and he sways, falling to the ground next to Vondur. The blue flames disappear, melting into his skin. However, Zoren extends a shaking hand and lays a cold finger onto Vondur's back, igniting him into flames. Zoren fully collapses, his hands fall flat onto Vondur and his eyes shut tightly.

The dandelions erupt into flames. Vondur screams in pain.

Orelia turns her back on him as she aids Linum, who rushes forward pulling Zoren away from the blue flames that quickly turn into a vile orange.

Yet, they do not have a moment of peace to tend to Zoren.

Charles yells, "Watch out!"

A ginormous shadow beast lands before them, clutching a clear quartz mirror. The beast has thirty red eyes and a large boiled green tongue. It has welts stretching up its decaying skin and talons longer than a person.

A woman draped in a maroon dress mutters, "Very well executed. I must admit I am impressed." Medaia appears before them in the reflection of the mirror, her dark brown eyes glitter with youthful energy, although she has been around since the formation of the legend. Her long black hair streams behind her, creating a dark halo around her head. "Now hand over the crystals, Linum, before anyone has to get hurt."

Zoren moans, his eyes are still pressed shut and his body contracts and stretches violently. Orelia crumbles onto the ground as well and clutches her chest, which heaves as she screams out in pain.

Charles roars, clutching his side and kneels onto the floor rocking himself, but he cries out, "Linum, do not give in to her!"

Linum stands and walks towards the mirror. She looks calmly into her adversary's dark eyes, "You look nothing like Judith."

"Judith never existed. She was just a shadow of my power. However, you whittled your way into my plot just as planned. You are rash and untamed and too willing to be deceived. My key that you crafted may not have given me what I desired, but it gave me something greater in that room of the poor Castle of Dalium."

Linum howls in rage, "The key I made for you? It gave you no such thing, you are bluffing!"

Medaia smiles shrewdly, "If only you knew Linum, how much I gained from that key you crafted. I still cannot believe that you thought it was a token of freedom. The key allowed me to gain you as an unwilling ally."

"Never!"

Medaia laughs, "Very unwilling ally. Did you ever think about what could have been planted? Did you ever think about what actually was robbed from the castle?"

"You put me into a trance and sent the shadow beasts."

"Yes, I did. While I do not have what I want as it was removed from that room before I had the chance, I gained a victory over you. Now I will reclaim what I had wanted from the start, for you have my desired object resting in your sword."

Linum observes Medaia, her dark black hair, and deep brown eyes appear vaguely familiar as does her voice.

"I know those eyes," whispers Linum to herself.

"What was that?" booms Medaia, her hands rise upwards casting her shadow against the floor.

"The crystal is mine and I do not fear you." Yells Linum who sheaths her sword and approaches the mirror.

"I am just a reflection, true, but I still hold great power."

"I do not fear you." Linum crosses her arms, her cheeks burn as red as a rose, and her lips press together firmly.

Her friends moan louder, but Linum keeps a steady eye on Medaia. The dragon-like demon growls.

"I do not fear you!" Linum charges at the mirror, but her feet are caught in a rose bush.

Medaia's eyes roll backwards and she begins to chant, causing the roses to grow and twist like a serpent, "Then fear this. Hand over the crystals, Linum."

Linum stretches forward, inching her body closer to the quartz mirror, although the rose bush pulls her back. "Never will I give into your darkness."

"I am not your enemy, Linum. I want to save this world, I want to rebuild the Kingdom of Dalium. I do not want to destroy any more lands. I just need the crystals and I will put an end to all the evil in this world. I will bring new life to Dalium using my own strengths to create the perfect kingdom and I will be a just ruler to the entire world. All will look up to me as they respect the Sun!"

Medaia's shadow stretches across the ground. It raises Linum's face so she may look into the crystal mirror. Medaia whispers, "Hand over what I desire and I will ensure there is no more suffering. You have suffered so much and so have your friends, but I can put an end to that. I do not wish to kill you." She smiles, drawing her lips into a crescent shape, and extends a hand through the mirror. Linum takes it and the rose bush creeps back down into the soil. "Good. Now handover the two crystals and everything will be just fine."

"I wish I could trust you," whispers Linum.

Medaia retracts her hand and glares at Linum, "I have had enough! Do you not understand? Life is like a rose. We all sprout, grow, blossom in our youth, but begin to wilt and eventually take one last breath before death. We are all beautiful in innocence and drunken with corruption by age. Birth by no means is a promise as it is not a seed's duty to sprout. Both could have fatal incidents leading to demise. And as such we live a flower's life. We rise, with beautiful succession then fall with or without grace. Such is our delicacy, such is nature, and such is life. But I can change that with the power of these crystals. I can reap what the Sun holds so dear and precious. Immortality is possible if you give up the crystals."

"To hell with immortality!" yells Linum who ducks as Asterian materializes and kicks at the quartz structure, creating a web of cracks all around the mirror. The demonic creature roars and Linum unsheaths her sword. Her blade glows a brilliant pink as the crystal of Dalium shines underneath the light of the Sun.

She bellows, "For the Sun!" Linum jumps onto Asterian's back and rides him into the sky. She charges at the monster that spits acid at her. The horrendous shadow beast traces her every move with its thirty glaring eyes. Asterian dodges, flying above the acidic spit. The beast raises its wings and takes off into the air, chasing after Asterian. Linum glances at it. The hideous shadow beast snaps its jaws together and attempts to bite at Asterian's tail.

"You must go faster," Linum urges Asterian. She grabs a hold of his wild mane. His wings glow a soft pink to match her crystal.

Asterian neighs in response. He bursts through the sky with lightning speed. The giant shadow beast remains close behind. Linum can smell the stench of its breath. Asterian slows down and dives underneath the beast. The monster's body is above Linum. She swings with her sword and cuts at its flesh. The creature roars in pain. Linum slices her blade all the way down to the horrendous creature's tail. The pink glow of her sword gives her the strength to cut through the thick hide. Asterian pulls up and Linum yanks her sword free. She stares into Asterian's galaxy eyes and understands what she must do. Asterian dives, heading towards the ground. The horrendous monster, although injured, chases after them with a renewed fury. Black sludge leaks from the deep wound inflicted on its stomach. It growls and spits its acid. Asterian swerves to the right to avoid the boiling hot acidic spit. The shadow beast blinks its thirty red eyes. Linum concentrates on it and it growls at her. The shadow beasts neck begins to swell. She spies the orange glow of flames building up in its mouth. Asterian is about to land before the cracked quartz mirror, but he shoots upright again. The monster spews its orange flames at the mirror. Linum hears Medaia shout in outrage. She smiles as Asterian loops in the air. He swings Linum below the shadow beast's horrendous neck. With a mighty swing of her sword she chops off the monster's head. Black ooze bursts into the air like a fountain as the beast melts into a puddle of ash, leaving the mirror standing on its own.

"My beautiful shadow beast. My wonderful creature!" croaks Medaia as she presses her hands against the surface of the cracked quartz mirror. She yells, "You will suffer for that. I will hunt you and your friends down with more powerful monsters and you will not have it so easy again. You will regret your decision to oppose me. You will regret this day and every day you live following this. No one defies me and you will learn that."

Linum stands. She points her sword at the mirror. Her brown eyes glow fiercely. She yells, "If life is a flower, then I choose to be the thorn in your side!"

"And so you will, but you will be hunted down at every turn until my shadow beasts have demolished your corpse. I will not rest until you are just an empty shell."

Linum closes her eyes and aims her sword at Medaia's reflection. She pictures herself in the cave, standing next to her. She feels the cold surroundings of the cavern, although she stands in Nomina. The pink crystal glows furiously beside the green crystal. Linum swings her sword through the air.

Medaia screams. Linum opens her eyes. She looks at the quartz mirror and sees Medaia clutching her hand. She is bleeding. The pink crystal glows furiously. Medaia's image begins to fade.

Medaia calls off her shadow beasts with a simple wave of her hand. Asterian kicks the quartz mirror, sending it crashing down on the rough ground and it shatters. Its fragments turn into a rose bush with no flowers, only sick twisted red thorns. Linum mutters under her breath, "Until we meet again" and slams her sword into her sheath. Asterian flaps his galaxy wings and disappears.

Zoren gasps for breath and Linum rushes up to him, helping him to his feet. He leans onto her for support as they hobble over to Charles.

Charles winces, still clutching his side, "You did it Linum."

Zoren smiles and actually laughs, "No. Medaia will be back."

"He is right, but we will be ready." She offers a hand to Charles and he takes it.

Orelia trembles on the floor. She pushes herself upright using the strength of her orchids to stand. "We have to get out of here, in case she returns."

The shadow monster's fly towards the Sun, causing an eclipse of darkness. They fade into thin air, creating a cacophony of horrendous hate filled screeches and growls as they melt to dust and travel threateningly on the viscous wind. The afternoon sky is streaked blood red and grey with departing clouds and the settling gloom of fog. Orelia shivers as the wind howls and rushes past them. Her orchids wrap around her exposed shoulders like a cape, revealing her blood stained white dress underneath. Zoren cracks his whip, causing a deafening sound to ricochet off the walls of the devastated wooden buildings. Screams still pierce the air, but the group runs past the shrieking fairies. They hurry from corner to corner, keeping a keen eye on the batlike monsters that are still rising from the ground and slowly fading away. Linum pauses, she nudges Charles and he gulps. They spy a young child scratching at the floor, trapped underneath the destruction of a nearby building. The boy holds onto a small doll. Linum rushes forward and lifts the lumber and Charles scoops up the small child. He bawls and cries, waving his hands in the air as his basil teddy bear wraps around him in comfort. His wings flutter and Charles lets go of him. They all watch as the boy floats away, searching through the destruction with wide eyes. He then smiles and flies down because he finds his mother and father searching through the ruin.

They hurry past the damaged structures, seeking a way out. They each take turns gasping at the remains and tragic sights of the disaster before them. The once great green fields with the endless array of flowers is now a barren wasteland. Orelia leads them through the dead crops and lifeless bouquets. But there is hope, for some of the flowers remain upright and healthy and not all of the trees are burnt down, in fact there are a few only singed and many others untouched.

"The buildings can be rebuilt," whispers Charles.

Orelia wishes she could say, *But the fairies' lives cannot be made new*, but instead she bites her lip and presses on, walking through the fields and letting her hands glide on the dried petals and smashed upturned roots.

They reach the ivy hanging from broken pillars laced with dim gold. The group marches down the cracked quartz steps to the edge of the island. The ground is only a miniscule green speck and the trees appear like ants.

Orelia warns, "I may only take one with me. I do not have the strength right now to carry two people."

Linum whispers to her eight-pointed silver star necklace, "Asterian, I need you."

Asterian materializes before her and bows his head.

Zoren instructs, "Charles you can go with Orelia." Zoren takes a step back and without hesitation jumps onto Asterian's back. Asterian rears anxiously, he dives off the floating island and begins to descend towards the ground.

Linum jumps off of the steps, falling straight towards the ground. She presses her hand against her star necklace, clutching it towards her chest and shuts her eyes. When she opens them she is the creature with skeleton wings, purple cracked skin, and blue talons. She plummets down from the sky and soars upwards and downwards riding the wind and circling around Zoren as he makes his slow descent towards the ground on Asterian.

"Hold onto my arm." Orelia warns as her orchids take the form of giant wings and knot a harness around Charles. She plucks a single purple orchid off her dress and places it on the small pile of dirt breaking through the surface of the quartz stairs. Orelia smiles as it roots itself, "This way I will always be connected to my home," she whispers to Charles as she flaps her enormous wings. She takes off into the air. Charles hangs from a strand of orchid's tightly fastened around his waist. They plummet towards the terrain below to catch up with the others. Linum reaches the ground first and makes her transformation back to her normal self. Zoren lands roughly since Asterian disappears as soon as they touch the ground. Zoren collapses on the grass with a thud. Orelia gently lands and Charles rolls onto the floor. She stretches out her hands and her orchid wings wrap around her dress.

They all look up to see the smoke rise from the green fields of the floating island. The Sun bends carefully over it as if it too were watching the devastation. As if in pity of the once great kingdom full of vigorous happy fairies and life, rain splashes from the sky. However, Charles, Linum, Orelia, and Zoren are kept dry underneath the shadow of the devastated island above. Orelia plants her hands into the ground and wails, creating a small patch of orchids. She stands back and observes the flowers. Charles, Linum, and even Zoren take a turn to approach her and tell her that everything will be better, but she only shakes her head in denial and pain.

A single flash of lightning strikes the ground nearby and Orelia squints at it, believing to have seen both of her parents in the brightness of the light. When the beautiful electrifying bolt retreats, she runs towards the darkened earth and gasps at the sight of a delicate marigold flower growing next to a cedar tree sapling. She smiles, and turns away to face her companions, and whispers to herself, "Everything will be okay."

Chapter 20
The Horizon

They run through the trees while carefully scanning their surroundings for monster's lurking in the dark. However, they only see their reflections in the clear water of the creek. Linum flies over the water and lands transformed on the other side. Orelia hovers over the gentle surface of the water. Charles follows behind Zoren, as they trudge across to the other side. Yet, Charles tumbles down into the water, he gets soaked and continues on dripping wet and curses at his luck. They rush past darker trees and narrow paths. Linum pauses in an open clearing and they begin to set up camp. The Sun glows faintly. They shiver in unity as the wind brushes over them and moans.

They wash their hands clean of blood and bandage their wounds with the herbs Orelia picks from the surrounding woods. Zoren catches two large trout that he tosses over a weak flame that they had to make themselves. Linum pokes a stick at the fragile embers while staring at the tender flesh of the fish. She whistles the tune of the Sun Blessed Everglades. Her black hair falls across her eyes and the single blue streak shines in the light of the flickering flares of the small warm fire. She watches the ash sway and dance in the breeze. Linum remembers the swaying roses from her nightmare from long ago. She recalls the flashing lights of the Crystal

Caverns. She shivers as the images of Penelope, Brandwyn, Pyro, and Irene stain her mind with remorse.

Medaia's words echo in her head. "*You will be hunted.*" She feels death stalking her behind the trees, in a far off cave where crystals grow in hatred and without the light of the Sun. She knows Medaia will be waiting for her and tracking her. Linum can feel her presence looming over her as the dark smoke rises. Through the flames she spies glimpses of the enormous shadow monster she killed and Medaia's familiar image in the mirror. She shivers, letting out a soft breath. Charles senses her unease and he touches her shoulder softly and offers a gentle smile. Linum shakes loose his hand and stares at the flames, wishing them to reveal her fate. The shadows are cast around them and Charles sighs. The green crystal glows for a moment in her sword.

Linum breaks the bittersweet silence, her voice rising over the crackling of the wood, "I have been given this quest by the Sun itself and look what it has done. All of you were innocent of it, but each of you have suffered on my behalf." They each look up at her, their eyes glittering from the light of the fire, she toys with the flames and continues, "And as much as I want to tell you for you all to get as far away from me as you can and quit on this quest... I cannot. The truth is that I need each and everyone of you to complete this perilous adventure with me, to save the world from darkness and despair. I tried for so long to remain aloof, but I learned from the crystal we are our strongest when we work together. I need you all, but it is your choice and I will not hold it against you if you decide to walk away. I have put you through the unbearable and unforgivable because I was given a fate by the Sun and–"

"So you think we will just give up now?" Charles questions and laughs, "I will accompany you on this quest until the bitter end."

"Linum, you may not trust me yet, but I am a loyal friend and will not give up on this quest either. Besides I need to avenge my mother and the Terrace Gardens of Nominia." Orelia flutters her wings with compassion and boldness.

Zoren shrugs and boasts, "You would not get anywhere without my help and I will not let you go anywhere with *my* crystal."

"So it is decided that you will all accompany me through the triumphs and tribulations of this mission to gather the remaining six crystals of the Sun and restore order to the entirety of Solenium?"

"Without a flicker of a doubt," answers Charles.

"Indeed," mutters Zoren.

"For the prosperity and well being of all, I will help you," replies Orelia with a sunny beam.

"Then we will face the trials ahead of us together!" Linum smiles at her friends. Asterian descends from the sky and neighs. "And of course we can not forget Asterian!" Linum laughs and heartedly sighs.

"So what kingdom are we heading to next, Linum?" Charles asks with a yawn.

Orelia speaks up, "Well the closest kingdom to the Terrace Gardens of Nominia is the Gardium Kingdom, then Miezul Noptilandia and of course the Crystal Common Grounds."

"No." Replies Linum with a stern voice, "We mustn't face Medaia, who lurks in those caverns, until we have the six other crystals. Miezul Noptilandia is too close to her domain. What is the farthest kingdom from here?"

Zoren remarks, "That would be the Horizonia Empire which is not far off from the Kingdom of Terraminionium and The Volcanic Village of Humberia, but of course before any of those places may be reached we must cross the ocean. However, we may not cross until we receive the blessing of the Gardium citizens to do so. Not to mention, a sea voyage will be perilous and daunting to undertake."

Linum shrugs and smiles, "Perilous and daunting? Sounds like a plan." She takes a moment to look at her friends. Asterian roars, Charles wrings out his puffy sleeved beige shirt, Zoren watches the tender flames, and Orelia smiles at the small wildflowers growing around them. "We may be a band of rapscallions like the thorns cut off from a growing rose, but we will save our land, the entirety of Solenium, from Medaia's dark powers of devastation. We will go over the horizon!" They watch the Sunset at the horizon line, illuminating the distant mountains in streaks of a warm orange and a soft pink glow. The group sets their sights on the world that remains ahead of them and beyond; Asterian takes off extending his galaxy wings towards the benevolent Sun and disappears in a flash of blue light.

ABOUT THE AUTHOR

Genesis Brillante is a young author who loves to read and write. Ever since she was able to grasp a pencil in her hand she had a story in her head. She grew up in a land of fantasy. During the day she daydreams of worlds she could create and at night she adventures in them. Genesis is creative, hardworking, diligent, fond of poetry, and a lover of animals. She is a keen reader and always finds herself diving into new stories. She began writing *Cut Thorn: The Sun Champion* when she was in the third grade and at age 17 she found the spare time to get it done. In response to the darkness of the COVID-19 pandemic she finished her book in 2020 to bring a little bit of sunshine into her world. The characters and plot have developed with her as she has aged and she is excited to finally share her story with the world. You can find her on Instagram @gjb.creates.